Buy Back
the Dawn

Buy Back the Dawn

Nicholas Garland

Richard Marek Publishers · New York

Library of Congress Cataloging in Publication Data

————
  Buy back the dawn.

  I. Title.
PZ4.K1965Bu   [PS3561.A754]   813'.54   80-13185
ISBN 0-399-90087-X

Printed in the United States of America

for N.B.K.,
mi corazón

One

Chapter One

The woman got off the elevator on the forty-first floor and hesitated as though she might change her mind. She was young but there was an authority to her appearance that made her seem older. In daylight her face projected a dormant sensuality, a vague suggestion of impatience for the night. It was impossible to guess her age; one would have said late twenties. Her smoky gray eyes and slightly thin mouth suggested a knowledge of the worst of life in the midst of life's best. It was this hint of a scenario in her startlingly beautiful face that had given her career its sudden thrust. In the next few months she was scheduled to become one of the most frequently photographed women in the world. She was nineteen.

The sudden closing of the elevator door put an end to her uncertainty. She turned abruptly and took long, quick strides toward the receptionist's desk. The receptionist had left for her break a moment ago and her temporary replacement had not yet arrived, so the desk was untended. The young woman adjusted her silk shawl and looked at her watch. She was, uncharacteristically, early for her appointment. She took a seat in the reception area of Temple, Norton, and Winter, Counsellors at Law, and waited. Her name was Toni Menard.

* * *

In a corner suite of those same law offices, Jeffrey Winter stood at his window looking out at a city aglow in the late afternoon sun of a perfect June day. He felt the city in his loins, felt the erotic dazzlement New York has for those lucky enough to straddle it. It was the height of arrogance, Jeff knew, to feel like a colossus. But Jesus, that was the feeling all right, and he loved it.

He stretched, yearning for a sofa and some Mozart on the stereo and Cathy Hayes to make love to. God, he'd almost forgotten to call her. He still didn't know whether he could get away in time to go to the Neil Simon opening with her tonight. It was sometimes a problem to be engaged to the hottest new television newscaster in New York, but mostly he enjoyed it. He took pride in her. She'd started late in the game, well past the age of thirty. But she'd made it fast, despite a few really hard knocks in her private life. Like a painful divorce. Like two kids who had little appreciation of what she was trying to do with her life. The kids were a real stumbling block in his relationship with Cathy. He wondered how that part of it was going to work. He liked them well enough, but they got in the way. Cathy understood that. What she proposed was that he keep his apartment even after their marriage. He'd move in with her; that would be their home. They'd use his apartment as a place to escape to. She wasn't at all averse to making love in the afternoon whenever they could arrange it.

He buzzed his secretary on the intercom.

"Jeff," his secretary said, "I'm on long distance. Can it wait or should I send one of the girls?"

"Buzz me back when you get off," he said.

Oh, Christ, he didn't need his secretary to place a call to Cathy. He looked up her new private number at Channel Seven and dialed it.

Cathy's male secretary answered the phone.

"Miss Hayes's office."

"This is Jeff Winter. Is Miss Hayes there?"

"She's out. Can she return your call?"

"I'll call back later."

"She won't have much time before going on the air. Will you be at your office at six?"

Jesus! The inquisition conducted by a twerp. "Tell her I'll call back at six."

He wondered where Cathy was. He guessed in a meeting. Why was it that whenever he telephoned a woman he loved and got no answer he felt an immediate twinge of anxiety. What fantasy was set off? Could Cathy ever be unfaithful? The way he knew he could be?

Beautiful women always distracted him. His enthusiasm for them was as eloquent as it was boyish. He was not a philanderer; he was just, on occasion, careless about fidelity. Since his divorce three years ago, he had enjoyed the full cycle of romance several times, savoring each of its phases from the first promise of passion to the last goodbye. He was hopeless that way. In that way he hadn't changed. It was always the same . . . the way it had been in Paris sixteen years ago with Johanna. He closed his eyes for a moment and thought of her. He thought of the last time he had seen her. Before he had to flee for his life. And for hers.

It was funny. He was planning to marry again. Someone really special, someone really good for him. He loved Cathy. But he wondered about the wisdom of it. So much in his life remained unresolved. Yet . . . did it really matter? He had learned to live from day to day, and he was quite comfortable. No dwelling on the past. No worrying about the future. The fact that there was so much to do in the present helped a lot. He was a successful attorney. Not bad looking. He jogged six miles every other morning, played a good game of tennis, was a connoisseur of haute cuisine and the ballet, and drove a white Mercedes like an inspired maniac; he was the sort of driver you could trust while enjoying the thrill of his scaring the hell out of you. He had no nearby parents and no children to put through school or take on weekends. Women quickly recognized that at forty-two he was a very good thing.

He buzzed his secretary again and got no answer; she was still on long distance. He wondered whether his four-thirty appointment had arrived. He dialed the receptionist, and a strange voice answered the phone.

"This is Jeff Winter," he said. "Who's this?"

"This is Toni Menard," the unfamiliar voice said, "your four-thirty appointment."

"Oh." He was momentarily flustered.

"There's no one out here. I picked up the phone."

"This office is falling apart today. Listen, if the intercom buzzes again and the receptionist isn't there, someone else will eventually pick it up. I'll be with you in a minute."

His intercom buzzed. His secretary, Linda, was off her long-distance call.

"Listen, Miss Menard's been sitting out there—" she began.

"I know," he said. "Bring her in."

11

He scratched his head. He began to review what he knew about Toni Menard, which wasn't a great deal. He'd seen pictures of her here and there; she was making it big as a model. But he didn't have the foggiest idea of what this meeting was all about. He waited. He was still flustered. He didn't know why. The door to his office was opened by Linda. Then Toni Menard came in, and Linda closed the door.

Toni Menard was tall and slender and had legs that moved against her dress like scissors clicking. Her face had the good bone structure called classical and planes that cameras loved. Her dark hair had been cut to dip forward with her every gesture and then to flow back into a state of perfect repose, augmenting her body's suggestion that movement itself could be witty.

For a moment Jeff thought his smile might get out of control. But he harnessed it into an appropriate greeting.

"I made this appointment four weeks ago," she said, extending her hand, returning his smile. "This was the first appointment your secretary could give me. I'm accustomed to that with dermatologists. But four weeks is a long time for a lawyer. Are you really that good?"

"I travel a lot," he said, sitting down and inviting her to do the same in one of the two facing wing chairs placed away from his desk in a corner near the window.

"You know," he said, grinning, "you produce an impulse in me I haven't felt in years. You're the sort of girl I would have whistled at in the street when I was a kid, before it became such bad form to whistle."

"Thank you," she said. "I really wouldn't mind if you whistled." He caught the vaguest hint of a European accent in her speech. "It seems so much more gracious," she went on, "than what passes for a compliment in my world."

"Your world?"

"I'm a model. I go to parties. The nice men are gay. The others think a compliment is when a stranger whispers in your ear how much he'd like to fuck you."

She opened her purse and felt around inside. She pulled out a cigarette, which went directly into her mouth. The hand that held the cigarette palmed a silver Cartier lighter. She lit up.

"I'm not as tough as I seem," she said.

"Surprise, surprise. Why have you come to see me?"

"You don't remember me?" she asked.

12

"Have we met before?"

"Yes."

"At the rate of one hundred and forty bucks an hour," Jeff said, "you shouldn't be playing games."

"I'm not playing games."

"If we'd met, I'd remember you."

"I was three years old when we met," she said slowly. She studied his face, but there were no signs of comprehension. He would keep on playing the lawyer, being gallant, patient and suspicious. But only for a moment more.

She was ready to shatter him now. "I'm Johanna's daughter," she said.

"*What?*" Fear stabbed at his gut. Over her shoulder he saw ghosts.

"Jeff, *look* at me. I *do* resemble Johanna, don't I?"

"Toni Menard?" he asked. "You're Johanna's daughter? You're Antonia?"

"Yes."

"Antonia Thornton?"

"Yes. Thornton didn't seem like a very good name for a model."

"*Johanna*'s daughter?" He was still struggling with it.

"I was three," she repeated, as though that explained everything.

"Where is Johanna?"

"My mother is dead."

His body grew cold. He could feel pain in all of his muscles.

"I thought you knew," she said.

"How could I have known? Your mother and I were never in touch again after that last day. When—how long ago did she die?"

"It was very soon after you left. An accident . . . She and my father went to the market. Only he came back."

"An accident?"

"A car . . . swerving around a corner. I've pictured it in my head thousands of times. In my daydreams I try to prevent it from happening. But," she said, biting her lower lip, "it happened."

"Where is your father?" Jeff asked.

"In Paris."

"What made you suddenly look me up now?"

"I saw the announcement of your engagement in the *Times*, and I wondered whether you were the same Jeffrey Winter. I took a chance

13

and called your office for an appointment. . . . You and my mother were lovers, weren't you." It wasn't a question. It was a statement that trailed off to someplace in her subconscious.

"Yes."

"It took me years to work that one out."

"Conrad never told you?"

"No."

"Not even in his rages?"

"He didn't have rages. What makes you say that?"

"I—" *Careful,* he told himself. She doesn't know what you think she knows. Oh, God. Then he mustn't tell her. He mustn't . . .

"You *what?*" She was confronting him now. What did he know about her father that she ought to be told?

"I remember Conrad as pretty hot tempered," Jeff said.

"Maybe he was hot tempered once, but not after my mother died. He turned cold and solitary. He sank into himself. Then later he turned mean."

"I take it you and Conrad aren't very close."

"Not the way we once were. We don't really see very much of each other anymore. Can you help me find an ashtray?"

There was one on the window sill. He got up and handed it to her.

"Thanks." She flicked off half an inch of ash. "I need to know about those months in Paris."

"Me and Johanna?" He lowered himself into his chair.

"Yes. You're smiling."

"Her name makes me smile." He hesitated. Then he asked, "Could you possibly have dinner with me tonight?"

"Yes."

"It's after five. Tell you what. Why don't you just wait around while I straighten up a bit, and we can go right out for drinks."

He thought about calling Cathy. She'd be on the air in twenty minutes. He decided to wait until later, when she'd be able to talk to him.

He started to move toward his desk. Halfway there he stopped to look at Toni again, deeply moved by the presence of Johanna's daughter. He reached out for her hand.

"Antonia," he said in more of a whisper than he intended. He closed his eyes, still holding her hand, trying to conjure for just a moment the child of three, but he saw Johanna instead . . . and Conrad, who swore he'd kill Johanna unless Jeff left Paris in twenty-four hours; Conrad was powerful enough in Paris in those days to do it and to get away with it, and there was no doubt that he meant it. So Jeff fled. But Conrad did it anyway. *He killed her anyway!* Jeff's anguish raced through his pulse as he held Antonia's hand. *This.* This was the thing he could not tell her.

"You're crying," Antonia said. She took his hand and gently kissed it.

They were sitting in the Grill Room of the Four Seasons. People had stared at them as they entered. Was she really that well recognized, he wondered, or was it just that she was so beautiful? Either way, he was pleased to be in her company.

"When did you change your name?" he asked her.

"When Scavullo discovered me. The sound is right now. It's sexy. Does your secretary read *Vogue*?"

"I don't know. I'll ask her."

"I'm in it this month. Take a look."

"What are you modeling?"

"Fernando Sanchez underwear. Satin and lace teddies. One of them has garters, and I'm wearing real stockings . . . You're looking at me as though I were talking dirty."

"Aren't you?"

"Come to think of it," she said. They both laughed.

The waitress came by, and they ordered a round of vodka martinis.

He began to count the ways in which Toni played the seductress. He understood that he was playing with fire and loving it. His response was to seek the safety of remembering that he hadn't yet reached Cathy. It was after six. He excused himself and went downstairs to the telephone.

When he came back he had the self-assured look of a man who could rely on his grasp of diplomacy.

"Cathy didn't decide to break off the engagement?" Toni asked as he sat down.

"Not yet."

"You're very good looking," Toni said. "I can see why my mother—"

"I was a callow young man of twenty-six. Nothing more. I didn't even have a budding career in those days. Your mother on the other hand— Oh, God, do you remember her at all?"

15

"I remember her at bedtime. I remember her perfume. I remember the way her body felt . . ."

"Do you remember her voice?" he asked.

"Was it like mine?"

"No . . . Oh, you have a lovely voice, but Johanna's voice—can you imagine putting on a brand new shirt of the finest silk, feeling its cool touch against your body, and then being stuck by a pin left in it?"

"Yes." She smiled.

"Johanna's voice was like that. Silk, with a pin. It caressed and then pricked. It was very arousing."

"I want to hear more."

"Yes," he said. "There's much to tell."

"Why did you leave Paris, Jeff? Did you and Johanna quarrel?"

"No."

"Then why?"

"It's a long story."

"I want to hear it."

"Some day," he said. "How were you able to remember my name all of these years?"

"My mother made a painting of your name and taught me to read it. On a miniature canvas the size of a paperback book. It was one of our many secrets. I still have it."

They were sitting side by side on a banquette facing two empty chairs. Her handbag was in the chair opposite her. She leaned over to pick it up.

She quickly found what she wanted; her sunglasses, and a scarf that she began to wrap around her head. Jeff thought her hands were shaking.

"What are you doing?" he asked.

"There's someone here I don't want to be seen by. Maybe this will work."

"I'd hardly call that a disguise," Jeff said. "Why don't you just say hello and get it over with?"

She removed the dark glasses and stuffed the scarf back into her bag. She was pouting.

"Is it a man you're avoiding?"

"Yes."

"You lead a busy life."

"I don't lead," she corrected him. "I follow."

"That's a wonderful line," Jeff said.

"I think I'm amusing you. I *hate* that." She began to sulk. Jeff wondered what the evening was all about; he grew depressed. In the void he saw Johanna. Dead.

Toni stopped sulking. "Do you see that man over there who looks like a fat Paul Newman?" she asked.

"He's the one you're avoiding?"

"Yes."

Jeff saw him a few feet away coming in their direction. What kind of nonsense is this, he wanted to ask her, but she was starting to leave the table.

"Goodbye, Jeff," Toni said, sliding out of the banquette. She headed for the stairs leading to the lower lobby and out to Fifty-second Street.

The fat Paul Newman walked past Jeff and, without even glancing in Jeff's direction, moved into the arms of an attractive blonde woman who kissed him on the mouth very hard and for a long time.

Jeff arrived home feeling headachy and hungry. The vodka martinis made his legs feel heavy, or maybe it was depression. His evening had been ruined. He'd stood Cathy up, sent her off to cover the Neil Simon opening without him, and was left with some unresolved erotic fantasies about Johanna's daughter. He loosened his necktie and threw himself down on top of his bed. The phone rang. He knew who it was.

"Hi," he said.

"It's Toni."

"What took you so long?"

"I don't understand."

"One of the advantages of being older is you learn how to predict the future."

"Jeff, I don't know what you're talking about. Can I come over to your place?"

"I'm in bed."

"That's okay."

"You want to get into bed with me?"

"It's *okay*."

"Come on over," he said. "Do you know the address?"

"I got it out of the same wonderful book that has your phone number in it."

17

"Where are you?"

"About ten minutes away," she said and clicked off.

The shower revived him enough so he could feel his pain. *Conrad, you bastard! You killed her! You killed her anyway!* He banged his fists up against the wet tiles while the hot water fell over his body. *Conrad! Conrad!* He was weeping now. What difference did it make? No one could hear him. Oh, Johanna . . . sweet, sweet, incredibly sweet Johanna. God, it was so long ago. He'd been married and divorced since then. And there'd been many, many others. But only one Johanna. The bathroom was thick with steam. In the steam an obsession was forming. An obsession to find Conrad. To confront him. He had to purge his guilt. How could he marry Cathy before he purged his guilt for the death of Johanna . . .

Toni would be there any minute now. Better sober up as best he could. He shut down the hot water and turned up the cold. He stood under it, getting colder, feeling his body revive. He forced himself to stay there as long as he could. He vaguely remembered stories about Nazis torturing people in tubs of ice. Torture, revenge, even death . . . could be aphrodisiacs. Did she really want to go to bed with him? Could he add the guilt of screwing her to his long list of other guilt? What was it she said? In my world a compliment is when some stranger at a party whispers in my ear how much he'd like to fuck me? He took the washcloth and applied it roughly to his groin. God, he was still drunk from those goddamn martinis and no dinner and from the news of Johanna's death. *Conrad!* He beat his fists against the tiles again. *Conrad, I'll get you for this, I swear.* Is that the doorbell? He turned off the water abruptly and listened. No. Not yet. He got out of the tub and began to dry himself.

The phone was ringing again. This time it was Cathy.

She was calling from the theater. He could hear the din of intermission in the background.

"You have an angel's voice," he told her.

"Only when I'm talking to you. Otherwise I sound like an imitation Barbara Walters. That's what they're trying to turn me into. And God knows that's no angel's voice. How are you, my darling? I missed you all through Act One."

"I'm lousy, lecherous, dishonest, and guilty of vile thoughts."

18

"I hope the lecherous and maybe the vile thoughts have something to do with me."

"I'd be a liar if I said they did."

"In that case I'm coming right over. Screw the Neil Simon play."

"Aren't you covering it for tomorrow's show?"

"I can do it without seeing the second act. Have you eaten?"

"No. I've had three vodka martinis and a shower."

"I'll be there in twenty minutes."

"So will Toni Menard. Ever hear of her?"

"The face of the year. One of her press agents has been trying hard to get me to interview her on my show. How'd she find *you*?"

"Well, I'm her second choice. We only got as far as drinks, but we did start to have dinner together tonight. What I told you when I stood you up was a crock. Do you recall my maudlin tales about Johanna?"

"Yes."

"Toni is Johanna's daughter."

"Oh." Cathy took a deep breath. "For God's sake."

"Will you be mad if I screw her?"

"How the hell modern do you think I am? I'm almost as old as you are." He could hear the control in her voice.

"I've got to go to Paris to find her father," he told Cathy.

"Jeff, what the hell are you talking about?"

"I'm going to—"

"I'm coming over," she said.

He stood at the phone naked, disoriented. God, it was nearly an hour since his last drink, and he was *drunker*.

"Cathy? You still there?"

"Yes."

"Cathy, please," he pleaded. "Don't come over."

"What *is* it, Jeff?" She sounded frightened.

"Nothing . . . Just . . . Okay?"

"Okay."

He heard a disconnect and then a dial tone. Cathy had hung up.

He put the phone back in its cradle, went to the closet, and put on a long terrycloth robe. In his head he saw Johanna. He felt her spectral touch.

The doorbell rang and announced the second arrival in his life that day of Toni Menard.

* * *

He sobered up the moment he saw her.

He felt charged by adrenalin and terribly shy all at once. He didn't quite have his balance as he ushered her in.

"I spoiled your dinner plans," she said. "But I brought you something nice." She followed him into the living room, opening her shoulder bag as they went, taking out a small round package, which she handed to him.

"Don't be fooled by the humble wrapping," she said. "It set me back forty bucks."

"It's got to be caviar."

"I hate sophisticated men," she said. "You can't ever surprise them."

"You've more than surprised me. You've swept me off my feet."

"So soon?" Her voice challenged him in a way that made his whole body tingle. She glanced around the room, at his books, his primitive American paintings, the old oak tables and Oriental rugs, then fitted herself into a corner of his sofa. "You're a man of taste," she said.

"Thank you. Can I get you something? A drink?"

"No. Come sit next to me. You're beautiful in that robe."

"You know," he said, sitting beside her, smiling broadly, feeling positively on the verge of giddiness, "you appeal to every puerile fantasy in my brain. You also smoke too much."

"Do you worry about things like cancer?" she asked.

"Sure I do. Tell me, who's this fat Paul Newman?"

"One of Conrad's spies," she said.

"Your father has people following you around?"

"Only this one nowadays. He goes wherever I go. It's become a joke between us."

"If he's such a familiar part of your life, why were you so frantic to avoid him?"

"I didn't want to involve *you*, Jeff."

"But he'd already seen me. And if he follows you everywhere, he probably knew you'd been to my office."

"He doesn't follow me *everywhere*. I do elude him from time to time. I don't think he knew I'd been to your office. Listen, you know what? I'd love a scotch after all."

20

He went into the kitchen for some ice and then to the refectory table that served as his bar.

"Cheers," he said, handing her her drink. He sat next to her.

"Aren't you having one?"

"No."

"Cheers then," she said. She raised her glass and peered at him over the rim of it.

"Your eyes are trying to tell me something," he said.

She lowered the glass. "Perhaps."

"Can you put it into words?"

"There's something I'd like to make you understand. I was three years old when you came along and took my mother away from me. Only three . . . Don't you think I'm entitled to know something *more*?"

"I didn't take her away."

"You really did. In those last weeks she belonged more to you than to anyone. You were the closest one to her. After the accident, Conrad refused to talk to me at all. You're my only link to her. You've got to bring Johanna back to me now by telling me everything. That's your penance."

"My *penance!*" Jeff shouted. His head was bursting with things he dared not tell her. *Jesus!* he thought. *Conrad killed your mother! That knowledge is my penance! That secret! Be careful, Antonia, or I'll share that secret with you one day! One day, after I've killed your father!*

He bolted from the sofa and went to fix himself a scotch. When he came back she was stretched out, lying on her side. She hadn't bothered to remove her shoes.

"Very pretty," he said. "When did you first start modeling?"

"I was sixteen. Conrad introduced me to Avedon."

"I thought you said Scavullo discovered you."

"Yes. Avedon photographed me. But Scavullo discovered me. Avedon was not impressed; he said I looked like a rancid child. Scavullo saw the same quality, but he liked it. He heightened it. He turned it into something very erotic. He never photographed my body. Just my face."

The room was in darkness except for one small lamp that cast a warm glow over her. Jeff looked at her, transfixed. She could have been posing for an erotic photograph even now; her cigarette smoke forming pink lamp-lit clouds that wafted above her, her surprisingly full breasts pushing against the thin silk of her man-tailored shirt, the curve of her hip long and high, the dark stockings, accentuating her legs, her face framed by rich brown hair. He saw what Avedon and Scavullo had seen. Every sensual message a woman could convey was in that mouth and those eyes. But his imagination shifted its focus. He wondered what her body was like.

He sipped his scotch and stood staring at her. He felt a bit dizzy. The feelings that flooded through him were intense and contradictory. He'd never really recovered from the loss of Johanna, but he had always believed he'd lost her to time and circumstance. It had never occurred to him that she could be dead. The fantasy that they would meet again had refused to die. He had confessed this to Cathy Hayes, and she understood it. It didn't seem too different to her from her own feelings after her divorce. But now there was the knowledge of Johanna's death for him to assimilate. And the need for revenge. It made his heart beat faster just to think about it. No wonder he felt dizzy. Staring at Johanna's daughter, he felt caught up in a pornographic moment, as though she had come there to be an object for his arousal. Something in the moment began to go against the grain of who he was or how he'd lived his life until then. He was a lover of women, not a user. He felt weak and clammy.

He shouldn't have had that scotch; it was too much for him after the martinis he'd had earlier, all on an empty stomach.

"Excuse me," he said.

He went into the bathroom, where he ran the cold water in the sink. He grabbed a washcloth from the rack in the shower, made a compress, and held it to his head, all the while looking at himself in the mirror. He looked different from the man he'd seen there this morning. This morning he'd seen a self-assured image, a man whose life was moving toward stability, a soon-to-be-married man. His reckless years were over now. This morning he had been glad of it. This morning . . . seemed light years away.

He knew it wasn't the alcohol that was making him ill. It was the shock of suddenly feeling out of place. That was really it. This morning his life had been in place, and now it *wasn't*.

Cathy had given his life a sense of necessity. Yes . . . necessity was exactly the right word. The trust between them was a necessary trust; it was part of their knowledge of each other. If he broke the trust, then that knowledge would become false.

The compress made him feel better. He removed it and dried his fore-

22

head. He opened the medicine cabinet and found a comb, which he ran through his hair. Not Redford. But better than before.

"Forgive me," he said when he returned to her. She was exactly as he'd left her. Her cigarette, which had burned down, had been replaced with a new one.

"You look better," she said. "Do you feel better?"

"I'm fine," he said.

She took his hand and brushed it lightly across her lips. She put his hand against her cheek and closed her eyes and slowly rocked her head from side to side. The dam burst in him, and all of his feelings came rushing to the surface. Sorrow and tenderness and lust got to him all at once. It was a potent mixture. He was aware of tension in every fiber of his body. Wanting her. Toni . . . Johanna.

But he held onto his connection with thought. It was her smile he needed to think about, the smile of a child applauding her own magic.

He touched her shoulder, then moved away from her, whispering, "Wait . . ."

Wait. The word echoed in his head. Did it mean there were possibilities in this situation? Possibilities for further betrayal? Would he make love to her?

Not now . . . Not tonight. That's what *wait* meant. But at some future time? No, he thought.

No, Toni.

No.

Chapter Two

The first night audience rose in an ovation for the new play, assured that it had borne witness to another Neil Simon hit. Although famous faces from the worlds of theater, television, fashion, and politics were everywhere in this glittering crowd, the face that had captured more surreptitious glances than any other belonged to a woman in a front box, seated next to a teenage boy. She was not a celebrity. But she had a presence that suggested, if not the stage, the platform of an eccentric teacher. There was something about her, some unmistakable aura of someone used to captivating an audience. She was, perhaps, forty. Her hair piled high added to her look of blowsy glamor. She was wearing an intricately designed floral caftan that was every bit as charismatic as she herself appeared to be. She went by the name of Sister Love. She was an evangelical minister on holiday.

During intermission she had scribbled a note to Cathy Hayes, whom the boy had pointed out to her. As the play concluded, Sister Love had handed the note to the boy, asking him to deliver it. Now, during the repeated curtain calls and while the audience was thunderously applauding, the woman left the box, quickly going down the short flight of stairs and then toward the exit. A chauffeur-driven limousine, hired for the night, waited for her at the curb.

Cathy Hayes, who had lost the battle against inner panic during Act Two, regained her calm as she joined the chic recessional moving up the center aisle of the orchestra. She had filled the seat next to her, the seat meant to have been Jeff's, with a six-foot-four television news researcher who happened to have been standing near her desk when Jeff called to break their date. The surprised young man had wanted to go home and change out of his brown turtleneck and Harris tweed jacket into something more elegant but Cathy said no, come as you are. She didn't want them to look like a couple. In a dark suit he'd be sufficiently dashing to generate some of that older-woman-younger-stud gossip. But dressed as he was, he'd lend credence to the simple truth. Jesus, the dumb details one had to be concerned with in this business, in this town. Yet these were the nuances that reminded her, whenever she needed reminding, that she was a success. Or, at least, on the way.

"How'd you like the play?" her unexpected escort asked.

"Oh, I liked it a lot. And you?"

"You seemed nervous," he told her, ignoring her question.

"You noticed that?"

"Uh huh."

"I was nervous."

"Funny. I thought *I* was going to be nervous. I've never been to an opening before. And I certainly never expected to be going to one with *you*."

They were making their way up the aisle. She thought he had a rather loud voice; something to do with his size maybe. He was making her self-conscious.

"It's a family problem I was nervous about," she confided, trying to whisper, hoping he'd do the same.

"Oh." He picked up the whisper. He lowered his voice and bent over her in a manner that seemed conspiratorial. "Your ex-husband?"

It was one of those questions that gets heard in a crowd, in any crowd, but especially in this one. Most of the conversation around them slowed down momentarily. She was surrounded by people who knew her, people she knew casually. They nodded; she nodded. Or they smiled, and she smiled. But there was no one there, at least no one she'd spotted, who would shelter her.

The evening had hardly begun. Next there was the party. Should she take her tall young man with her to the party? Or should she just quietly ditch him somewhere along Forty-fourth Street? Or should she forget the

26

party and go home and stay awake all night worrying about Jeff? Every time his name came into her consciousness she felt the panic again. Just the thought of his name caused her to fear losing him. All right! So I'll lose him. She looked at her watch.

"I'm going to have to get to the phone again," she told the tall young man.

"It's downstairs in the lounge," he confided.

"I know. I've been there."

There's Gene Shalit. Smile. Joan Mondale. Smile. Henry Fonda. Nod.

The lounge was empty. There was no line outside the phone booth this time. "I'll just be a minute," she said. The young man was sensitive enough to understand that he was being asked to retreat to a place from which he would be unable to overhear her.

Sitting in the phone booth, Cathy felt like a fool. Of course she couldn't call him. He was with Toni. It all seemed bizarre. But there could be no misunderstanding about what Jeff had told her. She lifted the receiver off the hook, put it to her ear, and dropped a coin into the box. She decided to call her housekeeper and check on the kids; it wasn't too late to do that. But before she dialed she tried to make up her mind about the party. Either she'd be home in fifteen minutes or wasn't to be expected until three in the morning. She began to dial, still not knowing what she'd say.

The young man was studying an old lithograph depicting the opening speech of King Lear when he sensed that he was being watched from across the lounge. He turned his head and saw a handsome boy of about sixteen wearing tight blue jeans and a brown velvet jacket. Blond, muscular, and probably gay; there was something unmistakable about the body language. The boy smiled and approached the young man.

"Hi," the blond boy said.

"Hello."

"You're waiting for Cathy Hayes?"

"Yes."

"Well, so am I actually," the blond boy said. "Do you mind giving her this?" He handed the young man a small, gray envelope on which Cathy's name appeared, written in brown ink. Then the blond boy walked back across the lounge and up the stairs. When Cathy returned,

27

her patient young man had moved from studying the print of *King Lear* to the next one, which was *Twelfth Night*.

"Want to come to a party?" she asked him.

"Are you kidding? Of course I do. God. New York; what a city."

"Where are you from?"

"Oklahoma City. From there to Montreal. I went to McGill."

"Yes," she agreed. "What a city. Come, I'll take you to the kind of party you've read about in gossip columns."

She took his arm and led him up the stairs. In his excitement he forgot to give her the envelope, which he'd tucked into the pocket of his Harris tweed jacket.

It had taken Jeff until now to recover, to regain confidence in his own stability, to be able to rely once more on his self-esteem. Until he had led Toni from the sofa to the table on which they were eating an improvised supper—he had endowed two omelettes with the caviar she'd brought—he could not be certain that he wouldn't spend the night in bed with her. Logic and reason, those familiar presences in his professional life, were of little use in his attempt to assuage the erotic anxiety that attacked the pulse of his conscience. But by the time they got to their coffee, his resistance regained its fortitude; he was able to reassure himself that his life would still be intact in the morning.

"Do you want to hear something funny?" Toni asked him.

He nodded that he did.

"For the first time today in over a month my horoscope was wrong."

"Oh."

"You probably don't believe in horoscopes."

"I don't know much about them."

"Some very handsome man—that part of it came true—was supposed to find me irresistibly attractive."

"You are very attractive, Toni. Beautiful."

"Thank you," she said softly.

"Do you really need my reassurance of that?"

"Johanna's a hard act to follow."

Oh, God, it was happening to him again. That terrible sense of *déjà vu.* That sinking feeling in his stomach. That sense of disorientation.

28

When he returned from Paris all those years ago he had known that his basic trust in life was gone, along with his romantic innocence. Certainty was gone, too. So was clarity. Everything he needed to sustain him was stuck back there. In the past. That was the beginning of his obsession.

"I can bring Johanna back to you, Jeff," Toni said. "Just as you can bring Johanna back to me. Isn't that what we both want?"

"Yes," he said.

"Jeff . . ." She reached out for his hand.

"Toni, I'm not sure what it is I want just now."

She took a deep breath and forced a smile. "That's okay."

The telephone rang and startled them both. He thought it was Cathy. He got to it on the second ring and was relieved that it wasn't.

He turned toward Toni. "It's for you," he said.

She took the call without any expression of surprise; she'd been expecting it. Jeff watched her; smiling as she said *hello,* animated as she said *yes, yes, okay,* pouting over a long-drawn-out *well maybe,* and finally impatient when she came to *ciao, ciao, yes, darling, goodbye.*

"Forgive me," she said to Jeff afterward. "I hope you don't mind. I gave out your number."

"It's in the book."

"It all has to do with my next assignment. You know the French magazine *Elle,* of course. Well, they're doing a spread called "Streetwalking," a fashion layout, naturally. We've done the New York shooting. Next we go to Paris and Lisbon."

"Was that your agent?"

"No. A friend of Conrad's, actually. He makes arrangements for me. Ned Longworth; you may have heard of him."

"Of course I've heard of Ned Longworth. That was Ned Longworth?"

"Yes."

He scratched his head and thought for a moment. "He moves in pretty elevated circles. Wives of former presidents for clients. He's also a damn good lawyer."

"I'll bet you're better."

She returned to the table. She didn't sit down; she wanted another sip of coffee. She drained the cup and looked at her watch.

"I'd better be going," she said.

"I'll go down with you. Get you a cab."

29

"I have to be in Paris sooner than I'd expected. Do you want to come?"

"What do you mean?"

Her eyes smiled at him. "I mean that would be the best way for you to tell me about Johanna."

"When do you leave?"

"Ned said the ten o'clock flight Wednesday morning."

"That would give me Tuesday to clear my desk. *If* I went with you. Tell me, would I recognize Paris after sixteen years?"

"Oh yes. The changes are startling. But you'd recognize Paris."

"Will you take me to Conrad?"

"I don't have to take you. Conrad's easy to find. Will you come?"

There it was. The turning point. He knew all evening that it was approaching.

There was a paradox about choices; something he had observed time and time again in his law practice. The more choices are delayed by thinking, the more they finally seem to be made by reflex.

"Yes," he said, "I'll come."

She stopped moving. Then she put her arms around him and pulled him to her. He felt her warm breasts against him and smelled the perfume on her neck. He kissed her. He loved the feeling of lust when it ached so softly, as it did now. He looked at her . . . the bearer of memories.

"You'll need a plane ticket," Toni said. "The flight may be booked solid, but Ned can do something. I'll ask him to take care of it."

Jeff gave her a puzzled look. "Ned Longworth also runs your errands?"

"He doesn't mind. Can you stay more than a few days?" she asked.

"I don't think so."

"What will you tell Cathy?"

"The truth."

"Does the truth include me?"

"The truth includes Johanna. Cathy is willing to grant me Johanna."

"Of course," Toni said. "That's easy. Johanna's dead."

"I'm going to marry Cathy. Do you understand that?"

"Yes," Toni said.

As they rode down in the elevator, he thought about the accidental

30

nature of most love affairs. And he fought the impulse to hold her in his arms once more.

The opening night party to which Cathy Hayes had brought the young man in the Harris tweed jacket was in full swing in a duplex penthouse apartment on Central Park South. It had been a perfect June day, and the weather had remained good throughout the evening. A three piece combo had settled itself into one corner of the huge terrace, where movie stars and politicians were now dancing with Broadway actresses and television personalities. Every now and then the young man, whose name was Max McClintock, would put his hand into his pocket and feel the envelope he had been asked to deliver to Cathy. But she'd either be on the dance floor or he'd be too busy asking whether that was really Mike Nichols over there or who was that Farrah Fawcett-looking blonde. So the envelope remained where he'd put it. Max was too shy to ask anyone to dance with him, and he'd twice refused Cathy. But he enjoyed going to the bar, and although he was pretty good about handling liquor, he was well on his way to getting drunk.

The combo had shifted, a few minutes ago, into a more conservative set and was now playing a fox-trot. Cathy was dancing with Ned Longworth. He had been at the theater earlier in the evening with Betty Ford, but she hadn't been able to come along to the party. So after escorting her back to her hotel Ned had come on by himself, had spotted Cathy, whom he recognized from Channel Seven News, and introduced himself.

"You're a very good dancer," Cathy told him. "You must dance a lot."

"What's the lyric that rhymes 'dance a lot' with 'Lancelot'?"

"Oh," Cathy said, "now I'm going to be tortured all night trying to remember."

"I hope not," he said. "I'd hate to be the cause of your having a bad night."

"Are you in the theater?"

"No; I'm a lawyer. I have clients in the theater. And elsewhere." He laughed.

He was a suave, good-looking, still-athletic man of middle age. There was a great strength to his body, of which Cathy was aware. She had called him a good dancer, but she was changing her mind about that now.

31

There was no suppleness to his movements, no sensuous grace, no soft-ness. Just skill and determination, and a self-assurance that came from years of practice.

"You're a strikingly original woman," Ned Longworth was saying to her.

She considered his compliment and dismissed it as slick. She nodded politely and began looking forward to the end of the fox-trot.

"Really," he continued, "I'm a fan of Channel Seven News. They're right in comparing you to Barbara Walters."

"Thank you," she said.

"I usually watch it in my office with a bourbon in one hand. Has it ever occurred to you that at half-past five half of your viewers are on their way to their first drink?"

"While the other half are preparing dinner. I get the feeling you're not a family man."

"I used to be. Divorced. The usual story."

"You called me an original woman. What do you mean?" Oh, God, she was doing it, her old Smith College frontal attack. She thought she'd given that up.

"I mean at a time when so many women are struggling to adopt male attitudes, you're not afraid to deal with important issues from your own unique perspective. You come on as a woman, an intelligent woman, reporting and responding to the news. That's why I watch. It's a fresh perspective you bring me. I happen to love it."

He's feeding me a line, she thought, but that doesn't mean I can't enjoy it. The music stopped, and they walked to the edge of the terrace and leaned on the railing together, looking north across Central Park.

"You must represent a lot of original women," she said.

"Each totally different."

"You're an extremely fortunate man," Cathy said.

"Yes, I think I am."

"So many men, I suspect, think originality, like great beauty, is bound to become destructive in a woman," Cathy said.

"Yes," he replied, turning his head to take in the view of the night-dappled city, "I know what you mean. But, you know"—and he paused—"destructiveness can be a strong aphrodisiac."

"An aphrodisiac for whom?" she asked. "The destroyer or the victim?"

32

"For both," Ned Longworth said. "That's what's so interesting."

Why is everyone in New York so full of interesting things to say at two in the morning, Cathy wondered, suddenly exhausted. I just don't think I can cope with one more interesting thing before getting some sleep. The three musicians began another fox-trot at that moment.

"Dance with me, and I'll explain," Ned Longworth said.

"Thank you, but I really should go home. I came on the arm of a young man. I'd better go find him."

"If your young man is the one I think he is, he disappeared through those French doors only half a minute ago. Is he the Harris tweed?"

"Yes."

"Well, he's gone to relieve himself. Which gives me another few minutes of your company."

"You were telling me about destructiveness."

"Was I? Oh well. There's a lot of that in this world, that's for sure."

"I somehow had the feeling you were going to say something with a little more depth."

"I like you, Cathy. Would you have dinner with me sometime?"

"Between my television show, two children, and a new marriage about to happen, I don't see how I'd have an evening free. But if I ever need a lawyer who can dance . . ." She smiled.

"Think of me. By the way, have the public-relations people for Toni Menard been badgering you about getting her an interview on your show? She's a client of mine."

Cathy's pulse was racing again. The anxiety she had conquered earlier in the evening had returned in one terrible eruption. Oh, Jeff, you didn't climb into bed with her, please . . . She felt chilled and a bit weak. She really had to leave now.

"Toni'd make a good interview," Ned Longworth said.

"What?" Cathy's focus was elsewhere. What was he talking about?

"Toni Menard."

"Oh, yes. Well, I'm seriously thinking about it. I haven't had anyone from the fashion world for quite a while. It could be interesting."

"*Newsweek* is doing a piece on her."

"I'll try to schedule her."

"It would be excellent timing."

"Listen," Cathy pleaded, "I'm really beat. I think I'm going to leave.

The young man I came with works at Channel Seven. If you should see him again, would you tell him I said goodnight? I enjoyed meeting you, Ned."

Then she realized that there were a hundred people on that terrace to whom she had to say goodnight. What was she thinking? She couldn't just make a beeline for the French doors and go through the living room to the foyer and into the elevator, which was the path she already imagined herself moving along. No. Deep breath. Reasonable smile. Now . . . First the playwright . . .

Finally, the host and hostess. When at last she could leave, she figured out that it had taken twenty minutes. But still no sign of her escort.

She got onto the elevator with several of the guests. They fussed over her and saw her into a taxi. Leaning back in the foul-smelling cab, she rolled down a window, felt momentarily on the verge of tears, and recovered her courage.

Max McClintock was still sick when he woke up Tuesday morning in his cluttered Morningside Heights apartment. The garbage trucks on West 113th Street between Broadway and Amsterdam were no noisier than usual this morning, but they seemed to Max to be part of a conspiracy to make his head ache harder. Oh, well, he thought between groans and bouts of nausea, at least they're picking up all that shit out there instead of letting it rot one more day. Jesus, what did I do to deserve this hangover?

He looked at the clock, aware that he'd never make it into the office on time this morning. Maybe he wouldn't make it in at all. Not the way he felt now.

It had been such a nice evening. And he hadn't really had that much to drink, he thought. So nice of Cathy Hayes to have asked me. Hope she got home all right.

Then he remembered his embarrassment, getting sick all over the bathroom floor, desperately trying to clean up the bathroom rug afterward, feeling dizzy and nauseated every time he looked down. God, he must have been in that bathroom until half past three. When they finally helped him out of there, the place was empty except for the host and hostess and some hired help. They offered him a room to sleep in. But he preferred getting home. As sick as he was, he enjoyed the ride through the park at that hour. As sick as he was, he knew that New York was still a magic place and he was glad to be living in it.

Try to get some more sleep. Those damn garbage trucks. Try . . .

At ten o'clock he awoke suddenly. He went to the phone and called his office. He called in sick. He *was* sick. It was more than a hangover. It felt like flu. He took his temperature.

Lying back with the thermometer in his mouth, he remembered the envelope still in his pocket, addressed to Cathy Hayes. Dammit, he thought. That's pretty irresponsible. Where was his jacket? Over there, on the chair in the corner, in a heap with his trousers, shirt, underwear, and socks. His clothes were probably a mess, he thought. He couldn't remember whether or not he had thrown up all over himself.

He looked at the thermometer. One hundred and two. What'd I tell you? It's no hangover. I knew it couldn't have been from drinking. I learned to drink at college.

One hundred and two! That's a lot of fever for an adult! Max McClintock was a true hypochondriac. He began to think he ought to be receiving medical attention, maybe even be hospitalized. Holy cow, it could be serious. He thought immediately of Legionnaire's Disease. He'd better call a friend. His best friend at the moment was Jeannie Christopher. He tried to remember her office number but couldn't. Where was his book . . .

He found his book. He found her number. He called her office and got her on the phone. There was panic in his voice. She said she'd get into a cab on her lunch break and come up there. He thanked her a dozen times. A dying man.

Before he fell back to sleep, he thought of the envelope. He had to remember to tell Jeannie Christopher to drop it off at Channel Seven News.

At one o'clock in the afternoon, Jeff rang the bell of Cathy's apartment. The harsh and irritating sound heralded a sadness that he felt first as tension around his mouth and then as a heavy weight in his chest. By the time Cathy came to the door, he was thoroughly depressed.

She looked lovely. He noticed immediately how the afternoon sun streaming into the room behind her lighted her pale auburn hair. She looked so right in the sunlight; he remembered making love to her in sunlight. Oh, Cathy . . .

"Hello," he said.

"Come in. I sent the housekeeper on a fool's errand so we could be alone. How are you?"

He stepped into the foyer, allowing her to close the door, and he awkwardly waited there to embrace her, wondering whether she would reject his gesture.

"Hey—" he said. He looked at her through his sadness, thinking that if she could see his sadness maybe she could forgive him for standing her up last night. It was a foolish thought that only depressed him further.

" 'Hey' ?" she asked. "You used to do a lot better than 'hey.' "

She gave him his opening. He took her in his arms. She didn't resist; she wanted him. She'd spent a desperate night thinking about him, throwing him out of her life and calling him back a hundred times. She kissed him long and hard, trying to read their future in the way he held her, in the way he breathed.

"Do you love me?" she asked him finally.

"Cathy, I do love you. I love you very much."

"Come. Let's go inside. Let's sit on the sofa. I'll get you a drink," she said.

He went into the living room. It was wonderfully cool there. The air conditioner was relatively quiet today, and its soft, steady hum seemed like an elegant sound in the white-and-blue room. He dropped onto the sofa like a wounded athlete, his long legs stuck straight out in front of him.

Cathy came in shortly with two glasses. She'd fixed him a scotch and water with exactly the right number of ice cubes.

"That looks good," he said.

She handed it to him.

"You sounded so frantic when you called me this morning," she said.

"I guess I was a bit frantic. I hope getting away from your office like this wasn't too disruptive."

"It was disruptive. But so what? Loving you is disruptive."

"Thank God you love me, Cathy."

"Jeff, what's this all about? What's happening?"

"I'm leaving for Paris for a few days," he said.

"Those things you were saying on the phone last night when I called you from the theater . . . you meant them all?"

36

"Yes. What I didn't tell you is that Johanna's dead. Cathy, Johanna's dead."

She searched for the appropriate response, the one he wanted, but she couldn't find it. She settled for "I'm sorry." It's sixteen years, she thought. Why is he still holding on after sixteen years?

"I killed her," he said in a dull voice.

"What are you talking about?"

"I was responsible for her death! Goddammit, Cathy, it's true. Or at least what I've got to find out is *whether* it's true. I've never told you the whole story. You know most of it. You know that Conrad threatened to kill her because of me. I tried to save her by going into an exile which for years I could hardly tolerate. I thought I'd die in my exile, without Johanna. I did that to save her life. But he killed her anyway!"

"Conrad killed Johanna? How do you know that?"

"She was hit by a car while walking with Conrad. It happened soon after I left Paris. Toni told me that. She believes it was an accident. But I know what happened. If it's true that Conrad arranged her death . . ." He stopped. Cathy was crying. *I'm sorry, Cathy, but it's my life you've bargained to share, and this is it, this is what it's really like right now. But there's still time for you. You can still get out.* He didn't say any of it. Instead he finished his sentence. "If it's true that Conrad arranged her death, I'm going to kill Conrad."

"Goodbye," Cathy whispered through her tears. "Goodbye."

"Goodbye? Do you mean that?"

"No . . . Of course I don't. But it's going to be goodbye anyway. It's going to happen." She moved very close to him and put her head on his chest, and she cried softly for a long time.

Then she stopped. She excused herself, went into the bathroom, and in a while came back with a dry face. She sat down next to him again.

"You know where the scotch is if you want another," she said.

"Do you want one?"

"No. Thank you. I've got to get back to my office."

"So do I. I've got time, though," he said.

"So do I."

"When did you tell them you'd be back?"

"After three," she said. "I thought we might make love."

He lifted her head and kissed her mouth. "I thought so too."

"Jeff," she said. "Are we about to lose each other?"

37

"No, Cathy, no. I promise you."

"Do you want to make love?"

"I do."

Afterward, when they lay drowsily in each other's arms, slowly drifting back to the realities of the afternoon, anticipating the children's return from school, thinking about the need to get back to their desks, aware that they were parting, Cathy remembered that she hadn't asked him the question. Did he sleep with Toni last night?

Did it still matter? Yes, dammit, it mattered a lot. Then another question occurred to her. Was Toni going to Paris with him? Or, more accurately, was he accompanying Toni?

She got out of bed, looking over at Jeff who was smiling at her. She went into the living room. Her head was too full of too many questions. But how could she not ask them?

Start with what you know, she told herself. All right. I know I love him. I know someone good when I see him. And I've more than seen him; he is good. Jeff is a good person. He's caught up in something beyond his control. Johanna! You must have been incredible! I hope your ghost isn't more powerful than I am.

She looked at her watch. It was ten past two. She'd better start getting dressed. She'd better urge Jeff to do the same.

There were too many questions, and whether he slept with Toni or not was, finally, not the most important of them. He's leaving tomorrow, she told herself. I won't see him again until after the past has grabbed him and he's survived it. I'm like Penelope waiting for her Ulysses. That sounds a bit grand, I know. But why deprive myself of grand emotions at a time like this? She smiled.

She went inside to tell him it was getting late.

Earlier that day, at a few minutes before noon, Jeannie Christopher had left her office at Fifty-third Street and Third Avenue and hailed a cab. She nervously got out her wallet and checked her cash. The drive up to 113th and Amsterdam was going to be expensive, and she had to have enough to get back. There wouldn't be time for the subway, not enough time to figure out where to change trains or how to cope with the Broadway line. She had to be back at her desk by one-thirty at the latest, and she didn't want to have to walk out on Max as soon as she got there. Poor guy was a nervous wreck. She knew how it felt to live alone and be sick. Don't worry, Max. Help is on the way. She stared out the window at the changing neighborhoods. Before long she was there.

The self-service elevator made her nervous, but she took it anyway, rather than run up five flights. She did some deep breathing and concentrated on anticipating the needs of her sick friend. She was sorry she hadn't brought him a flower. She wanted very much to walk in with a flower. When the elevator stopped at five, she thought of running down the stairs in search of a florist's shop. But she had no idea how far she'd have to wander, and her time was running out. Max needed her attention more than he needed a flower, she decided. She rang his bell.

At first there was no response. Then she heard Max weakly calling out, "Door's open. Come in."

She let herself in and adjusted the lock so no one else could enter. "Hi," she called out cheerily. She didn't see him. He wasn't in the living room.

The place was a mess. Not only was everything in disarray but everything smelled bad, including—when she finally found him in the bedroom—Max.

"Listen," Max said to her, "I think I need a doctor, but I don't know any."

"I have a doctor," she said. "A woman. She's in the Village. She sees men; she's an internist. She's really good."

"St. Luke's Hospital is just around the corner," he said.

"You'd have to wait for hours in the emergency room. I don't think that's such a hot idea. Would you like some tea?"

"Yeah," he said.

She brewed tea and put honey in it for him, and when he drank it he said he felt better. She found some cheese and crackers for herself; she hadn't stopped for lunch. Afterward, she took his temperature. It was still one hundred and two. He was out of aspirin, but she found some in her handbag. She decided to come back in the evening, and when she told him that, his face lit up. She said she'd sleep on the sofa. He felt terrific when he heard it; at least he wouldn't die alone. They decided to give the fever until tomorrow to break. If it didn't, she would take him to her doctor in the Village.

By the time Jeannie was ready to go back to her office, Max had fallen asleep. There was a pile of his clothes on a chair in one corner that had caught her eye earlier. The underwear she removed to the bathroom and dropped into a hamper. The jacket and trousers needed to be dry-cleaned.

39

She looked at her watch. She could probably find a dry cleaner on Broadway and take a cab from there. She rolled the Harris tweed jacket and the gray flannel slacks into a ball and put them under her arm. She noticed his billfold, card case, and keys on a nearby table, so she didn't stop to check the pockets. She left the apartment. In a shop on Broadway and 112th Street, a man named Gonzalez took the soiled garments from her with an agreeable smile, assuring her they'd be ready Friday. He gave her a ticket.

On her way back to the office, she began to think she should have checked the pockets anyway, just the way her father had always told her to when she was a kid running similar errands at home. She was sorry she hadn't done it. What if Max had written a poem on the back of an envelope while riding on the subway, or jotted down notes for a novel? She would never forgive herself if her carelessness was the cause of that kind of loss. She was starting to build up powerful feelings of guilt. She removed a small notepad from her coat pocket, eager to put it all down for her therapist.

Considerably crushed but still intact in a pocket of Max's tweed jacket was the envelope addressed to Cathy Hayes given to Max by the young stranger at the theater last night. It seemed for a moment, as Mr. Gonzalez picked up the jacket by both its shoulder pads and held it in front of him to examine the extent of its stains, that the envelope might be retrieved and perhaps finally delivered. But a customer came into the store just then, and Mr. Gonzalez dropped the jacket into a wire basket where it would remain until tomorrow, when it would be conveyed to a cleaning plant up in the Bronx.

Chapter Three

Ned Longworth had no difficulty getting Jeff onto the ten o'clock flight to Paris. The flight was booked solid; in fact, it was oversold. Nevertheless, Ned was assured that a First Class ticket would be waiting at the airport in the name of Jeffrey Winter. Magic.

It was all magic nowadays. Magic was Ned's reward for having worked from the time he was ten, for having lived his life as an American cliché. Poor boy. Big family. Mamma, Pappa, the kindly teacher who thought he'd make a good lawyer. The girl next door who married him young and worked as a secretary while he went to law school. Story book. Comic book. Bad movie. The most familiar of familiar chronicles. He'd lived it. He'd watched it. Seen "the wife" grow fat while his own muscle somehow refused to turn to flab. He'd watched all the others go nowhere while he went forward into opportunism, cynicism, political favor, and marginally criminal connections. They were all nice people, all of them, who made deals, who screwed their friends, who screwed around. They all had mothers and fathers and sisters and brothers. They all knew right from wrong; once. Once they were all virgins. Long ago. Until gray became their color; until their standards grayed out and their morality grayed over. So? So what else was new? Was he going to be a horse's ass and mourn the loss of innocence? He was still a nice guy at heart. Even his wife said so when she asked for the divorce. She was sure he'd be nice about the settlement, and he was nice. He had no enemies. Politicians came to him for legal representation, so did sports figures, publishers, ballet dancers, movie producers, photographers, pornographers, owners of discotheques, jewelers, and real estate developers. All of his clients were, like himself, people who'd recently made money. They all whored. He liked every last one of them.

Conrad Thornton had come to him for representation years ago. Ned and Conrad had become friends. Then, much later, Conrad came to him again, this time asking Ned to help Antonia. Ned said he'd give Toni all the help he could.

There was more to it than that. But he hated to dwell on that part. He refused to think about that part.

There was a knock at his door.

"Come in."

It was Jeannie Christopher.

"How's your friend?" Ned asked her.

"Oh, Max is all right. He's still got a fever, but he's all right. You men are all such babies. You're no different yourself when you're not feeling well."

"And how would you know that? You've never taken care of me."

"I've never slept on your living room sofa. But I've made your tea and fetched your Kleenex."

"Is it serious between you and this Max?"

"I'll bet nobody would believe that inflection if I were to repeat it. *Is it serious between you and this Max?* The answer is, I hope so. It isn't yet. But I'm really working on it. Thanks to your sexist tyranny, I met a really nice guy."

"Oh? I didn't know I had anything to do with it."

"Of course you knew. I told you. That evening about a month ago when you had me cancel my dental appointment because you insisted that I hand deliver the Toni Menard press kit to Channel Seven News? Do you remember that?"

"Vaguely."

"Your memory should be better than vague on that subject. Anyway, that was the night I met Max McClintock. I gave the press kit to him."

"You never told me that," Ned said. "You never told me you didn't give it to Cathy Hayes."

"I gave it to Max. He gave it to Cathy. I ran your errand. We all got what we wanted. I went out with Max that night. That was the beginning of what may turn out to be the nicest relationship I've ever had."

"No other secretary in town is provided with the opportunities to meet eligible men that I make available to you," Ned said in a voice that he thought suited the sexist tyrant she'd accused him of being. "Didn't you get terribly attached to Boris Shendler's page turner last year when I asked you to deliver Boris' New York Philharmonic contract?"

"Yes. I did."

"Is there a pattern that I should be seeing in all this? Does this occur every time I send you on an errand?"

"Yes," she said. "I fuck 'em all." She walked out of his office and slammed the door.

Ned shook his head and smiled broadly. He shouldn't have teased her that way. God, the world was so serious nowadays. It was getting harder and harder to make a joke. He buzzed her on the intercom.

"Yes?" She still sounded tense.

"Jeannie, I apologize. Can you come in here for a moment, please?"

The door opened, and she reappeared.

"Are the arrangements all made for Toni Menard in Paris?" he asked her.

"I guess so." She thought for a moment. "Am I forgetting something? Do I know what arrangements you're talking about?"

Then he became flustered. "Of course not," he said. "I beg your pardon, Jeannie."

He'd made all the arrangements himself. He'd taken care of everything himself. Just as Toni had insisted.

Toni didn't want to wait in the VIP lounge. She wanted to go to a bar on the mezzanine that was, she said, dark enough to hide in.

"Hide?" Jeff asked her.

"I want to burrow."

"Is a bar at Kennedy Airport a fit place to burrow?"

"I know that bar. I've burrowed there before, although never at this hour of the morning. Come with me."

He followed her up an escalator and across a short concourse and there it was; locked. It didn't open until noon.

43

They walked down a corridor bathed in sunlight that poured in through a glass wall, and settled for a fast-food counter.

There was no one there. They each took a stool. Toni smoked and hunched her shoulders.

"Are we burrowing?" Jeff asked her.

"I'll take you burrowing in Paris. It's really good there."

The counterman came for their order. Toni said she wanted tequila and tonic.

"Perrier," Jeff said. "With a straight Jack Daniels on the side."

The counterman grunted and showed them an expression that made clear his lack of appreciation of their jokes at this hour. They ordered coffee, and he moved away to get it.

"You haven't said a word about how I look," Toni complained.

"I've been meaning to. As a matter of fact if you'd waited another moment—"

"I'm sorry. That's something I have to learn."

She waited. But he said nothing, testing her patience.

"Well?" she asked, unable to contain herself any longer.

"You look smashing," he beamed. "Super. Gorgeous. A knockout. What more can I tell you?"

"That's enough. Thank you." She was struggling to untie the thin, black satin strings that were knotted together at her neck to prevent a feathered, bordeaux-colored cape from falling off her shoulders.

"Can I help you?" Jeff asked.

"Only if your fingernails are longer than mine."

He grinned.

"There. I've done it." She removed the cape and placed it on an adjacent stool.

"What is that cape anyway?" Jeff asked.

"Marabou. I modeled it in a Neiman-Marcus catalogue and then decided I couldn't live without it. I got it at a discount. It would cost you two grand. There's a longer version for three. Could you ever love anyone that much?"

"To spend three grand for a bunch of feathers? I must admit, I've never expressed my love in quite that way."

"But you're such a romantic man. Romantic men usually give extravagant gifts."

"Champagne and flowers. That's my speed. I used to bring Johanna

44

wildflowers in small bouquets. Once I brought her a ripe pomegranate because neither she nor I had ever eaten one. And because they were known as love apples."

The counterman put two coffee mugs down in front of them. Toni added cream and sugar. Jeff drank his black.

"Have you ever been in love?" Jeff asked her.

"Only with my career. With my father once. And with my mother's ghostly presence. Never with a reasonably eligible man. I'm still young, though."

"Yes, Toni." He laughed. "You're still young." He lifted his coffee mug. Out of the corner of his eye, he saw someone he thought he knew. Reflexively he turned around on his stool to stare. But it was too late. Whoever it was had already turned a corner. Jeff turned back to Toni. Then it came to him.

Should he say anything to her? He couldn't, of course, be absolutely certain, so why risk upsetting her. Yet something in his lawyer's brain insisted that he tell her, insisted that he watch her face carefully while he did.

"Toni," he said. He was afraid she might run off again.

"What is it, darling?" It was that high fashion "darling," that *Women's Wear Daily* endearment. She hadn't until now addressed him that way. He didn't mind it. He didn't like it either.

"Do you know who just went by? Who just walked down the corridor?"

"Who?" She didn't seem at all concerned.

"Your friend, the fat Paul Newman."

"Are you sure?"

"Yes."

"But, darling"—she began to be amused—"that really can't be. I assure you, it's just not possible."

"Okay." He decided not to press it.

He looked at his watch. "We'd better get going."

He asked the counterman for the check.

Their flight was uneventful. They drank champagne; they picked at their lunch; they slept.

Two hours away from Paris, everyone in the First Class cabin was startled by a shrill male voice calling her name. "Toni!"

45

She looked up and smiled broadly. "Streeter! I didn't know you were on this flight."

"To tell you the truth, darling, neither did I until a few minutes ago when I began to need the john. I wouldn't have found you were it not for the stress in my bladder. All the *pissoirs* in steerage—I'm flying steerage, darling—are occupied. So I bolted past the *mädchen in uniform* into first class, and here we are, united prematurely. Darling, I adore you, but I must pee before enduring further amenities."

"A member of your team?" Jeff asked, watching Streeter disappear into the lavatory.

"Streeter Cash is one of the top young fashion photographers in the world."

"Oh." It was somehow all he could muster.

Jeff put his head back against the small pillow the stewardess had brought him and closed his eyes. The afterglow of the champagne was still with him. He relaxed until, half awake, half dreaming, he let the images—undefined—come and go. Nothing concrete . . . just images. Then Streeter Cash was back, hovering over them like some giant bird, his long legs encased in skin-tight jeans, his torso puffed out by a quilted poplin vest adorned by cameras and light meters, which hung from his neck. His suntanned face was so well chiseled that his habit of gasping for air between sentences, which suggested imminent asphyxia, seemed to Jeff a mistake that should be corrected at once.

"Listen, darling," he said to Toni. "I'm going to be close to you on this trip, so behave. We're not only staying at the same hotel, but I've got the room next to yours. To be more accurate, you've got the suite, and I've got the broomcloset."

"Poor Streeter," Toni cooed.

"Well, you know, once upon a time, before that house became a hotel, my room and your suite were all one big apartment. Then they cut it up. Now you've got the penis, and I've got the foreskin, so to speak."

"Streeter," Toni said, "I'd like you to meet a friend of mine, Jeffrey Winter."

"Hodjadoo," Streeter sang out, bowing from the waist without extending his hand.

"Hodjadoo," Jeff repeated.

"Do you do civil liberties things?" Streeter asked him.

"What makes you think I'm a lawyer?"

"Oh, I can tell," Streeter said. "You know, I'm a very weird person.

46

And one of the things that's so weird about me is I can tell what other people do. Just by looking at them. Right, Toni?"

"Right. Really, Jeff, it's true. Wait'll you get to know him better. You'll see that it's really true. Is everything set for the shooting, Streeter?"

"Pretty nearly everything. I hope we have a clear day tomorrow. I want sunlight if we can get it. Get a good night's sleep. We start early. I'll slip a note under your door about where to meet us and when."

The thought of tomorrow made Jeff uneasy.

His heart began to race as they circled over Paris.

It was night. He pressed his face against the window and peered out in search of memories. The thrill of arrival was already attenuated by dread and confusion. Had he really come here to kill Conrad? To kill? How would *he* do that? He was sorry now that he hadn't planned his arrival for daylight. Perhaps in daylight the temptation to be deadly might have been more quickly tempered. He smiled at this wry thought.

They landed smoothly and after a while entered the terminal. Sixteen years ago he had come and gone by way of Orly. But Charles de Gaulle Airport was recognizable enough from all the movies he'd seen.

"Welcome to Paris," he heard in his head. But no one said it.

It didn't take long for Paris to grab him back. It happened as soon as they stepped into the taxi. The driver, who was barrel shaped and moustached, had his aging black poodle seated alongside him. Speaking very slowly, the driver told the dog in French that these handsome people were Americans who had come to Paris on their honeymoon.

As they sped toward the center of the city, Jeff lost all interest in comparing the Paris he remembered with the Paris of glass towers and modern roadways. The change had already begun to take place sixteen years ago. But it hadn't mattered to him then, and it wasn't going to make a difference to him now. As Toni had promised, Paris would still be recognizable. Sitting in the stuffy taxi, smelling the poodle, wondering whether lowering the window to let in some cool night air would outrage the driver, watching Citroëns and Peugeots and Renaults whiz by on their way to a traffic melee perhaps at the Place de la Concorde, he knew he was not a stranger.

Their hotel was on the Rue de l'Université, on the Left Bank. It was a small hotel, very old and, in an understated way, quite elegant. It was one of the places that Toni called home. Jeff had asked her in the taxi why she didn't maintain an apartment in Paris. It would be more economical, she readily admitted. But she liked the checking in and out along with other people who were doing the same thing. Also, someone else was always picking up the tab, and if someone else did not, she simply sent the tab to Conrad. So why shouldn't she live this way when she so much enjoyed it?

The concierge, the telephone operator, and the night porter erupted in greetings when they saw her. Their good cheer even spilled over in Jeff's direction. Jeff signed the register while they carried on their animated conversation. He heard Toni ask whether Streeter Cash had reached the hotel. He hadn't. Then Toni and the concierge moved one step closer to each other, bending forward to conspire. Their animated whispers would have projected into the far corners of a coliseum, so Jeff had no difficulty following the plot. Evidently the room that had been assigned to Jeff was on another floor. It was Toni's intention to switch Jeff's room with Streeter's. Now Jeff understood why she had made such an effort to elude Streeter at the airport. She hadn't wanted to share a cab with him; she had to get here first.

Ah . . . The concierge was smiling. It was done.

Jeff followed Toni and the porter into the tiny elevator, which took them to the second floor. Just a few steps down a narrow corridor they stopped. Toni entered her suite. Jeff entered his room. The porter brought their bags, gingerly accepted the tip Jeff handed him, coughed out *merci,* and left.

Jeff's room contained a single bed pushed sideways against a wall, a small armoire in front of the wall opposite it, a toilet and tub installed in a closet behind the head of the bed, and a small window at the foot. There were closed shutters on the window, which Jeff didn't bother to open. When he opened the armoire, its doors met the bed, filling up the center of the room. The room was immaculately clean and the few pieces of furniture were fine antiques, but there was no hope for charm in such a limited space.

Jeff unpacked. Then he went to tell Toni that Streeter got the better deal.

When she opened the door in the kimono made of paper-thin silk, her cigarette smoke floating around her like a seductive nimbus, its pungency mixing with her perfume's heavy scent, Jeff changed his mind. The better deal was not Streeter's; it was right here.

48

"Come in," she said.

She hadn't drawn the heavy draperies in her living room. Her suite, as Jeff's room, overlooked an inner courtyard.

"Nice," Jeff said, looking around.

"Would you like a drink?"

"Aren't you hungry?"

"Starved." Neither of them had done anything more than pick at their meals on the plane. She suggested the bistro in the basement of the hotel.

She went into the bedroom to get dressed. The impulse to follow her was stronger than his desire for supper. But he waited.

When they got downstairs to the candlelit, crypt-like room, they found an empty banquette in a corner. They were grateful to have it. They leaned back and ordered a carafe of red wine. At the far end of the room there was a piano being played by a very thin, elderly black woman who moaned ecstatically as she leaned over the keyboard. They looked at the menu and decided on the cassoulet. Then, apropos of nothing, she told him that Conrad was one of the richest men in the world.

"I know he's rich," Jeff said, "but aren't you exaggerating the extent of it?"

"No."

"Has Conrad discussed his affairs with you?"

"There's not much about Conrad I don't know," she said.

"Just how close to him *are* you?"

"You know," she said, looking softer and more beautiful, "I don't really understand that myself. I see him when I come to Paris. I speak to him from New York or Lisbon or wherever I am. But how close are we? I don't know. The problem is there's not too much about him I like any more. His friends are unsavory. His women are bad. He's—you know, he's not old, he's just a few years older than I imagine you are, Jeff. He's mad about power. I think power is his last defense . . ."

"Against what?"

"Dying. The thing we all fear. Still, I wish it could be taken away from him. I'd like to see him without it. Is that cruel?"

"Depends. Are women just as much attracted to him as ever?"

"He buys them."

"He was exceedingly handsome once. He must be still."

"I don't think I'd call him handsome."

"Oh, come on."

49

"I'd call *you* handsome."

The way she kissed him just then plunged him into turmoil.

The swift, soft placement of her warm mouth on his sent waves of pleasure through his body. He moved his mouth away, then brought it back again. Away. Back. Achingly. Tantalizingly. Piercingly excited. The withholding of tongues added a tension that was unbearable. Soon. Not yet. Soon. Now! Their tongues darted, thrust, entered, probed. Her eyes were closed. He closed his. Then violent images rushed across his darkened field of vision.

He approached his betrayal of Cathy as though he were etherized. He'd gone through the entire day without letting Toni near his emotions. He kept telling himself that Toni wasn't dangerous, that he could be close to her, make love to her, and walk away from her. It was what he wanted to believe.

"Take me upstairs," Toni whispered.

The violent images flickered away. In their place there came a flash of memory . . .

Shortly before he met Cathy he'd been teaching an evening course at N.Y.U. One night a student stayed after class to find out whether he was interested in going back to her place. He was. She undressed in a way he would always remember, pulling off her clothes with the quick innocence of a child heading for the bath. He hadn't been able to decide whether her candor was commendable or just careless; in any event, it was unexciting. But when he woke up next to her in the morning, she was uncovered and still asleep. And when he looked at her body in the bright, early light of day, he saw droplets of her own moisture clinging like dew to the curled ends of her pubic hair. It was an incredibly beautiful thing to see.

"Jeff?" Toni's entreaty was still unanswered.

"Yes," he said. "Yes, let's go up."

They left without eating.

In the elevator they clung to each other. The elevator lights were yellow. His lust felt embalmed.

In the suite she wanted too much to be a magician. But he didn't need her wonderful feats to tempt the blood to pump faster into his erection. He had to slow her down.

She was still partially clothed when he took her by the hand and led her to the bed. He undressed her. He lay down beside her and began to kiss her body.

50

When he entered her, she clung to him. To his surprise, she was uncertain about letting go, until he reassured her with his skillfully controlled strength and with his kisses. He never stopped kissing her all the while he moved inside her. He made no demands of her; she had only to receive his kisses. He was aware that a wild expectancy was building in her flesh.

But there was something else. Some other tension he didn't understand. Perhaps some fear . . . Whatever it was, it caused her to cry out, "Jeff, stay with me, stay, stay . . ." as she dug her fingernails into his back, into his buttocks.

Inhaling her breath, tasting her lips, stroking her, letting his eyes feast on glimpses of her dancing nakedness, he said he would stay with her. And when he said it, he felt the contractions of her orgasm and the rush of his semen into her.

Shortly after four, he was awakened by voices coming from across the inner court. A man and a woman. The man was gruff and American, the woman shrill and English. They sounded drunk and quite angry. They were fighting, but Jeff couldn't tell about what. The man kept calling her a bitch, and once he called her a son of a bitch. The woman always replied with the same phrase, "You're low, very low. Dirt is what you are." Again and again; a stuporous litany.

Then all at once, silence from across the court. Maybe the concierge had rapped at their door. Maybe they just tired of their disagreement. But Jeff was thoroughly and unpleasantly awake now. Images out of the past were washing over him. Images of Conrad and Johanna . . . Could he get back to sleep? He looked over at Toni, sleeping undisturbed. She'd heard nothing.

He remained awake until just before the sky lightened. He kept thinking, today was the day he would see Conrad.

Toni was up at seven. She wanted three hours to bathe, have breakfast, do her hair and make-up, dress, and be mentally set for the shooting. Streeter Cash, true to his word, had left a note under the door urging her to be ready to be picked up by ten o'clock.

Jeff stayed in bed until Toni emerged from the bathroom. He pulled on his trousers and started to sneak back next door where all of his things

51

were. He asked Toni to call room service. By the time he returned, having bathed, shaved, and dressed, breakfast was being set up in her living room.

He thought the croissants inferior to those he got at a French bakery in New York, but the coffee was remarkable and so was the pot of chocolate. Toni listened to him with amusement; her gastronomic demands, she said, were never at a peak at this hour. "My senses awaken at noon," she told him.

"Your sense of nervousness is plenty awake right now," he said.

"I'm always like this before an assignment. It's stage fright. You seem pretty tense yourself."

"It's stage fright of a different kind. I'm waiting for you to give me Conrad's address."

"I wrote it down for you." She handed him a small piece of paper that had come from a pad provided by the hotel. She had written an address on the Rue de Rivoli.

"You can walk from here," she said.

"I'll take a taxi. My legs feel like rubber."

He watched her get dressed. Watching her was more erotic than the revue at the Crazy Horse. He told her that.

"That's because you're a man of refinement," she replied.

"When will you be back?" he asked her.

"I don't know. If you get back before I do and you're impatient, wait for me in the bar in the basement."

He kissed her and said goodbye.

There was a taxi parked outside the hotel. He got in and read the address to the driver.

Getting out of the taxi, Jeff glanced across at the Tuileries Gardens, listened intently, and heard the sound—the large dissonant chord made up of the voices of children kicking soccer balls, roller skating, running. They'd spent one night at a hotel not far from here, he and Johanna, and when he awakened in the morning he heard that sound through the louvered window. It was winter then. He remembered the wonderful softness of the large bed, the goosedown quilt, the enormous pillows. He remembered the mirrored armoire they'd stood in front of, undressing each other. But most of all he remembered hearing the voices of children

52

that morning long ago as he awakened entangled in her limbs, hard and eager to push between the moist grasses at her groin, thirsting for her mouth, craving her breasts. He remembered those sharp, small voices lifting up on the winter day, cutting through the chilled air, sounding a counterpoint to his desire, awakening her smile, and bidding good morning to their need for pleasure.

"Monsieur!"

The driver was trying to get his attention, to give him his change. Jeff told him to keep it and got out of the cab.

He was standing in one of the arcades along the Rue de Rivoli where tacky souvenir shops alternated with expensive boutiques. He saw a doorway with a number corresponding to what was on the piece of paper. He'd never asked her whether it was a hotel or a house Conrad lived in. He'd somehow gotten the impression it was a hotel, and his expectation was of coming upon something small and expensive. But the hotel he entered was more modest than anything he might have associated with Conrad's style; it was the sort of hotel that catered to Europeans traveling on a budget. The lobby had a musty smell, and its furniture was most likely of late nineteen-forties vintage; seedy, with no redeeming charm. The concierge was a man of about sixty, of medium height and not terribly distinguished in any way but one: he would be recognized as French in any part of the world before he uttered a word. There was something unmistakable about his attitude, about the aloof bearing of his thin, bird-like body. At the moment, he was arguing with a middle-aged German couple who were insisting they'd been cheated on their bill. It was apparent to Jeff that however much the German couple might rage, they were not going to win this argument. Toni had told him that Conrad lived in apartment B on the top floor. He walked directly into the elevator; the concierge either hadn't noticed or chose not to be interrupted.

The top floor was six. The elevator ascended slowly. The pounding of Jeff's heart filled his throat, his ears. He had never fainted in his life, but he thought he might faint now. The elevator stopped. Jeff grabbed the brass handle of the inside gate and pulled it back. He pushed open the outer door and stepped off. There were two apartments. A and B. There was no name plate on either. He stopped in front of B.

There was no bell and no knocker. Jeff rapped with his knuckles. And waited. No one came to the door. The relief in his chest was sudden. His breathing began to return to normal. But he remembered Toni saying

53

every move of his would be watched and reported to Conrad. He had somehow assumed that Conrad was expecting him. Jeff knocked again. He was still knocking when the door began to open.

The man who stood there in a yellow bathrobe, ashen, slack-jawed, in need of a shave, his hair thin and gray, his eyes distorted by the thickest lenses Jeff had ever seen in a pair of frames, was plainly not Conrad. Jeff looked at the man's face and backed away, begging the man's pardon. *"Excusez-moi; pardonnez-moi; pardonne."* It was all some crazy mistake, some bizarre error of Toni's. She'd doubtless given him an old address; a place Conrad had once lived in. But why? And why hadn't the man in the bathrobe gone back inside and shut his door? Why was he still gazing out inquiringly after Jeff? The man had the terrible aspect of one of those frightening beggars who come at you out of some doorway with the piercing eyes and scary effect of a witch.

The elevator finally got back up to the sixth floor, and even as Jeff got onto it, sliding the inside gate into place, pressing the lobby button, he could see, could still feel the man staring at him. God, he hoped the sun was still shining. He needed the warmth of sunshine to rid him of the chill now sliding through his body. He wondered whether the concierge and the German couple would still be arguing, and of course they were. He walked past them for the second time without their noticing. He walked out into the Paris sunshine.

He found his way to the Quai de la Mégisserie and walked down the steps to the crowded embankment. He couldn't get rid of the chill, nor could he resolve his bewilderment. He saw a place to sit on a bench next to a young couple. But his mood was not the same as theirs. He wanted the sun, but this wasn't the place for him to be right now. He looked at his watch. It would be hours before Toni would get back.

He walked back up the steps and found a taxi. He decided to return to the hotel. He needed to lie down. He went to his room.

He was awakened by the sound of her voice.

He bolted up and called her name. But he realized that he was alone. Then he heard it. The same two voices that had awakened him in the middle of the night. The gruff American man and the shrill English woman, coming from across the courtyard. Toni was with them.

She had told him that except for Streeter Cash there was no one else she knew staying at the hotel. All the others who'd come to Paris for the shooting were staying elsewhere. He looked at his watch; it wasn't quite noon.

He went to the window, which he'd opened, and looked out. In the room across the courtyard, the shutters were flung back and the windows were wide open, but the light was peculiar and so was the angle; he could see nothing. He could only hear them. And now what he heard was Toni saying goodbye.

He went into the corridor and walked in the direction of the room she'd be coming out of. He waited. In a moment, smiling brightly, she was running into his arms.

It felt surreal. Like a ballet by Béjart. She led him in a *pas de deux*, back to her suite.

"Darling, I'm so glad to see you," she said. "Now you can buy me a fabulous lunch somewhere. The shooting was cancelled, after all my hard work this morning. Look at me. I'm dressed for a magazine layout, not for lunch. I'll change."

"The shooting was cancelled?"

"Postponed. Until tomorrow. Streeter's crew was delayed somewhere."

"I didn't know you had friends in the hotel."

"Neither did I until I was on my way out to meet Streeter. I bumped into them."

"Who are they?"

"Business acquaintances of Conrad's I haven't seen in years. Boring, boring people."

"Noisy, too. They woke me up at four this morning, screaming at each other."

"Oh, darling. No wonder you're so edgy. Did you see Conrad?"

"I'm edgy because you gave me the wrong address."

"No, darling, I didn't. That address is correct."

"Then Conrad has changed one hell of a lot." He described the man who came to the door.

"That was Conrad," Toni said.

"What?"

"We all change, Jeff."

"That man appeared to be over seventy."

"Conrad is aging badly," she said, lighting another cigarette from her endless chain.

"That's not the picture you painted of him last night," he snapped. His blood was boiling now.

55

"Perhaps I was remembering him as he used to be," Toni said.

"Listen to me," he shouted. "You're going back there with me. We're going back there together."

"I can't go with you. I've promised those awful people across the court that I'd meet them. I'm already late."

"Goddamn liar! You just got through asking me to take you to lunch!"

"I don't want to go with you, Jeff. I'll see you later."

He watched her leave. He didn't attempt to follow her. His head was throbbing. He went to the mirror and smoothed his hair. He adjusted his necktie. He put his jacket on, went downstairs and once again into a taxi, back to the same hotel in search of Conrad.

This time the concierge stopped him before he could reach the elevator.

"Monsieur Conrad Thornton," Jeff said, expecting the concierge to tell him there was no one in the hotel of that name.

Instead the concierge beamed broadly and explained that Monsieur Thornton had just a few minutes ago gone out.

"When will he be back?" Jeff asked in English. The concierge's English was more adequate than Jeff's French.

"With Monsieur Thornton one never knows," the concierge said.

Jeff still found it hard to believe that the man he'd seen earlier was really Conrad. "Tell me," he asked the concierge, "does Monsieur Thornton wear eyeglasses?"

"*Mais oui,*" the concierge explained. "Very thick ones. Monsieur Thornton is almost blind."

"*Quel age*—? How old would you say Monsieur Thornton is?"

"He told me his age once," the concierge said, "but I did not believe him. Yet, from the number of beautiful women who come and go, perhaps I should believe him. He told me he is forty-six."

Conviction settled in Jeff's brain like lead. It had to be Conrad. Forty-six was his age. But how was it possible? He thanked the concierge and walked out into the street as though he were entering a maze.

Aimlessly he walked. He found his way to the Ile de la Cité. He followed the tourists and the pull of his memory to the Cathedral of Notre Dame. That's where he'd first seen Johanna. That's where he wanted to be now.

56

Up the stairs. How many? Did it matter? He climbed upward in line behind a score of tourists, in search of the gargoyles.

"These are not the originals, you know." It was Johanna's voice, sixteen years ago. He could hear her now as clearly as he'd heard her then, that rich, resonant, theatrical voice that made him shiver in his first adoration.

"I thought they were," he had said.

"No. The originals went crashing to the ground one by one, or at least they started to. They got loose after six hundred years. These are the well-attached replacements. The originals were medieval, of course. But these aren't brand new; they were made in the nineteenth century."

He was perspiring now and out of breath. He was almost there; at the observation deck from which he'd see all of Paris. And the gargoyles. And he would hear her voice.

He stepped outside. The magnificent view thrilled him and buoyed his spirits. After his eyes had their fill, he stopped seeing.

He stared out over the city and remembered his first arrival.

Chapter Four

The wind rose up and blew the strands of her long blonde hair across his chest, into his mouth, and over his eyes. She was standing that close to him; her hair smelled of perfume and earth. She said, "Oh, I'm sorry," pulling her hair back. But in a moment the wind rose up a second time, and it happened again. Either it never occurred to her to move a few steps away or she simply chose not to do it. She was hypnotizing him into speechlessness.

They wore heavy coats; it was a cold day in January. But neither of them wore a hat. She liked his face and wanted to paint his portrait; she told him that in their first few minutes. He said very little. Her green eyes, her high cheekbones, her full lips, her mesmerizing voice, and something about her long, sensuous hands worked their way into an image that fevered his brain. Jeffrey Winter, at the still boyish age of twenty-six, was having a sexual epiphany on a terrace high up in the Cathedral of Notre Dame; smitten by love at first sight. She'd already told him her name was Johanna Thornton. He'd seen the wide gold wedding band on her finger. She was babbling on about her little girl. And the damn fool, two years out of law school, felt himself getting an erection.

"Listen," she said, "I've told you all I know about the gargoyles, and I'm really freezing now. I think we'd better go inside."

"Okay," he said.

"You're new in Paris," she said as they went down the stairs.

"I arrived this morning. And you?"

"I live here."

"Then you weren't up here sightseeing."

"No. I told you I paint. I needed to look at the view in this light. I would have made a sketch hadn't you come along."

"I was already there. It was you who came along."

"If you're going to insist on literalness, I'm going to leave you when we get to the bottom of the stairs."

"Honest," he said, "I'm not a stickler for fact. And I really could use a friend."

"Good. I want to introduce you to my husband and daughter, who are waiting in the nave. I *was* flirting with you, but I wasn't serious. We need an American friend just now. All of ours seem to have disappeared for the winter. Okay?"

"Okay."

He saw the child first; darker than her mother but unmistakably Johanna's daughter. Then the powerfully built man in blue corduroy and an army overcoat emerged from the shadows behind the child. He smiled at Jeff. He understood that Johanna had found him.

They went back in a Citroën to an apartment in the Opéra Quarter.

"We live in the shadow of the Ministry of Justice," Johanna said.

"Or between Chanel and Schiaparelli is another way of looking at it," Conrad added.

It was clear to Jeff from what he saw through the window of the speeding car that they were heading into one of the more fashionable sectors of the city. Which surprised him. He somehow thought they were poor.

The apartment seemed cramped, although there were at least six rooms. Antonia ran off to the room they called the nursery. There was a separate dining room and a small but comfortable living room. There was a master bedroom somewhere and a kitchen that he hadn't yet seen, and there turned out to be a guest room in addition, which they quite surprisingly offered to him rent free if his funds, which they correctly guessed were limited, should run out.

They drank brandy while he drank wine. It was four in the afternoon, and they insisted that he stay for dinner. They would all move into the kitchen shortly, Johanna explained, where Jeff and Conrad would keep her company while she cooked. Jeff felt warm and happy, and his spontaneous lust for Johanna had abated into something comfortable. All around him, on every wall, were her nudes and still-lifes, all in the same range of earth colors, so the flesh of the women and the flesh of the fruit were all one flesh; it added to the warmth of the room and the warmth of their company. He began to like Conrad.

"Where do you paint?" he asked Johanna.

"I have a studio. Elsewhere. Not far from here. I'll show it to you."

Jeff was looking at Conrad when she said that. Conrad's easy smile seemed suddenly frozen into place. And there were additional signs of tension around his eyes.

They were from Boston, although Johanna was originally from New York.

She had worked as an advertising copywriter in Manhattan while attending classes at the Art Students League at night. Conrad Thornton had a small agency of his own in Boston. He had advertised in the *New York Times* for a general assistant who could handle layout and write copy. The ad mentioned that the job could lead to a partnership. Johanna took the train up to Boston and stayed there. Eventually she would get Conrad to leave and try Paris.

They were piled into the Citroën, heading for the country. Conrad was driving. Johanna was in the front seat next to him with Antonia on her lap. Jeff was in the back seat with cartons of paint, paper bags full of food, some odd bits of clothing that had been tossed into the car at the last minute, and an assortment of playthings brought along for Antonia. They were going to Normandy for five days. All Jeff knew was that they were building a house. Literally, building it. With their own hands.

What they hadn't told him was that the house was merely an appendage to a seventeenth-century château they owned in the countryside between Évreux and Caen. The house was a studio for Johanna. It was the building of it that mattered. Johanna and Conrad, once they deposited Antonia with the two maids who lived on the estate, could literally turn their backs on their newly acquired affluence and proceed to the more basic labors of laying a floor and raising a roof.

Actually most of that was already done. The job at hand was painting, both inside and out. When Jeff realized that he'd been conscripted, he began to wonder whether the scheme behind their sudden and unexpected friendship hadn't been, from the beginning, to pick up cheap labor. He told them that, and they laughed. Even if he seriously suspected them of ulterior motives, Johanna's warm glances and sudden light touches on the back of his hand or on his shoulder would have dispelled any such notion.

Living with them was like moving into a seductive landscape where he knew none of the rules. Their life together was charged with an erotic energy that identified itself in the loud sounds of their lovemaking in the middle of the night, or in the way they worked at their chores half naked in the winter sun. The real foreign country Jeff had come to was the lives of the Thorntons. They exchanged lascivious glances, screamed American obscenities at each other, retreated into long silences, and reminisced about a time when they were as innocent as Jeff. He wondered whether these allusions to a loss of innocence had something to do with the way they made their money.

There was a road that wound in a nearly perfect circle around the château. There was a place along it where it joined two other roads, but one could stay on it and circle endlessly around the château. It was from this road that Jeff heard sounds that awakened him abruptly on the second morning of his stay there. He sat up in bed and listened to a voice that was unmistakably Conrad's shouting above the roar of engines and the clambering of two cars. Jeff went to the window and got a better idea of what was going on.

The Citroën, driven by Johanna, was obviously having some undiagnosed motor trouble. It was being pushed by a large American car that looked like a Buick. The driver of that car was Conrad. The idea was to get the Citroën's motor to turn over. *Merde! Don't brake! Just steer! You dumb cunt!*

From a dead halt in front of the château, the two cars would start moving again, the Buick pushing, the Citroën mercilessly pushed. *You fat prick! You're pushing too fast! Slow down. You can't push me on a dirt road at forty miles an hour! Jerk!*

But Johanna might just as well have been shouting at a wall. Conrad's blood was heating up. This was one more primal ceremony. He pushed her harder, harder, then he would brake and watch her roll to a halt. Then he'd come up from behind her and bump her and push her again. And they'd disappear around the bend. Jeff at the window watched and waited for the return and saw it all happen one more time. And it *was* really sexual. The car behind was fucking the car in front, very hard, and both drivers were getting excited. Then there was an explosion of voices.

Jeff leaned out the window and peered up the road. He saw that Johanna had braked suddenly, and Conrad, with no time to stop, had plowed right smack into her; the Buick and the Citroën had locked fenders. The front of the Buick and the back of the Citroën were meshed in a triangle that pointed up off the ground.

They came out of their cars shouting. They ran at each other with clenched fists, ready to pummel. They wrestled and fell to the ground. Finally they rolled over onto their backs laughing uncontrollably, two overheated beasts. Jeff had never seen anything quite like them before.

The next day he was sitting alone with Johanna on the hard winter ground in a field to the side of the château. They had some privacy there; Antonia was off in her room napping, and Conrad was down at the new construction painting walls. They were supposed to have been there painting, too. But they found an excuse, and they wandered off together.

"Do you have a girl friend?" she asked him.

"You've asked me that before."

"You ought to have a girl friend," she said.

"I would like to, but I think it's something I just have to let happen."

"I wish I could make love to you. Without making Conrad mad."

He stared at her. Her eyes were the most improbable green. Not as deep as emeralds, but he could only think of emeralds to compare them to; he had the good sense to keep it to himself. He knew she might laugh at him, because she was an artist and the job of an artist was to find new ways of comparing things and to disparage the old. He wondered whether she'd ever done a self-portrait. He asked her.

"Yes," she said. "Several."

"I'd like to see them. I'd like to see how you've rendered your eyes."

"Purple," she said. "My eyes are purple. In all of them."

For a split second, staring at her, he saw her eyes purple, and he smiled in sudden rapture, enchanted by the way she'd changed his perception.

"My breasts are vermilion, my belly green, my thighs—"

"Are velvet," he said.

"We're doing color, not texture." She laughed.

"Brown, then."

"My God, that's marvelous. You really understand that?"

"Well, yes, I think I do. Do I get to see the self-portraits?"

"Yes. They're in the studio in Paris. Conrad won't be too happy about my taking you there."

"Why?"

"Because of what you'll see there. As an artist I'm very involved with sex. I think about sex all of the time; it's what I want to paint. I haven't yet found out how to do it. Do you think about sex a lot?"

"When I'm with you I do."

"I'm very much in love with Conrad. You know that?"

"Yes."

"We're like two panthers in heat together. What I wish I could give you, Jeff, is some of that experience. I think it's as sublime as any spiritual message I know of. It's worth passing on. It's what I want to pass on in my paintings. Do you understand what I mean?"

"All I know is if you want to seduce me, I wish you'd do it and stop driving me crazy."

"That's vulgar!" She reddened; she was furious at him. He considered the possibility that she was going to strike him. "Dummy!" she screamed, "you *do* misunderstand; I knew you did."

"I'm sorry. I guess I do. I feel like a sixteen-year-old kid around you."

"You think love is nothing more than animal instinct."

"Who said that?"

"I believe you just did."

"No, no, no, no, goddamn it, no. Most of the pleasure we take in love is the work of the imagination. Even a dummy like me understands that."

"You *know* that? You *really* know that?" Her voice was a choked whisper; she knelt on the ground in front of him like Joan, the Maid of Orleans, acknowledging for the first time the messages of her angels. If she weren't so achingly beautiful, so passionately serious, so incongruously young beneath her earth goddess make-up, he might have been distracted by the melodrama. But he never for a moment perceived it as theatrical. He was touched by it; he understood that they were falling in love. He would have kissed her just then, lifted her tenderly from her kneeling position, held her in his arms lightly, and whispered in her ear that his flesh was on fire. But a noise from below the crest of the hill made that impossible. The noise was coming from Conrad.

64

"Aaaaaagh! Aaaaaagh!" Pale as a ghost, naked except for jockey shorts, a pair of army boots, and socks that rose up to his knees, Conrad came flailing up the hill, weaving unsteadily from side to side, his muscular arms outstretched, his eyes shut tight like Oedipus blinded, his firm alabaster thighs looking powder blue in the waning winter light, his barrel chest thrust forward. Seeing him this way, even the most stone-hearted stranger would have paused to ask from what disaster this anguished warrior was now returning.

"What happened? Conrad! What happened?" Johanna was on her feet, running toward him. Only a few steps behind, Jeff tried to imagine what accident Conrad might have been in. There was no bleeding. Just that incredible head-to-toe pallor.

"Oh, my God!" Johanna screamed.

With a considerable thud, Conrad had fallen into a dead faint onto the cold ground. A slain mammoth. Jeff noticed white paint splattered on Conrad's forehead, hands, and legs.

"There aren't any windows in that studio," he said to Johanna.

"No. Just a skylight."

"Paint fumes," Jeff said.

Conrad was showing signs of reviving.

"It's airless in there," Jeff said. "The ventilation system isn't in, and he probably had the front door closed. He was overcome by paint fumes."

"Fuckin' paint," Conrad was mumbling under his breath, coming to. "Fuckin' paint— Oh, my head; oh, I feel nauseous. Johanna, Johanna . . ."

"Here," she said, stroking his hands, then his chest.

I'm not sure I want to be here, Jeff thought. I'm really not sure I want to be here.

There was Conrad, on the cold ground in his jockey shorts with Johanna bending over him, moaning over him, stroking him. Jeff had the distinct feeling that they might at any moment start to make love. He excused himself and left.

He headed back to the house. He hoped he'd be able to find a bottle of scotch.

The next day they were invited to a cocktail party by a German art dealer who maintained a villa about ten miles away. By now Jeff felt as though he'd known Conrad and Johanna Thornton forever. They were like old friends, yet he had no idea what they did for a living. He decided to ask them.

"Investments. Real estate mostly. Some nightclubs," Conrad said.

"Nightclubs?" They were in the Cirtoën on their way to the party.

"Yeah," Conrad said. "Paris is lousy with nightclubs. When we get back I'll take you to one of them that I own."

"You mightn't like us anymore after that, Jeff," Johanna said. She sounded serious.

"Why?"

"Because it's seamy and you're refined. Because Conrad's work and Conrad are two very different, very separate things."

"She means I mix with the underworld," Conrad said very matter-of-factly. "What she won't tell you is how much it excites her that I do. I'm a powerful man in Paris, Jeff. Better not mess with me."

It wasn't a menacing statement. It was just a cock-of-the-walk kind of remark. Conrad loved to flex his muscles, all of the time. Johanna's ego was in her painting; Conrad's was in his strength. Jeff had lain awake all night trying to figure out his bonding with these two. The first answer he'd come up with was the only one he had when he fell asleep. They represented what he secretly wanted: sex and power. That's why he clung to them as though they were long-lost kinfolk. They *were*, in fact, lost kinfolk; lost from his own genteel background over several generations. There was an energy in them that he found enormously attractive. At that moment in his life he needed them for sustenance; they were the force he'd been searching for.

"I won't mess with you," Jeff said ingenuously, leaning over from the backseat to rub Conrad's shoulder. Conrad took one hand off the wheel and extended it to Jeff in a handshake. Johanna lit a cigarette and muttered under her breath that she looked forward to drinking hard at the party; it upset her to think that Jeff had been intimidated by Conrad.

The problem with drinking hard, for Johanna, was that she couldn't tolerate alcohol. She could manage wine well enough, but hard liquor made her drunk by the time she finished her second drink. This evening, she began with a double vodka, which she imbibed standing in the smallest of several enclosed gardens—greenhouses, really—that surrounded the villa. Then she drank another double vodka. Halfway through her third, she passed out.

The smallest garden, although it had been set up with its own bar and bartenders, was not where any of the action was. Most of the guests assembled in the largest, glassed-over garden, where there were two bars and a string trio that was now playing Schubert. Some of the overflow went into the second, middle-sized garden. But the setting for Johanna's swoon was inhabited by only a handful of people, who were not at all disposed to fussing over her loss of consciousness. Johanna, therefore, cold and supine, was left to her own devices, with only Jeff in attendance. It was going to be his job to revive her. Conrad had disappeared into the thick of the main garden crowd about half an hour ago.

Jeff knelt beside her. Moonlight came through the glass roof, bathing them both in its glow. The only other illumination was from candles. It all looked unreal; a stage set for a fantasy by Jean Anouilh. Some mad countess ought at any moment to emerge from the wings followed by a dashing, youthful Louis Jourdan.

"Johanna," Jeff whispered. Her forehead was the color of clay and felt pasty. "Johanna." Jeff was going out of his mind with exaggerated responses. He felt love in his heart. *Felt* it. He felt it so much he knew he could touch it with his hand. Then could he also pluck it out? It was an indelible moment. He would always remember the purity of his anguish on the floor of this make-believe garden, this fake addition to some rich man's house; one more fantasy that money had built. But why dwell on irony now? With Johanna lying on the floor like some bewitched princess waiting to be kissed. . . . By a frog? He began to smirk, to laugh. That was a funny concept. God, he was drunk, too. He had to be drunk, laughing like that while she lay there, the object of his love, his unrequited passion. He felt the bartenders staring at him now. Well, let them know he was crazy, he didn't care. They were all crazy. That was their secret.

He knelt over her, grabbed her under her arms, and tried to lift her. She was heavier than he could ever have imagined. He knew that if Conrad were there he would have scooped her up and carried her off like Rhett Butler carrying Scarlett. Goddamn animal Conrad.

He tried again and this time succeeded in getting her into a sitting position, in which she partially recovered. She was awake now, just drunk. He got her to her feet, asked a bartender the shortest way to the driveway, and started walking her toward the car. He thought he'd leave her in the Citroën and then go back in to find their coats and to find Conrad.

He had his arm around her so she wouldn't get a chill. She seemed to get stronger on her feet as they approached the driveway. They were walking across an enormous lawn on which there were several benches. It was a cold night, but she wanted to sit on one of them. He said no, not without a coat. She promised not to die of pneumonia. They sat down, his arm very tightly around her, her head on his shoulder.

"Everything will work out when we get back to Paris," she said.

"I don't know."

"Yes. It will. That's what I had to tell you."

"Johanna, I'm falling in love with you, Johanna, I—"

"You've been in love with me for three days," she said.

"Yes, it's true."

"*True* is a beautiful word."

He kissed her on the mouth then. There would never be another kiss like that one. It was all breath at first; their lips hadn't really made contact. Their mouths clung to each other with a warm space still between them, like two souls suspended, one on top of the other. It was the most tantalizing moment of his life, and when, at last, their mouths did touch, softness gave way to passion as they sucked at each other's lips and tongues, trying to slake a desire that could only be made more acute. They pulled apart. Out of breath. Hurting in the gut. Knowing that unless they found release in each other's arms in Paris, they would explode.

"Take me to the car now," she asked.

They got to their feet again. They walked slowly. Their bodies had grown very warm, close together. They were still clinging to each other when he reached down to open the door of the Citroën. He helped her into the front seat. Then he went back for their coats and to tell Conrad where she was.

More.

He needed to remember more. All of it. Their whole story. But not here. Not yet. His back hurt and he felt drained, exhausted. How long had he been standing here? He looked out one last time at the view from Notre Dame and said goodbye. He would never come up those steps again. Never. Now he had only to walk down them.

When he got back to the hotel he found the door to Toni's suite open. The telephone was ringing, the voices from across the courtyard were raised in a new argument, and Streeter Cash was sitting in a corner of the living room waiting for him.

First the phone. It was the switchboard operator explaining that there had been two calls, one for him from Cathy Hayes in New York, the other from a Ned Longworth in London. Did he wish to call New York now? In a while. Thank you. Cathy's face flashed in front of him; his only reliable love. He thought of the word *steady*. It was a good word.

Then he thought about the other call. Ned Longworth certainly moved around. He turned from the phone and said hello to Streeter. There was something about Streeter that was not entirely unpleasant. Could it be charm?

"It's the toughest, most excitingly glamorous, and—although I know you won't believe this—most disciplined profession in the world," Streeter said.

"What is?" Jeff asked.

"The fashion photographer's model."

"Oh. Toni, you mean."

"Do you know how many there are like her?" Streeter asked.

"Thousands?"

"Thousands of aspirants, maybe. But in her league? Maybe twenty."

"I'm not sure I understand what Toni's league is."

"When she really moves into it, which I figure is at the most a year away, she'll be making between a grand and a grand and a half a day. That's what it's worth to have a face the camera not only loves but creams itself over. And *I'm* the one who gets to wipe the lens!" Streeter gasped. "Here, she asked me to give you this." He handed Jeff an envelope. "I can save you the job of reading it, though. She left Paris."

The man and woman across the courtyard were fighting over which of them was going to pack their second suitcase. Hearing their voices reinforced Jeff's anxiety.

"Who needs television?" Streeter said.

Jeff tore open the envelope and read the brief note. The location for tomorrow's shooting, it said, had been changed from Paris to London. Well, that was easy enough to check out. All Jeff had to do was ask Streeter. As long as she was going to be in London, it said, she could catch up with Scavullo, who was there for a few days, a meeting they'd both been trying for, unsuccessfully, for months. She begged Jeff's forgiveness

69

and understanding, adding within parentheses that she'd fallen in love with him. Jeff stopped there. It was so fake. It felt so alien. "Please, please understand," he read on. "I *must* see you again in New York, if only to say goodbye. Lisbon's been cancelled." She signed it "Antonia."

"Why aren't you in London with the rest of them?" Jeff asked. "Aren't you the most important member of this team?"

"Precisely, dear boy. *I* am the real star. Toni is merely the body. I shall depart in my own good time. Except for the flight from New York on which we met, I never travel with the cattle. I'll leave sometime this evening. I have a heavy date in Paris at five that I've no intention of missing."

"So it's true that she's gone to London," Jeff said. "Must be hard for her agent to keep track of her."

"She's done a really unusual thing, you know. Instead of going to Eileen Ford or Wilhelmina or any of those top agencies, she uses a lawyer."

"Ned Longworth." Jeff was more emphatic than he needed to be.

"That's right," Streeter said.

"But how can a busy lawyer possibly spend the time it must take to promote her, keep her in circulation, and get her bookings?"

"I don't really know," Streeter said. "She claims she makes her own contacts and just uses the lawyer to do the paperwork. But there's a rumor circulating that someone in the John Casablancas agency moonlights for her. I don't see how that's possible. In any event, Toni is fast reaching that pinnacle where everyone wants her. How she got there so fast is her secret. But Scavullo helped; I think her father helped. Just take a good look at her. She's *got* what they're all looking for now. She's not your typical American skinny-marink model; she's more European, more individual. She's a willow branch made of iron. She's got tits and hips; but it's her face that makes the camera come. I mean *come*. What more can I tell you?"

"I think you've told me enough. Listen I don't mean to be rude—"

"You've got calls to make. So have I. I sort of like you. Does that make you nervous?"

"Not at all." Jeff smiled. He shook Streeter's extended hand and said goodbye.

Jeff went with Streeter to the door. Just as he was about to close it again he became aware that his neighbors from across the courtyard were emerging into the corridor. Their voices were unmistakable. They were just around the bend. If he waited there on some pretext, he would see them at last.

Streeter, thank God, decided not to wait for the elevator but to head down the stairs, so Jeff could loiter there without arousing Streeter's curiosity.

He waited. He was prepared to duck back inside his room the moment he saw them. Their footsteps were heavy; they were obviously carrying luggage. They had stopped fighting. In fact they had stopped talking to one another altogether, for the time being. He saw the woman's shoe, then all of her. And then the man. He knew them instantly.

Somehow he wasn't as surprised as he ought to have been, although none of it made any sense. His head was reeling as he stepped back into Toni's suite and closed the door. He felt disoriented and, for some reason, afraid. He was shaking deep inside himself, and he didn't know why.

The man was the fat Paul Newman. The woman was the same blonde he had first seen at the Four Seasons Grill.

He went to the sofa and sat down. He picked up the phone and told the operator he was ready to place the call to Cathy Hayes in New York.

In New York it was mid-morning.

In his apartment on 113th Street just off Amsterdam Avenue, Max McClintock was still suffering from symptoms of the flu, although his morbid anxieties about dying young were considerably alleviated by the ministrations of Jeannie Christopher. He lay in bed remembering last night, when his fever had dropped to one hundred and a half and she had wanted to make love. The idea had at first worried him.

"Do you think it's safe?"

"How do you mean?"

"With a fever?"

"Haven't you ever made love with a fever?" She was incredulous.

"No. I think I'm too weak."

"The fever really helps," she said.

"Helps?"

"Yes. It more than makes up for any weakness you might feel. A fever is terrific for lovemaking." She was undressing at his bedside, watching him writhe under the covers, looking for signs of his arousal.

"Is that really so?" He felt guilty now, like a small boy, because all

71

afternoon as he lay there impatiently waiting for her return from her office, he had kept having incredibly varied erotic fantasies. He'd spent much of the afternoon, in fact, stroking a single ongoing erection. He was nervous about being able to repeat that miracle of longevity in her company.

She was naked. He'd seen her naked before. She was adorable. He looked at her face, impish and grinning. She moved toward the bed slowly. He thought, from the way she was approaching him, that she was going to rip off the covers and jump in alongside him. But she didn't do that. She didn't touch the covers. She bent over him instead. Her breasts lightly brushed the part of his bare chest exposed above the top of the blanket. She placed her cheek, feather lightly, on his cheek. Her face was as warm as his, and so smooth. Her face felt wonderful. His body was ready for her now. There was no longer any doubt in his mind about his stamina. He threw back the covers and grabbed her wrist.

"You're right about the fever," he said.

Later, he told her about the gray envelope addressed to Cathy Hayes, which he was certain he'd left in the pocket of the Harris tweed jacket she'd taken to the dry cleaner.

"It's too late for me to run down there now," she said. "It's after seven, and he'll be closed."

"Dammit," Max said.

"Was it something important?"

"I don't know."

"Can't you just tell Cathy the truth about it? Do you remember who it was from?"

"I have no idea who it was from. Somebody—some gay boy—came up and handed it to me while she was making a phone call the other night at the theater."

"Maybe the cleaner noticed it and set it aside. I'll step in tomorrow and ask him."

"I can do it," he said. "I think I can go back to work tomorrow."

"I think you should wait one more day."

"I don't know."

"I think you should stay in bed tomorrow and go back Friday."

"Will you stay in bed with me?"

"All right," she said. "But I'll have to call my office. Ned Longworth's in London, and someone has to cover."

"I think I love you, Jeannie."

72

"I think I love you, too."

That had been yesterday. As he lay in bed next to her this morning, waiting for her to awaken, he began to think about the letter again.

He eased himself out of the bed, managing not to disturb her, and went in search of her handbag, which he quickly found. Rummaging through it, he came upon the dry cleaner's receipt, which had a phone number on it. He called.

A letter? The cleaner had no idea what he was talking about.

He got back into bed next to Jeannie; she hadn't stirred in all this time. He stared at the ceiling, wondering whether he should, after all, say something to Cathy Hayes. He still couldn't make up his mind.

In a large dry-cleaning plant in the Bronx where the work from small, independent dry-cleaning establishments all over the city was done, a workman named Jerome Sheehy found a gray envelope that had fallen out of one of the thousands of garments being processed. This sort of discovery was not unusual, for which reason a Lost-and-Found department had been set up, where, depending upon the degree of honesty or diligence of the workmen, such diverse items as letters, wallets, loose bills, photographs, keys, jewelry, condoms, bank books, address books, and gloves were brought to await inquiries.

Jerome Sheehy was honest enough but not especially diligent. As it happened, he found the gray envelope on the floor only a few yards away from the Lost-and-Found department, so he figured what the hell, he might as well bring it in. It would be a good excuse anyway to make one more pass at Yvonne Smith.

"Found a letter," he said.

"A tisket, a tasket," Yvonne Smith responded, grabbing it from him. She absolutely killed him with her wisecracking; she broke him up. He loved women who wisecracked. He claimed it turned him on.

"Can I drive you home after work?"

"No, thanks. I brought my Rabbit."

The banter continued in that fashion for a full three minutes, during which time Yvonne recorded the retrieval of the gray envelope, turned out some of the lights in the Lost-and-Found department, which she was about to abandon for a coffee break, kissed Jerome Sheehy squarely on the mouth, picked up her purse, and said to the wildly perplexed suitor, "Keep trying, Sheehy. I have a secret yen for you after all."

Then she dropped the gray envelope into a box full of other envelopes of various sizes and colors, and ushered Sheehy smartly out the door.

The operator had been unable to get through to Cathy Hayes, so Jeff told her to try Conrad's hotel.

The call was placed. A telephone began to ring.

"Monsieur Conrad Thornton, *s'il vous plait*," Jeff said.

"Hello?" It was the concierge.

"I would like to speak to Monsieur Conrad Thornton," Jeff repeated. "Has he returned? I was there earlier inquiring about him. I spoke to you."

"Ah." The concierge did indeed recall.

The concierge explained that Monsieur Thornton had left Paris and was not expected to return for one month.

"Did he go to London?" Jeff heard himself begging. What was this, anyway? A game of hide and seek? Was Jeff planning to follow him there if the answer was yes?

"No, Monsieur. He did not go to London."

"Where *did* he go?"

"I am not at liberty to say, Monsieur."

Jeff hung up. He was sweating. Dammit, it was hot in the suite, suddenly. He could feel his heart pounding. He was exhausted. *What the hell was going on?*

The phone rang. It was the operator. The call to Cathy Hayes was going through.

Never had he wanted her, needed her more than now. She was his sanity. God, he'd actually come to Paris with the idea of killing somebody. It was beyond believing.

"Hello? Jeff?"

Her voice . . . She was going to be his salvation.

He told her he was getting the first available flight back to New York.

TWO

Chapter Five

When he came to Paris in January 1962, the French were feeling prosperous; everyone was on a buying spree. At first Jeff thought the ebullient mood was due to the possibility of peace in Algeria. But then as *plastique* bombs began to burst in the city, it became clear that the issue of a cease fire was creating as much anger as approval, so the good mood had nothing to do with the outcome of the Algerian crisis. Even after Brigitte Bardot was threatened by *plastiqueurs,* Paris remained optimistic. Regardless of whether one thought de Gaulle was right in trying to settle the war or whether one thought he was selling out, one went on spending. It was a good time for commerce of any sort. All Conrad ever spoke of when he, Jeff, and Johanna sat together over a drink or a meal was the opportunity to make money.

Conrad never talked calmly about money; he expostulated. He exhorted. He was as pedantic about his cynical code of economic opportunism as Johanna tended to be about art. In the first few days of knowing them, Jeff felt naive. But after listening more carefully to their various speeches, he decided that Conrad and Johanna, in their own separate styles, sounded like children. The biggest difference between them was that Johanna's dreams were pure and Conrad's were not.

77

"You're a lawyer," Conrad told Jeff. "I can use a lawyer. Why don't you come work for me."

"You've got a lawyer."

"I've got three lawyers."

"Then what do you need me for? Anyway, I'm here to be a bum."

"Then what can I do for you? Do you want to get laid? I can introduce you to some of the best ass in Paris."

Being patronized this way ought to have bothered Jeff. It didn't. He was amused. At twenty-six, he had no prospects whatever and few prejudices. With nothing to defend, tolerance came easily.

He had come to Paris on a small inheritance from an aunt who loved him. His mother, when he told her what he was doing with her sister's money, merely said, "Oh dear, this isn't going to be the rake's progress, is it?" To which his father had added, "Twenty-six is a bit late for this kind of behavior, Jeff. Nevertheless, better now than at forty."

He wasn't entirely a bum. He'd done very well at Columbia Law School. He hadn't made Law Review, but he'd stayed at the top of his class. Offers from important firms appropriately awaited him upon graduation. He accepted one of them and worked at it for two years, until he felt he needed to breathe. There was an urge inside him he couldn't quite figure out. That's what brought him to Paris.

Perhaps he shouldn't have moved in with them. It had all been decided so quickly, coming back from the country with Antonia on his lap, the Citroën even more crowded with bundles and cartons than on the trip out. Conrad had said, "We'd like to take you in as a non-paying boarder," and that was it. Jeff had kissed the back of Antonia's head and said, "Okay." Then he asked, "Is it okay with you, Antonia?" Understanding perfectly, she had expressed her delight with a series of giggles. Jeff felt inexplicably happy; he thought he loved everyone in that car just then. His feelings about Johanna didn't seem in any way a betrayal, because nothing had happened between them except a lot of conversation. He told himself it would go no further, and he honestly believed it. The attraction he'd felt in the country and the promise of passion she had extended were temporarily forgotten behind the semblance of camaraderie that warmed their journey back to Paris.

What Jeff didn't understand was that moving into the arena of their struggle would make him a part of it. Conrad did nothing to disguise his need to possess Johanna absolutely, to control her sexually and physically, to dominate her work, which meant trying to manage her soul. Jeff's participation in this struggle, more than the attraction between him and Johanna, would change them from a casual trio of new friends into a tense and volatile triangle.

When Johanna and Conrad fought with each other, they were relentless. They didn't care about the neighbors, the concierge, the maid, Antonia, the cats, or Jeff.

Tonight their quarrel began on the way home from a Truffaut movie Johanna liked and Conrad didn't, and it escalated as they drove home. Jeff had decided at the last minute not to go with them; he wanted to get to sleep early. And that seemed to be part of the problem; they were getting used to Jeff's presence as a safety valve.

They calmed down enough to come through the front door quietly, aware that it was nearly one in the morning. Conrad headed straight for their bedroom, tore off his clothes, didn't bother with a robe, and marched out first into the kitchen and then into the living room in search of Johanna.

His appearance infuriated her. His naked body in that eclectically appointed apartment, cluttered with paintings, art nouveau lamps, biedermeier tables and Victorian sofas, seemed an incongruity to her; that's what she screamed at him.

"These rooms call for a hairy man or a soft man or for the female form. Mine," she shouted. "I've asked you not to run through them with your white, shiny skin. Your body is wrong for this decor. It goes best with Swedish modern or provincial furnishings. Run naked in the country all you want to. Let me be the one to run naked here."

"I'll run naked wherever the hell I fuckin' please. You drank too much wine at the movies." They had bought a bottle of cheap Algerian white to go with their popcorn. But it was Conrad who drank most of it.

"Johanna . . ."

"What?"

"I want to make love to you."

"No."

"Why are you withdrawing from me?"

"Because you're doing ugly things for money."

"The new club?"

79

"I hate it!"

"It's no different from the other clubs. Is that what this fight's about?"

"I never liked the other clubs. I especially dislike this one."

"Ned Longworth and Irene are coming over for the opening. Did you know that?"

"Good for them. As long as you're not planning to invite them to stay here."

"I would have if Jeff hadn't moved in."

"One more reason, then, to be grateful for Jeff."

"I thought you liked Ned and Irene."

"They're okay."

"I have a wonderful idea," he said. His voice grew soft. It made her soften. She stopped being angry in order to listen to him.

"What's your idea?"

"Let's make love," he said. "Then let's wake Jeff."

"To join us in bed?" she asked, her voice heavy with irony.

"I'll bet you'd like that."

"Oh, shit, Conrad. You know what the real trouble is when you lose your integrity?"

He knew the answer before she gave it. But he had to listen to it anyway.

"You begin to imagine everyone else has lost theirs as well," she said. "You've crossed too many boundaries. That's why I find myself withdrawing from you."

"Make love to me," he begged.

"And then wake Jeff? What will we do with him?"

"Take him out in the Citroën and show him Paris at four in the morning."

"It's only a quarter past one," she said. "I don't know if I can keep awake that long."

"I'll keep you awake." He grinned his most boyish grin. He looked incredibly young. She felt herself drawn to him again; she could never resist him when he looked so beautiful.

She fell into his arms. Her fluttering hands touched his shoulders and then like snowflakes fell down his back and kept falling. "When you're pure. Like now. Like now. I love you so. I hate your need for power. I hate it."

"I—want to keep my power over you, Johanna. That's all."

"Then be tender," she whispered. "Be pure. That's the only way." She wept against his chest, and then she kissed him, knowing how glad she was that he was naked. As long as she remained clothed he would have to deal with the feeling that she held the power. She wondered how long he could tolerate it; she would love him for as long as he did, and perhaps she would go on loving him afterward. When she got ready to undress they would be equal. And the pleasure they would be giving one another would obliterate the struggle.

Oh, how she loved him when he was like this. "Conrad," she whispered, caressing his body, "Conrad, Conrad . . ."

Conrad made good his promise. He made love and rested with her, trusting her with his gentle side. Then it was time to awaken Jeff.

They couldn't agree on the best method of doing it.

Johanna was in favor of simply opening his door, going into the bedroom, and shaking him. But Conrad opposed this, out of jealousy. He told Johanna—laughing, holding her, kissing her ear—that he thought there might be too great an erotic impact from such an encounter. He meant every crazy word of it, but he told it to her in a way that charmed her, wooed her, made her tingle. Conrad had the imagination of a satyr, and he imposed it in its entirety on Johanna. Having provoked her lust earlier, he worried about it now, never considering the fact that she was satiable. He could never believe she wasn't perpetually hungry, the way he was. What if he weren't around to satisfy her hunger? He always wondered about that. What would she do then? There was her work, of course. He would go on approving of her work as long as he could read into her paintings a private code, a message about the strength of their passion. But once she began painting for the outside world, once the energy for her art could no longer be attributed just to their love, he would begin to feel crazy. He already understood that Johanna's imagination was something he couldn't own, and he raged inside himself because of it.

All right then, they wouldn't simply open Jeff's door. But how about knocking on it?

They tried. Not too loudly. If they knocked too loudly, they'd run the risk of disturbing Antonia or the maid. They tried three times with no success.

There was a balcony outside their bedroom window that touched a smaller balcony outside Jeff's. Why not go out there, climb over, and rap on one of the large glass panes? It seemed like a good idea. Except for the fact that it was cold out there and they were dressed in bathrobes.

The charm of their dilemma began to wear off. Johanna was no longer willing to laugh at Conrad's craziness. She was beginning to see it as the shaping up of a confrontation. But, oh, hell, if they were going to have fun at four in the morning, if they were going to do something agreeably foolish, then she didn't want to wreck it. She suggested that they try knocking on Jeff's door one more time. Conrad told her to do it. He stood behind her, kissing her shoulders.

This time Jeff stirred. It took him a moment to come to the door, and when he opened it he was only mildly startled to find them there. He was wearing red pajamas.

"What's going on?" Jeff mumbled.

"Get dressed. We're going to show you Paris," Johanna said.

"What?" But even as he asked, he understood. "Oh," he said, yawning, "okay." He knew them well enough now to be able to deal matter-of-factly with most of their schemes. He looked at his watch. "Okay," he repeated. He liked driving through cities at this hour. During the day you could hear a city's hardest breathing, but at four in the morning you could feel its resting pulse. Seeing Paris now would be like taking the hand of a sleeping lover.

In ten minutes they were assembled in the living room, ready to leave. Conrad insisted on bringing a bottle of champagne. He filled a huge bucket with ice cubes and got some glasses. Then he reconsidered and took a second bottle. Now he was ready.

It was a reckless drive even though they weren't speeding. Conrad drove so slowly that Johanna said it felt like rowing.

"It's the champagne that's altering your perception," Conrad said.

"No, it's not the champagne. It feels like we're going through Paris in a rowboat."

They drove past the Place Vendôme and then along the Rue de la Paix singing *row, row, row your boat,* and then past the Palais Royal singing *oh how lovely is the evening, is the evening, when the bells are gently ringing,* and when Conrad insisted on *genitally* ringing, they laughed. They were drunk not so much on champagne as on the night air and the idea that they had more freedom at that moment than most of the world. They drove across the Pont Neuf savoring the view as they went, and then to the Church of Saint Sulpice, past the Luxembourg Gardens, then

82

back toward the Seine and across it once more, and suddenly out toward the Gare de Lyon.

"Where are you going?" There was something about Johanna's voice and the fact that Conrad didn't answer her that made Jeff feel sober and cold. Furthermore, they were no longer driving slowly. Conrad was deliberately speeding, while under his breath, without a trace of gaiety, he sang the words "Gare de Lyon" to the tune of "Chattanooga Choo Choo." He sang and drove with the same disturbing air of exaggerated menace.

They kept driving. Past the railroad station. "Would you believe there's a marvelous restaurant in there?" Johanna said in a flat voice, in an effort to ignore what she knew was happening. She still hoped Conrad might change his mind. But they drove on.

When the car did finally come to a halt, they were somewhere in the eastern end of Paris, parked outside a gray frame house that looked as though it could have been imported whole from the wrong side of any midwestern American city. But why had Conrad come here?

Conrad and Johanna stared at each other coldly until whatever it was that seethed inside them evaporated like air going out of a tire. Then they leaned their heads together, ignoring Jeff, who couldn't bear being with them any longer. There were tears in Conrad's eyes. He started the car. Johanna sighed in exhaustion.

"Look, you two," Jeff finally said, "the next time you want to do something like this, do me a favor. Leave me home." Then, unable to contain his curiosity, he asked, "Whose house is that you stopped in front of?"

"A ghost lives there," Johanna said.

"Yes," Conrad said. "The ghost of a dead boy. Right Johanna?"

"Bastard!" she hissed. "I hate you."

"Well, folks," Jeff said, "I want to thank you all for this exhilarating excursion."

In her studio she was like the Johanna he'd begun to fall in love with in the country. The lines of tension that he saw in her face most of the time they were in the apartment were gone. She seemed younger, more beautiful, more sensual. She dared to be on fire again.

They had come in secrecy. Conrad had to be at a business meeting all day. Jeff had found out about that at dinner last night and as a result lay awake until morning wondering whether he and Johanna would at last be together in Paris in the way they had vowed that night in Normandy. Jeff's nervousness made him sullen at breakfast, but Conrad was so involved with his plans for the day that he took no notice. Johanna, having a pretty good idea of Jeff's state of mind, did her best to avoid conversation with him. But Antonia, thinking perhaps she had done something wrong, focused on Jeff's quiet behavior and demanded to know whether he had a stomachache. At last Conrad bolted from the table, grabbed his briefcase, which he'd parked in a corner, kissed Antonia, kissed Johanna, grunted something in Jeff's direction that sounded like "See you, kid," and left. It was then she asked him if he'd like to visit the studio.

"If it's such a secret that we're here, how come you invited me in front of Antonia?" They had arrived only a few minutes ago. The studio was cold, and they hadn't removed their coats. There was a huge fireplace along one wall with a large stack of wood next to it. Johanna was starting to gather some logs for a fire.

"Because Antonia and I share secrets. If I tell her it's a secret, she won't tell her father. We're that close. And she's only three. I know it's sort of using her, but I want her to be my ally for life. This is her basic training. I want her to be prepared to join me, the two of us pitted against Conrad if it ever came to that. Are you shocked?"

"Yes."

"I'm sorry. I've got to learn not to be so blatant. Do you think I can build a fire without kindling?"

"If you've got plenty of newspaper."

"I don't."

"Well, you can't just put a match to those logs and expect something to happen."

"Not even if I douse them with kerosene? I've got lots of kerosene."

"You'd get a blaze for a few minutes, but not a fire. You sure there's no newspaper?"

"Wait a minute." She ran to the tiny toilet in the far corner and there on the floor she found a stack of *Le Monde*. She picked up all of them. "Enough?"

"Fine," he said. "We'll roll them up tightly, and we're in business."

Soon there was a good fire, and they stood before it warming their hands and feet. Jeff was grateful for this distraction; it gave him a chance to absorb what he saw when they'd walked in. All those blatant, aggressive nudes on the walls, on easels, leaning against chairs and tables, had taken his breath away momentarily. He was ready to approach them now.

"There's such an incredible concentration of energy in this room," he said.

"I *explore* in this room."

"I can feel that. And your curiosity."

She laughed. "I grew up in a Norman Rockwell home. If you've ever wondered what those people look like without their clothes, you'll find the answer here."

"I always saved those thoughts for cheerleaders."

"Then you've missed the point about the body." She was frowning at him. "While I was dreaming of painting those Norman Rockwell people, you were just thinking of getting laid."

He could feel a flush of embarrassment in his cheeks; she obviously thought he didn't understand her seriousness. He was desperate now to persuade her that he *did*. But it had to be with something real. Then it occurred to him.

"Was there bright light in your childhood?" he asked.

"How do you mean?"

"When you were happy, did you *see* it as bright light?"

"I love you!" she screamed. "That's fantastic! You're right. It was just like that!"

"For me, too," Jeff said. "We used to go to a place in Maine each summer that was covered by fog most of the time, but when I'd feel happy I'd tell everyone the light was shining, and they'd look out expecting to see the sun and tell me I was wrong."

"If you just made that up, I'm going to hate you forever."

"Do you always fight when you talk about your work?"

Now it was her turn to be flushed. "Yes," she said. "Yes. I do. I—I get belligerent. I can't help it. Jeff?"

"What?"

"You'll get used to me. I'm sorry. Come . . . I'm going to show you things in this closet. Paintings I know I can trust you to see. Are you ready?"

"Not yet," he said. "I'm still looking at these."

As he looked at her work, academic, struggled over, robust as well as sensual, he began to understand that she was searching for the biological vitality in the naked form and not for some idealized abstraction.

"Jeff," she said, "it all comes down to this one thing, really. When sex is used as a defense against reality, you're dealing with corruption. Pornography is like that. That's what I see in Conrad's clubs. They've figured out a way of lighting the girls' asses in the show so the girls look bruised, as though they've been spanked. Those girls and certain paintings by Whistler are one and the same as far as I'm concerned. One vulgarizes the erotic and the other sentimentalizes it. And they're both for people who want to defend their sensibilities against reality. I'm not awfully good as a painter yet; maybe I'll never be. But I want to look at the truth. Do you understand?"

"Yes."

"I don't think there's ever been a time in my life when I haven't known my own mind and feelings. When I was a teenager I would have gone naked with any boy who would have gone naked with me for the knowledge of it and the joy and not to make me dirty. But they were afraid of sex, those boys. And probably afraid of death, too. I think it's the same fear. Some day I'm going to paint a corpse—don't tell Conrad." She laughed in a tight way. She felt warm and she was tense again and there were tears in her eyes and she couldn't stop talking.

"I've always been uncomfortable with people who aren't serious in the same way I am; people who are afraid of sex and of death and of certain triumphs of the spirit they can't tolerate. My paintings are *free* of corruption. A fact that Conrad doesn't understand. His own capacity for corruption is so overwhelming he thinks I have that capacity in me, too. He can't see the difference! He can't see that I'm attracted to his energy and his wildness and even to his anarchy but that I'm repelled by his corruption. He distrusts my painting because he thinks what I show on canvas is the same as what he shows at his clubs. He wants to harness me and control me because he believes in that way he can control himself."

The warm, sweet smell of her was exciting him. He was desperate to hold her, and afraid of his own yearning, knowing how she'd despise it at this moment. He was moved by her words and spirit and at the same time weighed down by massive feelings of desire for her. He was standing at a tilt; he felt off balance. He took her hand, and the two of them sat on the floor in front of the fire.

"Jeff . . ." she said.

Without his willing it, his mouth was on hers. Lightly.

She didn't pull away.

Without his willing it, his lips brushed over her cheek.

"Small kisses are the best kind," she said in a voice that was no more than a whisper. "Oh, Jeff."

He came back. For one more small kiss. He found the place he was looking for on her neck. They were still wearing their heavy coats, sitting there in front of the fire, and now they were much too warm. Jeff began to take his coat off.

"There are more things I want to show you," she said.

"I know."

They got to their feet, and he put his arms around her. She embraced him with a hunger that surprised him.

"I want to make love to you," she said. "But not here. Not here. I've never made love here. I couldn't now. I don't want to now."

He went on kissing her.

"There'll be a time for us. But not here."

"Oh, God, Johanna . . ."

"Please . . ."

He continued to kiss her.

She pulled away.

"Will there really be a time for us?" he asked.

"Yes."

"*Will* there?"

"Yes."

"Okay," he said, letting go of her. "Okay."

She took a moment to catch her breath. Then she went and opened the door of a huge walk-in closet. She turned on the light and invited him inside. The closet was lined with racks designed to hold canvases in a neat file. She easily found the one she was searching for. She removed it from its slot and carried it back into the better light of the studio.

"Recognize this?" she asked him.

It was one of the self-portraits she had told him about in the country. But what she hadn't told him, what she couldn't possibly have prepared him for, was how good a painting it was. It was the best work of hers he'd so far seen. He took the canvas from her. It was large enough so that when he held it by its edges his arms were stretched out to their full length on either side of him. He set it down on an easel in the middle of the room. Then he stood in front of it, letting the painting induce in him the same feelings that had washed over him the first time he saw her.

"It's much better than your description of it," he told her, smiling broadly in his delight. He told her how the painting made him feel enormously happy, for it was in fact a song to her body that she'd put on canvas. He would have gone on, but she stopped him.

"Come, there are more."

She led him back into the closet. While she searched, so did he. He found something that at first puzzled him.

"I was beginning to think you did only nudes," he said.

"Oh." She stopped what she was doing. "You found the house."

"Yes." It was making his blood run cold.

"I'd forgotten it was there. Well? Do you think it's a good painting?"

"I don't know." He began carrying it into the studio.

"I wish you wouldn't. I'd like you to put it back."

"Oh, come on, Johanna."

"Shit! Can't you just do as I ask?"

"Okay, then," he said, replacing the canvas in its rack. "That's the house Conrad drove us to the other night, isn't it?"

"Go to the head of the class."

"Listen," Jeff said, "I'm getting a very uncomfortable feeling."

"Good. You're on the right track."

"Conrad said something about the ghost of a dead boy."

"Yes. He did say that."

"I don't feel death in the painting."

"Because you didn't *look*. You're not at the head of the class any more."

"Was there a dead boy?"

"I don't know!"

"Johanna—"

"Can we go? Can we please go?"

She held him at bay—she would answer no question—until they got to lunch.

"Paris has a very good Italian restaurant called San Francisco. Okay?" she asked him.

He hesitated.

"I've got money," she said.

"Okay."

88

When they got there, they sipped Campari and soda, perused the menu, and made small talk.

The waiter appeared. They ordered.

"Jeff," she said, reaching across the table for his hand, ready to answer his questions now, "when Conrad and I first arrived in Paris determined to make a go of it, I found out I was pregnant. I didn't tell Conrad for a long time because I knew how conflicted he would be. We both wanted a child, but we knew we weren't ready. When I finally told him, I said I'd be willing to have an abortion if I could find someone to do it I could trust. That's when Conrad took me to the gray frame house you saw the other night, where he left me while he walked the streets fantasizing his revenge against the abortionist were I to die." She paused for another sip of her drink.

Did she know that she was challenging Jeff's innocent soul? Could she know that he'd contracted no sins in his youth to repent of and that she seemed for just a moment the embodiment of all of those sins his mother once warned him against? Jeff tried hard to go on smiling at her, but his eyes were burning and his mouth was dry. She was his biggest life experience; he was in awe. He fought the need to evaluate her morality. He repressed his father's reproving voice, and he fell more deeply under her spell.

"Well," she said, "as it turned out the abortionist was a kind and skillful doctor. I was okay. And I was very lucky. Then, a little more than a year afterward, Conrad and I got lucky financially. I didn't have to work for him any longer. I could go back to painting. It also meant I could become pregnant again and this time have my baby. And so Antonia was born. Conrad filled my hospital room with flowers, with champagne, and with denizens of the Paris underworld. And six months after I came home with Antonia, he urged me to get pregnant once more. He said he wanted a boy. I said I wasn't ready. One night, drunk, he told me he was certain that the child I had aborted was a boy. An obsession had built in him that he couldn't shake, and along with it the conviction that we had to replenish our lives with another boy child. I began to be afraid of him because whenever he would get angry and lose control, he would repeat that I had killed our son. Sometimes I felt sorry for him. Mostly I was just furious. As time passed, his obsession lifted, or so it seemed. Nearly two years went by without a single accusation. Then we took that drive the other night. That drive was his way of reminding me the obsession is still alive. Oh, God, Jeff . . ." She opened her eyes as wide as she could in an effort to stop her tears.

Jeff's heart ached. He shared her sadness. He looked at her adoringly.

"You're on the side of life, Johanna," he said.

She laughed. "I'm hardly an earth mother, if that's what you mean."

"Aren't you?"

"No. Earth mothers are brunette, not blonde. Haven't you ever noticed?"

"My experience has been too limited."

"Take it from me."

"But you *are* on the side of life."

"I think I could be as destructive as the next one if I were provoked."

"I will never provoke you. I swear it," he said.

Johanna laughed again. A deep, wonderfully throaty laugh. She was laughing when the waiter arrived with their lunch.

Chapter Six

As the sun rose over the cold city, Ned Longworth was hurrying back to the Hôtel Meurice, hoping to get into his pajamas and into bed before his wife awakened. Irene was such a heavy sleeper that Ned had every reason to believe he'd make it. He had told her the latest he'd get back was two. Two was an hour that made her nervous, but since circumstances were extenuating, she accepted it. Sunrise, however, would be quite another matter. For Irene it would be the difference between feeling sympathetic because Ned had stayed up half the night working and feeling stabbed by a visceral suspicion that where he'd really been was out whoring.

Ned Longworth's French wasn't good enough to convey to the driver his desperate wish for speed. But not even a taxi that could fly would affect his fate now. How Irene would respond to his return by daylight was a matter for the gods.

There were two things Irene knew about Ned. One was that he was no angel; the other was that he truly loved her. Since Irene, at the age of thirty, was beginning to read books, and in particular the books of Theodore Reik, she was learning to deal with ambivalence. The deeper her reading, the more she understood that love's definition was elusive. This insight, more than religion, gave her the ability to cope with the contradiction between her husband's avowals and his capacity for sleeping around. It was a friend of Irene's, a recent convert to the analyst's couch, who put her on to reading Reik. This same friend, after commiserating with Irene one rainy afternoon about Ned's low-keyed infidelities, apologized for giving cheap advice. "But I adore cheap advice," Irene had said. "It's so overwhelmingly sincere."

Irene had agreed to come with Ned to Paris on the condition that he behave himself. As a matter of fact, she looked upon the trip with romantic expectations. She bought herself a wardrobe of lingerie designed to appeal to Ned's low taste. She had managed the purchase in New York without a trace of nervousness, her stoic determination making it amply clear to the saleslady that this was not a case of hanky-panky so much as a noble effort on behalf of marriage. What the saleslady missed was the glint in Irene's eye. At thirty-four, Ned was definitely worth arousing. Irene took the garments home fully expecting to get her money's worth.

She was in fact asleep when Ned came into the bedroom. And she did, as he had predicted she would, stir in response to his getting in between the sheets. She opened one eye and groggily called him a bastard.

"You're wrong," he protested.

She sat up and groped along the surface of the night table for her cigarettes.

"What the hell kind of a business meeting takes until half past six in the morning?"

"I was in arbitration with Conrad and Arthur Lamb, that's what," Ned said, really upset now because for once he was on firm ground. He was telling the truth.

"Arbitration? At a nightclub? I thought tonight was the show's final rehearsal and a last look at all the details before the opening. That's what you told me at dinner."

"At dinner I didn't know."

"Bullshit," Irene said, putting out her cigarette. "Bullshit," she repeated, pulling up the covers and turning her back to him in bed.

Frustrated, Ned tried to sleep. Maybe at breakfast she'd let him tell her what happened.

There was in Paris a young woman, a girl really—she had just turned sixteen—by the name of Charlotte Medley-Tripp, the runaway daughter of a wealthy upper-class English family. Because she had been trained in ballet, she could dance in a Paris nightclub instead of turning to a pimp or a rich American. Her too-full body, with its tendency to overflow the confines of a leotard—a detriment in a sedate London dancing school—was a distinct advantage at a club such as the one Conrad was about to open. And that was where she found employment. In keeping with a tradition begun at a rival club, the Crazy Horse Saloon, her name was changed. Purely for the sake of amusement, Charlotte Medley-Tripp was to be known as Charlotte Russe.

It was Conrad's idea to surpass the Crazy Horse's reputation for sexy shows featuring beautiful women. The Crazy Horse's success was due just as much to brilliant showmanship and witty production numbers as it was to nudity, and the dance numbers there were approached with as much seriousness as anything at the ballet, all of which Conrad fully understood. But the quality he was after at his new club was much more blatant. He'd pull in tourists and Parisians alike for a show they'd remember. He expected to make a fortune; that's what he promised his backers, who were inclined to worry about their return even while enjoying the sexual promise implicit in their investment. Conrad called the club L'Aphrodite.

Charlotte Russe became a featured dancer in a number called "The Midas Touch," which depicted in song and dance the plight of the woebegone king in his bedchamber. Charlotte would enter the scene in the nude, and then as Midas fondled her breasts, thighs, or buttocks, those areas, with the help of clever lighting, would turn to gold, reducing the king's lust to frustration. The premature ripeness and startlingly perfect roundness of Charlotte's young body caused her entrance, at every rehearsal, to become a moment of agonized adoration for everyone watching her. Her appearance was in itself a confrontation with desire. She elicited from men and women alike fantasies that ranged from tender to rapine. Those first few seconds during which everyone in the audience sucked in a breath and dealt with the shock of his or her own lasciviousness were a test of self-control. Only after a long while did the flush fade as each observer assimilated the impact of Charlotte's sensuality, made even more intense by the fact that Charlotte herself had no awareness of it. She was still a nice, reasonably innocent, disinherited British girl; a quasi virgin.

There was one spectator at every rehearsal who, despite his familiarity with Charlotte's performance, could never quite calm down afterward.

The flush on his face did not fade, nor did the pulsing in his groin abate. He was eroticized by Charlotte to the point of trauma. He could not eat for hours after seeing her. In his bed he lay awake sleepless, night after night. He dreamed of holding her.

His name was Arthur Lamb and he worked for Conrad. Arthur was Conrad's accountant. He was thirty-six years old and conservative in dress. He dealt with investors, with banks, with employees' salaries, with working capital, with budgets. Arthur Lamb was also, every now and then, a baby-sitter for Antonia. Although Johanna didn't like him very much, she succumbed to Conrad's argument that anyone he could trust with his money she could trust with their child. Arthur was not a bad-looking man. He was a bit overweight, but he had a square jaw, blue eyes, and a rather handsome face. He didn't appear to be the sort who could become unhinged by a sexual obsession.

If sex were all that Arthur sought from Charlotte there would have been no crisis; some deal, doubtless, could have been arranged to put him in possession of her. But Arthur's dream was more perverse. He dreamed of introducing her to astonished colleagues as his wife. He imagined removing her photograph from his wallet and watching envy flare up on the faces of men at bars or on trains. He dreamed of buying her flowers on their anniversary and bringing her to meet stockbrokers who would plan an annuity for her old age; for she, being twenty years his junior, would surely outlive him. So, with dreams such as those, Arthur Lamb would not be satisfied merely by a night in bed. He wanted her in marriage, blessed by the Lord, forever.

The crisis came backstage, after the morning rehearsal. He blurted out a proposal. Poor Charlotte, who knew him only slightly, smiled at what she thought was a compliment, then asked him to excuse her so she could change. She was naked, except for the high-heeled sandals, headdress, and arm bands that were her costume. He invited her to lunch. She said no.

Looking worried, Arthur went into his tiny office to check his memory about something. Although the costumes were minimal, they were made of expensive materials such as feathers and satins and lace, leather and semi-precious fur and rich velvet. Furthermore, they'd been designed by someone who, vaguely associated with Schiaparelli, charged outrageous prices. Despite their brevity, the costumes were a substantial investment. Just how big, Arthur Lamb was checking to see.

94

When Charlotte passed by Arthur's office a short while later, wearing blue jeans and a sweater, scrubbed free of make-up, her hair in pigtails, looking no older than her true age, her fresh youthfulness only incited him further. He sprang out of his swivel chair and ran after her with a repeated plea that she join him for lunch. This time, clothed and less vulnerable, she acquiesced. They went off to the nearest brasserie, where Arthur ordered a carafe of red wine and raised his glass in a toast. To our future, he said.

Over the third glass of wine, she admitted that she liked him. He seemed a decent enough sort, she said, unlike the ruffians who hung around the club thinking they owned the girls. Arthur wasn't a pincher or a feeler. Charlotte said she'd sleep with him if that's what he wanted.

But Arthur's need was tempered by a grander design. One night of sex was not the compensation he sought. He wanted her for a lifetime. He told her he loved her and advised her to marry him.

Never had the question of marriage seemed so purple a matter. She said no. She said, furthermore, that that was final. She asked whether they could order their lunch immediately, since the next rehearsal was at two. The final rehearsal was at seven that evening.

The two o'clock rehearsal ended at four-thirty, and everyone left the club. At half past six when Charlotte returned to the dressing room, she could not find her costume. Furthermore, neither could any of the other girls find theirs. All of the costumes were missing. Conrad, after being telephoned by the distraught choreographer, came to the club and searched. Everyone looked with him. They looked everywhere. The costumes were not to be found, and Arthur Lamb was not in his office.

When Arthur returned, he told Conrad in a private meeting that he had removed the costumes to a room in a house miles away. He would bring them back only on one condition. That condition was Charlotte's agreement to marry him. The club was due to open in twenty-four hours. A huge publicity effort had gone into the opening, and it seemed to have been successful. Brigitte Bardot and Roger Vadim were said to be attending. Prince Rainier was rumored to be coming, although no one believed that Princess Grace would come with him. The opening of L'Aphrodite might yet be a major event. But without those costumes there would be no opening. Conrad thought of two possibilities. The first involved turning Arthur Lamb over to one of the investors for an interrogation. The second was to persuade Charlotte to wed the son of a bitch. Conrad leaned toward the latter idea. He decided to get hold of Ned Longworth, his New York attorney who had just flown in for the opening and was also an investor. He would ask him to arbitrate.

Ned had taken Irene to dinner at Lassere, or so the doorman at the Hôtel Meurice told the flunky that Conrad had dispatched to determine Ned's whereabouts. Conrad looked at his watch. It was eight o'clock. Late in terms of what needed to be done. But too early to disturb Ned and Irene. They would just now be arriving, not yet enjoying their first aperitif. Irene, who wasn't overly fond of Conrad to begin with, would certainly not take kindly to an interruption at this point, not on her first night in Paris. Okay, dammit, the earliest he could disturb them would be half-past ten. Conrad told the musicians and the girls and the propmen to take a break until ten forty-five. He wanted everyone back in the club by that hour, even though the only parties to the dispute were Charlotte and Arthur Lamb. Charlotte was allowed to leave with the others; there was no doubt in Conrad's mind that she'd return by the deadline. But Arthur was detained by some goons who engaged him in an enforced game of poker in an effort to kill time.

At ten-thirty Ned Longworth was savoring the enraptured look on Irene's face as she ate the last of some perfect raspberries. He looked forward now to an *eau de vie de poire* with his coffee and then perhaps a short stroll with Irene; a kiss on the back of her neck, his arm around her as they walked, and then to bed. She was a good and comfortable wife for him to have. Tonight would be a sort of second honeymoon. God knows, Irene needed the reassurance from him that he still cared. It would be nice. But when the telephone was brought to their table, both Ned and Irene understood that their hopes for the evening were being wrecked.

When he told her he had to go to the club, she asked to go with him. When he refused, she wondered whether he hadn't in fact planned to get away from her into the bed of some whore. She remembered the lingerie she'd brought and winced over the artifice she'd been willing to employ to hold him.

All Conrad had told Ned was that there was a problem with the final rehearsal and that Ned was needed. What Ned actually thought was that they wanted his advice about one of the dance numbers. They've probably got something going there that's so raunchy, he thought, they want a legal opinion. He began to look forward to it. He had a taste for illicit experience. That's what he sensed now. A moment ago he had been aroused by the sight of Irene eating raspberries. Now he was looking forward to the display of flesh and the lure of fantasy. He paid the check. Irene applied some lipstick and told him two A.M. was his absolute deadline. He agreed.

It took until eleven forty-five for Ned to be ready to begin an arbitration between Arthur and Charlotte. Since their dispute involved everyone, everyone was invited to sit in a large circle of chairs placed around them on the stage.

Arthur Lamb spoke like a madman. He pleaded, cajoled, told anecdotes about his mother's real estate holdings near the Costa Brava that would one day be his (she owned a modest fish restaurant and the small parcel of land it was on), and rambled on in whispers and asides about his passion for Charlotte. Charlotte merely giggled, protesting that she felt like a slave on an auction block, and grew flushed in response to sensations of excitement this confrontation produced in her body. Suddenly, however, she understood that the cards were stacked against her. Ned pointed out that there were really only two possibilities. Either Arthur Lamb would be beaten until he produced the costumes, or Charlotte would agree to become his bride. From the way everyone stared at her, it was clear they all considered the second choice more expeditious. She didn't stand a chance. Well, she'd show them. She'd give them an event to remember. She said she needed time to think it over.

At three o'clock, when they all stopped for refreshment, Ned considered telephoning Irene. But waking her, he decided, would only reinforce her doubts about him. Better to risk sneaking in at whatever hour, unnoticed.

At four o'clock, things didn't seem much improved. Arthur Lamb was more manic than ever and Charlotte more obstinate, claiming she still needed time to think. Everyone else was struggling to remain awake. And there was still all that work to be done. The retrieval of the costumes was just the first step. They still had to rehearse.

At five o'clock, Ned Longworth asked to see Charlotte privately in Conrad's office. Twenty minutes later the two of them emerged, Ned looking triumphant, Charlotte smiling sweetly, intermittently giving Arthur shy and loving glances. The arbitration was settled; Charlotte had agreed to the marriage. But how had it been done? That was still Ned's secret.

Arthur drew a map showing where the costumes were and handed over

97

some keys to various doors. All of this Conrad gave to one of his men, who was dispatched to bring everything back.

Conrad took Ned into his office and demanded to know the secret of his sudden success.

"I figured a girl like Charlotte is basically a very insecure person, right?"

"Right?"

"Hungry for some sense of importance, right?"

"Right."

"The guy she'd marry has to offer something to improve her status even if just a little bit, follow?"

"I follow."

"Well, what's Arthur Lamb got to offer?"

"I dunno."

"Neither did I. But I'm thinking. And then it hits me."

"*What* hits you?"

"Have you seen a movie called *The Hustler*? An American movie."

"No. It's showing somewhere in Paris, but I haven't seen it."

"But you know who Paul Newman is."

"Yeah, he's the one who didn't want to fuck Elizabeth Taylor in *Cat on a Hot Tin Roof*."

"Right."

"What the hell has this got to do with anything?"

"Just be patient."

"Go on."

"The first thing I asked her was whether she'd seen *The Hustler*."

"Had she?"

"No. But she'd heard about it. She'd been reading about Paul Newman in a magazine. I asked her whether she happened to have the magazine with her. She did. In her handbag. I figured there'd be pictures. I asked her to get it." Ned paused for effect.

"All right. Then what?"

"The resemblance between that son of a bitch Arthur and Paul Newman is uncanny. She stared at the pictures in that magazine and just kept on looking. Same jaw, same blue eyes, same nose, same everything, except that our boy is a bit on the pudgy side, a sort of fat version, but to a yearner like Charlotte the resemblance is all that counts. There's her status, you see. It's by proxy, but who cares? She can tell everyone that her husband looks exactly like a famous movie star. I think Paul New-

98

man will really have to continue making it big to make this marriage last. But in the meantime Charlotte is hooked. Brilliant?"

"Brilliant," Conrad agreed. "There's one thing more, though."

"What's that?"

"I want this presented to Arthur in a way that puts him deeply in my debt. Can you do that?"

"I guess so. Why?"

"Because I want him deeply in my debt, that's all. He's been useful to me. He even baby-sits. He's been somebody I can trust. Somebody who'd do anything at all for me. I want to keep it that way. In my debt. Okay?"

"I guess so," Ned said.

"Oh, and one other thing."

"What's that?"

"We've got a houseguest, a guy named Jeff Winter. You'll see him with Johanna at the opening. When you talk to Arthur, tell him to make a real effort to stay out of Jeff's path. I don't want them to meet. Shouldn't be difficult; Johanna can't stand Arthur anyway. I'm not even going to tell Johanna what happened at the club tonight. Okay?"

"Okay."

Conrad slapped Ned on the back, and the two of them laughed.

Eighteen hours later, the club L'Aphrodite had its opening.

The uppermost question in Jeff's mind as he sat there absorbing its ambience was whether or not this den of iniquity was to be taken seriously. He had to turn to Johanna to ask if it was one big joke or truly as wicked as it seemed. Johanna assured him of the latter. The pimps at the bar were real pimps, and the half dozen or so whores seated at small tables scattered around the room were real whores. They were all essential ingredients of the living decor. The idea, she explained, was to bring the street life of Paris indoors; a self-consciously expensive equivalency of the sort of dive one could find in less attractive parts of the city, but a place to be taken seriously on its own terms for all of that. The extra ingredient here was a show that borrowed its potency from the Crazy Horse and then developed a mind all its own. The show, triumphantly successful with tonight's gala audience, had ended an hour ago.

Conrad had been busy backstage and in the front office most of the evening. He made one appearance to be introduced to Peter Lawford and another to pay some protection money to a local tough, but he remained out of sight much of the while. Johanna kept out of the limelight and was, in turn, left uninvolved in the grand events except as a spectator, just as she and Conrad had agreed. To a stranger passing Johanna's table, it would have seemed that she and Jeff were lovers, a nuance that did not escape Conrad's quick eye. At one point he whispered into Ned Longworth's ear that Ned should keep an eye on Johanna. But it hardly mattered, for from Ned and Irene's table, Johanna and Jeff could not be seen unless Ned were to stand up and call attention to the fact that he was observing them.

So the growing tension between Conrad and Johanna over Jeff did not register on Ned at all. Ned would return to New York in a few days unaware that a storm was brewing, and in the months to come he would know only what Conrad would tell him and nothing more. Ned and Johanna had met only once previously, and their meeting tonight was very brief. So Ned's impression of Johanna was ephemeral. The fact that Conrad had asked him to keep an eye on her had no real impact on him whatever. Conrad was the sort of man who, either directly or indirectly, kept an eye on everyone he could.

After the club closed, the dancers and musicians, the waiters, some of the investors, two of the whores, the girls from the cloakroom, and Ned and Irene stayed on to drink champagne, exchange good wishes, and assure each other of steady work and plenty of money for years to come. Arthur Lamb and Charlotte sneaked away quietly before the celebration began. Jeff and Johanna remained at their table, oblivious to everyone.

"You know what I discovered tonight?" Jeff asked.

"What?"

"That I've got a talent after all. A talent for appreciation. I've been looking at you. I've been watching what your eyes do as your mind changes subjects, and how your mouth works."

"I've been wanting to kiss you."

"Not here."

"I know. But, I've been doing it all evening anyway, in my mind. Have you been getting my kisses?"

"I think I have. I'm very warm."

"Do you *want* to be in love?" she asked him.

"Does it happen by wanting?"

"Do you want to *let* it happen?"

"It's already happened," he said.

"Are you willing, then, to be unhappily in love with me?"

"Why unhappily?"

"Just look around."

"Are you in love with *me*?" he asked.

She laughed. "No man has ever asked me that before, not even Conrad. Am I in love with you?" Her eyes were already answering. "Yes," she said.

"Well?" he said, as though proving a point. "Why should we be unhappy?"

She laughed again. "Oh, God," she said, "I can't think of a single reason."

Chapter Seven

They said goodnight to Jeff and went to their room.

They started to undress in silence. Then Conrad turned on her.

"Everyone in the club tonight could see that you've got the hots for old Jeffrey."

"Can we try very hard not to go on with this?"

"Sure we can. . . . I want to fuck."

"If you weren't drunk and ugly you'd be comical."

"Listen, I mean it. I want to fuck."

"Then you'd better put your clothes back on," she said.

"That's not the way it's done. That ain't the way."

"You can head right back out the front door and find yourself some woman for hire. Cause it won't be me."

"Oh, it will, it will, my lady. It will."

"You don't stand a chance."

"Don't I?" He had removed his suspenders. Now, grabbing her wrists, he encircled them with the elastic and pulled the suspenders tightly around in an attempt to bind her. It was a clumsy arrangement, but it made his point potently. Her stomach caught fire. Until she freed herself, which took only a few seconds, she felt like a drowning person fiercely struggling for the surface. He waited for her to be free, then threw her onto the bed.

"I want pussy. And do you know why I want pussy? Cause it's time to make another baby. My son! Do you hear me?"

In a blind rage that was just one purely reflexive movement, she kicked him, causing him to howl. He grabbed himself and danced around the room.

Jeff got into bed naked, already half asleep, half dreaming of Johanna, conjuring her into his arms. His body was tense and hot. He felt muscles flexing everywhere. Then he heard her scream.

Jeff bolted up and waited. He expected to hear Conrad next. Booming. Threatening. He waited.

"No! Get away from me! I'm going to call for help; I don't give a damn who hears me, do you understand? Crazy bastard! You must be out of your mind!"

Where was the maid? Surely she was hearing this. Why wasn't Antonia crying out in the nursery? Was everyone in the apartment sitting up in bed in impotent terror just as Jeff was? Not knowing what to do? Did he dare to intervene? What the hell was the proper etiquette for a houseguest overhearing his host beating his hostess? He could imagine Johanna's fury at him if he intruded. He could cope with Conrad. But he knew that Johanna would find it intolerable were he to do anything other than mind his own business.

"I hate you!" she screamed. "Hate you! Hate you!"

Jeff put on his clothes as quickly as he could. He was shaking. He had to get out of that apartment.

He put on the same clothes he had worn to the club earlier. He had no idea where he would go, stumbling around the city at half-past five on a wintry morning. Within minutes he was out the door and down the stairs.

"Please," Conrad pleaded. "Please, please, please." He was crying. Defeated by her. In pain. Begging her not to leave him.

"You disgust me! I want to vomit! You're an animal!"

"Please," he said. "I beg you. Please . . ."

"I hate your litany! Stop it."

104

"Then talk to me. Please . . ."

"I'll never forgive you for this. Never," she said.

"Johanna, I—" He grabbed himself at the groin. "Oh! Goddamn it, you hurt me!"

"Good," she said. "My mother always told me the best way to handle a rapist was a good swift kick in the balls. Now I know mother was right about something."

"Your mother's a cunt. A ballbreaker."

"Charm will get you nowhere."

"Funny."

"What do you want to talk about? What could we possibly say to each other now?"

"I could tell you I'm sorry."

"But you're not sorry. You would have raped me if you'd been able to."

"And you would have enjoyed it."

"Fuck you, Conrad. Listen, I'm walking out on you. I mean it. I've had all I can take."

"Don't, Johanna. Don't—" He was crying now. Heaving. He was still drunk on champagne.

Johanna trembled. She tried desperately to control the shaking, but it wouldn't stop. Conrad was on the floor waiting for his pain to subside, his face white and pasty. He looked terrified.

"We're a pathetic sight," Johanna said. "Do you still think there's something for us to talk about?"

"Yes. Yes, I do. Give me the chance. Will you?"

"Sure." She said it without conviction.

But he had no idea where to begin. "Listen. None of that shit about my being jealous of Jeff was serious, just before."

"For Christ's sake, Conrad!"

"No. Listen. Please. You said you'd listen."

"To sense. I won't listen to anything crazy. You would have raped me!"

"And you kicked me in the balls! In the balls!" he screamed.

"Good! Good! I'd do it again. Right now if you like. Just try me, if you don't believe me!"

"I should have tied your feet instead of your hands. That was my big mistake."

"You're a loser, Conrad."

"No," he said. He seemed to collapse even further; a big mass of a man suddenly crying, worrying her, causing her sorrow, and finally repulsing her.

"Johanna?"

"What?" Her voice was dead.

"Can we have another child?"

"You know the answer to that."

"No?"

"No."

"Never?"

"I don't deal in never. But probably never."

"Listen," he said. His voice trailed off. He appeared to be falling asleep right there on the floor in front of her.

"What is it?"

"I've got to go away," he said.

"Where to?"

"London. New business in London. Come with me."

"Not on your life."

"Got to leave in three days," he told her. "Come with me. Take Antonia."

"No."

"Will you be here when I come back?" he asked her.

"I'll be here."

"Can I trust you, Johanna?"

She knew exactly what that meant.

"Answer me," Conrad whimpered.

"You can trust me." She stood up.

"Where are you going?"

"To sleep. You can stay there on the floor if you like."

He got into bed soon after she did. She retreated to one corner and slept there all curled up. He didn't dare come near her. But in the morning, when she awoke, they were lying very close and her hand was in his. It took her a moment to remember her anger. But even then she had to acknowledge the strength of the attachment that would bring their bodies so close. She waited. Then she took her hand away. He was sound asleep still. She looked at him, deliberately recalling her anger. She sat up slowly so as not to disturb him. "Bastard," she whispered, carefully getting out of bed. She put on her robe and looked at her watch. It was half past ten. Antonia would be out for her morning stroll with the maid. They'd be on their way to the market. The apartment would be quiet. She wondered whether Jeff was still sleeping.

She opened her bedroom door with great caution, praying there'd be no creaking sound. Then she closed it behind her. She walked down the hall and stood outside Jeff's room. She had no idea he'd gone out at the height of their quarrel and then come back in. She heard him moving about, probably dressing. She knocked. She had come to tell him the news. Conrad was going to London.

"Three days," Johanna told Jeff.

"How can you be sure?"

"I looked in his appointment book. He leaves Sunday night and has a late afternoon flight back on Wednesday."

"Okay." Jeff exhaled a long breath. "I guess we can relax. All we have to do is survive until Sunday. How many more meals do we have to eat together between now and then?"

"Concentrate on your food and on Antonia; that should help."

"Just make sure there's plenty of wine on the table."

"He asked me if he could trust me." Lying to Conrad had made her thoroughly miserable.

"Johanna—we don't have to do this. We don't have to cheat on him. We can wait."

"Can we?"

"Yes. I could leave Paris for a while."

"But you're not leaving. I don't want you to go. I'm in love with you."

"I'm in love with you, Johanna."

"We'll go to a hotel on each of those afternoons."

"And on one of those nights stay over? Can we arrange that?"

She began to laugh.

"What?" he asked. "What is it?"

"It doesn't matter what we do. Conrad will know. Are you prepared for that?"

"Prepared? I love you Johanna. I don't know what else to say."

The days that followed were days of unexpected calm in which, despite their tensions, the three of them fell into a pattern of easy friendship once

107

more. They told stories and shared reminiscences, filling in for each other details of the past as though to create a bond of shared history. The heat went out of their bodies. The thing about innocence when it exists in the imagination is that it can be recaptured whenever the mood is right. Not only was the mood now right, but their enthusiasm for it could not have been greater. They knew disaster was coming. This was their way of forgetting.

"I'm going to tell him about your mother," Conrad said.

"Grandma?" Antonia's face lit up in a beautiful smile. They were finishing dinner; it was way past her bedtime. She'd been so quiet they'd forgotten her.

"You go to sleep, sweetheart," Conrad told her, "and I'll tell you the story another time."

"Stay up!" she pleaded.

But Conrad bellowed the name of the maid, who came to remove the child.

"The story you're about to hear," he said by way of introduction after Antonia was gone from the room, "is not suitable for the ears of a child."

Johanna had no idea what he was about to tell. She leaned back, prepared to be entertained.

"Kiddies," Conrad began, "do you remember the year nineteen-fifty-six?"

They nodded. They did. Conrad continued.

"It was all of six fucking long years ago except we didn't do much fucking in those days. Johanna, you see, was a virgin. And that's the name of this story."

"I didn't want to be," she protested.

"Sshh! You're giving away the punch line."

"The name of the story should be 'The Reluctant Virgin,' " she added, helpfully.

"Or 'The Frustrated Virgin,' " Conrad said, correcting her.

"I was a good girl who loved life; it was all very confusing, you see." She turned to Jeff, once more the mediator. She had to convince him. It was as though she and Conrad were drunk. Only they weren't. They were just at it again, at each other again, the same stupid, aggressive, obscene dance of courtship. Damn them. Jeff poured himself another glass of wine and made an effort to listen.

108

"You were a good girl," Conrad said, "and you had the hottest untouched twat in town."

"Listen, folks," Jeff said, embarrassed, sounding a bit more high-strung than he intended, "I'd like to hear the story about Johanna's mother. Okay?"

"You're hearing it," Conrad said. "This is the story."

"Oh."

"The year was fifty-six. We met in April. Do you remember, Johanna?"

"Yes."

"You were nineteen and going to the Art Students League. You were painting naked bodies even then."

"I was going to school at night. In real life I worked at an ad agency."

"I've heard this part of it before," Jeff said a bit impatiently.

"I ran my own agency in Boston," Conrad said. "She came up in answer to an ad I placed. You know all that?"

"Yep."

"Nearly four months passed between the time I offered her the job and the time she moved to Boston to begin working for me. You don't know that."

"Okay," Jeff said. "Please begin."

"Well . . . We met during the first week in April, and I fell in love with her. She went back to New York on the train, and I knew I couldn't wait until July, when she would begin work, to see her again. I had her résumé. I knew her phone number and where she lived. So . . ."

"He came to see me."

"And slept at the Y."

Conrad told Jeff of one particular weekend late in May when, to his and Johanna's total surprise, he was invited by Johanna's mother, Alma Berg, to sleep not at the Y but under her roof.

It rained that weekend, one of those steady, warm, soft spring showers. Johanna loved to walk in the rain without an umbrella. But Alma required the reassurance of a hairnet, rain bonnet, plastic raincoat, floral imprinted umbrella, and galoshes before she could even think about the short distance from their front porch to the dress shop she and her husband Stephen owned. Normally she would drive the car to the shop with Stephen beside her. But on this particular Saturday, Stephen had been

109

sent on ahead to open the shop alone, and he had taken the car with him.

This was a special day. Conrad Thornton, the handsome young entrepreneurial gentleman in the advertising game, having arrived from Boston the night before, was at that very moment having his breakfast in Alma's dining room. Johanna, who had had breakfast with her mother earlier, was in the kitchen frying eggs. Alma was in the front hall trying to tie a knot in her rain bonnet while making small talk.

"Did you sleep all right?" Alma called to Conrad.

"Like a baby," he grinned.

"Hope the television didn't disturb you."

"Not at all."

"I was watching a play with an actress who could pass for Marilyn Monroe's twin sister," Alma said with the air of someone convinced she was sharing an important insight.

"A lot of actresses, I guess, are trying to look like Marilyn Monroe," Conrad said.

"I don't see why. Oh, I know she makes a lot of money and all, but there's no real talent there, if you ask me. I guess I know what Joe DiMaggio thought he saw in her, but to tell you the truth I feel sorry for him now. When you run a business like mine you meet all types, believe me, and after a while you begin to understnad that what really counts isn't—"

She stopped suddenly and turned to stare in his direction, while her mind raced ahead. Her rain bonnet securely tied beneath her chin now, she padded across the floor in her galoshes to the dining room table and sat down next to him. He got the feeling she might hang her umbrella from his arm.

"You're in advertising," she said to him. It wasn't a question. Advertising was, after all, a focal theme in the relationship between Conrad and her daughter. Furthermore, one of the reasons she approved of his courtship of Johanna was the fact that he owned his own agency.

"What I'm trying to say," she continued, "is that someone like Marilyn Monroe must mean something very different to you from what she means to me. You see her the same way they see her in Hollywood. If it sells, it's got to be good. Am I right?"

"Well, I guess you're right."

"Too bad," she said. She looked at her watch, got up abruptly, and went into the kitchen to tell Johanna that the cleaning woman, "the girl" as Alma referred to her, would be along in five minutes, so Johanna needn't bother with the beds upstairs or the dishes in the sink. Then, blowing Johanna a quick kiss, Alma returned to the dining room, nodded goodbye to Conrad, and headed for the front door and out into the rain at last.

Johanna came into the dining room a moment later with Conrad's eggs, which she'd been deliberately holding, keeping them warm in the pan. "What was she saying to you?" she asked, setting them down.

"Oh. We were having a philosophical discussion about Marilyn Monroe, that's all."

"Philosophical or moralistic?"

"Moralistic." He grinned. "She started a sentence way back whenever that I'd love to hear the ending of. She said that after a while in a business like hers you begin to understand that what really counts isn't—And then she broke off. What comes after 'isn't'?"

" 'Sex.' I've heard it before."

"I thought it was 'sex.' But that seemed too easy."

"Filling in my mother's sentences isn't in the same league as doing the *New York Times* crossword puzzle; I think you better get that clear right now."

"I've got it. I've got it," he said.

"Do you know why they left at different times this morning?"

"No. Alma likes to sleep later than Stephen?"

"So we wouldn't be left alone."

"We're alone now."

"The housekeeper who normally comes here twice a week has been engaged for the rest of the morning and the entire afternoon, by which time they will have returned. Dammit, Conrad, they won't let me lose my virginity."

"We can have a threesome with the maid," he said. "It's a terrific way for you to break in. How old is she?"

"Young enough."

"Terrific! Listen, when I was in the army there were these two girls in San Antonio—"

"I don't want to hear it. Okay?"

"Okay."

"Are you serious or just kidding?"

"Serious," he said.

"Really serious?"

111

"Yes." But he began to laugh. And she laughed too. Her relief was enormous. But so was her curiosity.

"You *were* kidding."

"About you, me, and the maid, yes. About me in San Antonio I wasn't kidding."

"You slept with two girls at one time?"

"In the army it was something to brag about. I was a braggart."

"Still are," she said.

"Still am. So?"

"What do you do when there are three of you in bed?"

"First you'd better find out what happens when there are just two," he said.

"Do you really love me?"

"Yes." His voice was so soft it melted her. "I love you very much."

"Then I want you to teach me," she said. "But Conrad?"

"What?"

"After you teach me I'm going to want you to marry me, do you know that?"

"I figured out as much."

"If you still love me after we make love, will you marry me?"

"Maybe."

"And give me half of the advertising agency?" She threw her arms around him, nearly upsetting his cup of coffee in the process. She was shrieking with laughter, and beneath it there was a possessiveness he already understood. She sat in his lap and this time did upset the coffee. She kissed him. Then she pulled away. "There's one thing more," she said, cleaning up the mess she'd made on the table.

"What more could there be?"

"Just this. There'll never be anyone but the two of us in our bed. Understand?"

He was running his hand up her skirt.

"Stop that!"

The doorbell rang. She went to answer it. It was the housekeeper.

After Conrad's third cup of coffee, they left the table together. "Will you take a walk with me?" she asked. "I'll show you Yonkers."

He grabbed her wrist. "Listen," he said. "Can we borrow a car?"

"There's no one I can borrow a car from on Saturday."

"We could rent one. There must be a motel somewhere between here and Manhattan. We could be back by five."

"Tonight; we'll figure something out. I promise."

"Are you kidding? Those walls are so thin up there they might as well be curtained partitions. And those goddamn creaking floors. Can't they afford carpeting? Doesn't anyone ever have sex in this house?"

"Probably not," she said. "I don't know."

"Oh, Johanna," he said. "Fucking is so nice. You'll see."

"Is it the same as making love?"

"What the hell are you talking about? Of course!"

"Are you sure?"

"Yes."

"Then don't say fucking. Say making love. I'm still a virgin." She wasn't smiling. She meant it. "You better be nice to me, Conrad, or your ass is going to be in a sling."

"There's something just a little off about your slang, Johanna. You don't quite have the hang of it."

"That's all right," she said. "I hate vulgarity even when it's my own."

They took a walk, and she pointed out the houses her friends lived in and where her parents' friends lived. She took him to her parents' dress shop, where they happened to arrive at a moment when her father, who did the tailoring, was on his knees in front of a stout customer who had just bought a tent of a dress that required a new hem. Stephen had a mouth full of pins, so all he could manage from his humble position was to look up at his daughter and at Conrad and wave. Alma was on the phone ordering lunch from the local delicatessen. She waved at them too. The shop was small, and when two women emerged from the dressing rooms at the same moment for their first glance at themselves in the three-way mirror, the place became unquestionably overcrowded. Conrad and Johanna waved back at everyone, smiled, and left.

The shop was in a residential part of Yonkers, not in the downtown section, and as they continued their walk, Johanna pointed out more houses of people she grew up with.

"How come you never went to college?" Conrad asked suddenly.

"I read a lot. I go to the Art Students League for painting classes. I've learned the advertising business in a very short while. I'm employable, as you yourself have recently noticed. Why go to college?"

He thought for a moment. It seemed like a good answer. But for a girl like Johanna it wasn't quite good enough. So he repeated the question.

She gave him a puzzled look. Then she gave him the answer he expected.

"They wanted me to go to New York University and live at home. It's a big commute, but it's possible. Friends of mine do it. But living at home for as long as it would take to get a degree was something I couldn't bear the thought of."

"Are you really in love with me?"

"You're the right opportunity. Is that what you mean?"

"Are you in love with me?"

"I think so. I'll have a better idea after tonight," she said, smiling. "Do you really think it's possible to make love in that house?"

"You were the one who said you'd think of something to make it possible."

"Yeah." She put her arm around his waist. Then she put her head on his shoulder. "I'll surely try."

They stood still. She raised her face. He kissed her lightly, sweetly, on the mouth. She clung to him. "I'll come to your room when I think it's safe," she said.

They walked for hours, stopping for lunch and then, much later, at a noisy bar for a beer. They walked so far they had to call a taxi to get home.

They survived the cocktail hour with Alma and Stephen. And dinner. And *Lawrence Welk* in the family room. They survived the *News* and the *Late Show.* Somehow, it got to be half past one, and everyone finally went upstairs to bed.

An hour and a half later she came to him. Naked beneath a long, white terrycloth robe. Carrying an old towel to put on the bed to protect the sheet; she had already thought of how she would remove it from the house in a brown paper bag and leave it in some trash can in Manhattan.

She came to him on fire; melting. She imagined herself a femme fatale, coming to harness his lust and press it into service. The risk tonight was not really hers, but Conrad's. That was the secret she carried in her heart.

"I've got to talk to you," he whispered.

"Let me get into bed with you first."

"I'll put the light on."

"No, don't! It shines into the hall under the door."

"Listen," he said, "this isn't turning out exactly the way we had imagined."

"What do you mean?" She was under the covers now. She could feel the warmth of his body.

"I can't find my condoms."

114

She bolted up. "What?"

"They're gone."

"What do you mean?"

"Hey, keep your voice down. You'll wake your fucking mother."

"Tell me what you mean."

"I told you. They're gone."

"Your condoms?"

"Yes."

"From where? Where were they?"

"In my suitcase."

"How many?"

"What difference does that make?"

"I want to know whether it was a tiny thing that got lost, which one or two condoms would be, or something larger, like a dozen in a box."

"You've got it."

"A dozen in a box?"

"Right."

"You're sure they were in your suitcase?"

"Jesus! Yes!"

"My mother went through your things and removed them! I'm sure that's what happened."

"Alma?"

"I have only one mother, and her name is Alma. She came home at some point while we were out walking. And she did it then. She took your condoms."

"I don't believe it," Conrad said.

They fell into a sullen silence while their bodies got warmer. Their hands touched. Then their arms and legs. And he was on top of her, in agony, asking her what they should do.

"If I get pregnant, you have to marry me. Okay?"

There was enough moonlight coming through the window for him to see her body, and he went wild with desire for her. He also remembered that he had to deal with her virginity, which meant there was going to be a kind of clinical aspect to the proceedings. But he'd do the best he could.

Their first time together was a chore for both of them. Afterward, they rested. Then they tried again, and this time found bliss. After that, they slept.

When Johanna returned to her room at seven in the morning, certain

115

her parents were still asleep, which was their usual Sunday morning habit, she understood that her mother had been on the prowl. Johanna's bed, which she'd left so rumpled when she got out of it hours earlier, had been made, a sign from Alma that she knew what was going on.

Enraged and guilty, Johanna went into the shower. After a while she came out and got dressed. While she was combing her hair, she heard her father going out the front door on his way to play golf. She wondered whether Conrad was still in his room sleeping; she wanted to tell him about Alma making up her bed in the middle of the night. It was eight o'clock. She went downstairs.

Her mother was sitting at the dining-room table over a cup of coffee and the Sunday *Times*. Conrad, in a robe, barefoot and disheveled, towered over her.

"You shouldn't have taken my condoms, Alma," he was shouting. "Alma, do you hear me?"

Johanna backed up to the bottom of the stairs and grabbed the banister for support.

"You son of a bitch, get out of my house!" Alma screamed at Conrad.

"He'll get out of your house, don't worry about that!" Johanna screamed back. "And so will I?"

"Tramp!" her mother whimpered.

"Tramp, tramp, tramp," Conrad sang in a ridiculous baritone. "That's my favorite song. Sigmund Romberg, isn't it?"

"Here!" Alma shrieked as she removed his box of condoms from the bulging pocket of her apron and flung them at him.

"We screwed without them, Alma," he shouted. "Left you a bloody towel as part of the bargain."

"Conrad, I hate you!" Johanna hooted. But it didn't seem from her tone of voice that she hated him at all. She was enjoying his unrelenting energy. He loved life the way she did and the way her mother and her father did not. She didn't take her mother's tears too seriously when they began to flow. Conrad was plainly her hero in this comedy. God, it was funny. And wonderful. "Conrad," she shouted. "I love you!"

Then she turned to her mother and tried to embrace her and calm her.

"Get away from me," Alma snapped.

"Mother, don't cry."

116

"Get away!"

"Mother?"

"What? What do you want? Get away."

"We're getting married."

Conrad looked as though he might go through the floor.

"Only if you got pregnant!" he bellowed in protest. "That's all I promised."

"No. I'm talking about your earlier vow. Remember? If you still love me after we make love will you marry me? That's what I asked you, and you said yes."

"I said maybe."

"Do you still love me?"

"Yes! Yes! Goddamn it!"

"Mother?"

"Are you really getting married?" Alma asked.

"Yes," Johanna answered.

"Oh, darling," Alma said, perfectly dry-eyed now. "That's wonderful news. Your father will be so pleased. That's wonderful news. Conrad?"

"Yes?"

"That's wonderful news."

"Thank you," Conrad said.

"Wonderful news," Alma repeated.

Conrad was on his hands and knees somewhere under the table. They didn't ask him what he was doing there, because they knew. He was trying to retrieve the condoms Alma had flung at him across the room. He found them. He crawled out and stood up.

"Wonderful news," he muttered, and went back upstairs.

Applause! Bravo!

Conrad's story had cast a strange spell over all of them. A glow irradiated the table, making Jeff feel decidedly uncomfortable. It disconcerted him to have to deal with Johanna's courtship by Conrad.

"Oh, God," Johanna said. "I'll never forget those condoms as long as I live."

"Do you see much of your parents?" Jeff asked.

"They're dead. My mother died of cancer shortly after we were married. And my father fell asleep at the wheel of his car about six months after that." She brushed back some hair that had fallen over her eyes. "Jeff, don't you have a story?"

"Not as good as that one."

"Tell it anyway."

"Maybe tomorrow," Jeff said.

"Tomorrow I'll be gone," Conrad reminded him. And the room froze into silence.

Chapter Eight

Antonia's nightmare grew out of an anxiety created by Conrad over his departure. She couldn't understand why she and her mother hadn't gone with him. It seemed like such a nice trip, flying in a plane for just an hour and arriving in a foreign country that her great-grandparents had once lived in. Conrad had explained all of that to her, sitting on her bed, showing her a map, pointing out the body of water the plane would fly over, and drawing a circle around London, where the plane would land. Of course she had asked him the inevitable question, "Can Mommy and I come too, Daddy?" And he had told her how much he wanted them to come and that Mommy had said they couldn't.

Something in his tone left a cloud of doubt, planted an unspoken fear. Johanna became aware of it from the questions Antonia had asked her all through the morning, before Conrad's actual leave-taking. So it wasn't a complete surprise that Antonia awakened from her sleep that night crying. That bastard, Johanna said to herself, holding Antonia, rocking her, comforting her, that bastard doesn't mind upsetting his own daughter in an effort to manipulate me. When Antonia fell back to sleep, Johanna contemplated her affair with Jeff with a new determination.

The next morning, before Jeff awoke, Johanna telephoned the Hôtel Continental to reserve a room in the name of Kruger. Mr. and Mrs.

119

Herman Kruger. She reserved it for two days. She couldn't wait to tell Jeff the names she had invented for them.

They ate a large breakfast, intermittently joined by Antonia who seemed to be suffering no bad effects from last night's dreams. Johanna told the maid to take Antonia to the park in the afternoon if the weather was clear, and to broil two lamb chops for her supper. Johanna explained that she and Mr. Winter would be gone until sometime late tonight. "Oh, if Mr. Thornton should call, please tell him we've gone to Versailles and then on to dinner at"—it suddenly occurred to her that he might telephone the restaurant—"just tell him we weren't certain where we'd be having dinner."

They packed a bag in order to respect the convention of checking into a hotel with at least one suitcase. And as long as they were actually packing, Johanna found things to take along. A black dress in case they did go out later, or maybe she'd just try it on for Jeff and let him remove it from her body. Stockings. Shoes. A hairbrush. She went into his room and asked him whether he'd like to take a white shirt, a tie, a suit, any or all of the above. He wondered which was better, a suit or an extra pair of trousers to go with the jacket he was wearing. They knew they weren't making much sense. Her hands were shaking. His were merely cold.

In the taxi—they could have walked, but a freezing rain had begun to fall—he complained about becoming lazy. He wasn't working hard enough at becoming a tourist, he said.

"Was that really your plan when you came here?"

"Well, I thought I'd absorb some culture."

"I think you're actually serious."

"I am. I want to be a typical American in Paris."

"I thought, to coin a phrase, you came to find yourself."

"That too."

"Well?"

"I found you instead. Falling in love has proved to be very distracting."

"We could just go to the movies and then go home," she said.

He grabbed her shoulders. Then he encircled her with his arms and pulled her against him. He kissed her until neither of them could breathe.

When he pulled back, he laughed, embarrassed by his own clumsiness. But she laughed too, so it was all right. She knew how gentle his kisses could be.

"I want to lie naked next to you," she whispered. She put his hand on her breast and held it there while she kissed his neck. "Oh, hurry," she said into his shoulder, willing the taxi to go faster, "hurry, please hurry."

Their driver coped with the impossible traffic as best he could. It was a short distance they were traveling. Although it seemed to take forever, they soon were there.

While Jeff was signing the hotel register, Johanna saw Arthur Lamb. In a tweed porkpie hat that fell down over his ears, he looked considerably less like Paul Newman. The first sight of him caused a small, hot explosion in her stomach. But then she quieted herself. She thought through her predicament and decided to hell with it, to hell with Conrad and his whole fucking squadron of goons. There was no escaping them. She had given Jeff fair warning, and he seemed willing enough to run the risk. Why alarm him now? She decided to say nothing. While Jeff's back was turned, she stared hard at Arthur and quickly gave him the finger, a gesture that did not go unappreciated in the crowded hotel lobby. Arthur stared back dumbly as she and Jeff walked arm in arm toward the elevator.

They were shown to their room by a bellboy, and then, from nowhere, a housekeeper appeared to point out the towels, the bidet, and the light switch, which controlled all of the lamps in the room and was known as *le général*.

There were large French windows that overlooked the Tuileries Gardens, where despite the winter rain there were children playing. They looked out the windows, possessing the scene, making of it their special memory. The bellboy and the housekeeper recognized the attitude, having witnessed it hundreds of times before, and without a trace of cynicism or impatience, retreated from the room.

They removed their coats and threw them on a chair. Her skirt and blouse fell away, and she was naked. It was wonderful to find her body so quickly. He inhaled her warmth all at once. The suddenness of her beauty made him shiver even as the blood overheated in his loins. He kissed her mouth and then her breasts and then her mouth again while she lay back on the incredibly soft bed and opened her body to him. He seemed to have so much to remove compared to her, an undershirt and shorts and socks and shoes with laces, but when he was naked neither of them could remember what it felt like to be clothed. On top of her, inside her, he didn't notice that his mind was no longer with him, no longer the friendly

121

observer, for there was nothing to observe. There were no parts, no parts at all; that was what was wonderful. No parts; no bodies even. Just the two of them in their wholeness receiving each other. Returning the gift, then receiving it back again. Oh, God, it was beautiful. Where was his mind now? Somewhere inside her mind, because what he felt was somehow interchangeable with what she felt. That was what was so remarkable about their wholeness. She was feeling the same thing exactly, and where her feelings began and his ended they could no longer tell. And it was building. There were small sounds that came from their blood and their breath and their rushing together; then one sound that grew and grew. When they came, fully and together, it was with a layered and slow-building intensity. They absolutely knew they were in love.

They didn't sleep. They made love a second time. This time she rode on top of him and asked him to admire her breasts, and as she rode, her chest grew flushed and her hair flew, and she told him how good his cock felt inside her and she came quickly, before he did, changing her position on him as she came so that instead of sitting straight up she leaned over with her chest on his chest, bending over him to make exactly the contact she wanted, and she shrieked and bit him, and he laughed in pleasure, happy, so happy to see her enthralled. And when she finished coming, he asked her to sit straight up again and ride him slowly, and he told her what a beautiful cunt she had, because that was what she wanted to hear then. The time had come for those words, and they spoke them as though they'd never been spoken by lovers in bed before, and their lust was full.

They made love a third time. This time he got behind her. She bent over, on her knees, and he touched her between her thighs and kissed her round rump. The smell of their lovemaking was pungent now. He studied her in her submission. He felt freer in his lust now because she couldn't see him. His brain was working, and he knew hers was also. He entered her from his position of dominance. He was fucking her. Enjoying the spectacle. He came quickly, and so did she, and just as quickly he rolled her over onto her back and hurried to embrace her, to kiss her, to hold her hand, to drive away the twinge of guilt he felt, to obliterate the possibility that they had already lost the innocence of their first coition. She was smiling, and her eyes were softer than any eyes he had ever seen. There was an unimaginable beauty in her face. He told her that. He told her that *he* ought to be the painter, not she, so she could be his subject. She loved his words as much as his mouth, which she kissed over and over. Then she said that since she was the painter and not he, he would be the subject, and that she would paint him naked and wet from their lovemaking, to immortalize their juices. The idea made him nervous, but the image seemed heroic. He smiled as they both grew sleepy.

They slept in each other's arms, and when they awoke she felt a response to him in her skin that was like a quiet ecstasy. It had been good before, but too frenzied, too rushed. Nothing earlier had matched this feeling. They weren't making love, but she felt closer. All of her feelings were softer than before, and more erotic. She told him about it. She wanted him to go on lying there next to her without possessing her. He said that what she really wanted was love with a clearer conscience. She thought about it, and she had to agree. But then she thought of something that spoiled it. If she and Jeff were lovers in a state of good conscience, then she and Conrad had to be enemies. It was the first confrontation in her head with the fact of enmity. It frightened her.

They didn't mean to spend the night there. Their plan was to return to the apartment before midnight, as a defense against the claim that they had run off together. Of course it was foolish. What difference did it make now? Arthur Lamb was a witness to their afternoon adultery; they might just as well have stayed on through the night. But then there was the matter of Antonia. In the morning, Antonia would rap on Johanna's bedroom door and want to know that her mother was there.

They weren't back in the apartment five minutes when the phone rang. She knew it was Conrad before she answered it. She had asked the maid for her messages when she and Jeff came in, and the maid had said there weren't any. Conrad hadn't called. He knew without inquiring that she wasn't home, so why waste a call from London. Apparently, he also knew the precise moment she and Jeff would return.

She let the phone ring five times—Antonia was too soundly asleep to be disturbed—before she answered it.

"Hi," Conrad said. His voice was clipped, tight.

"Hello, Conrad. How're things?"

"Things? Funny your asking about *things*. You should have asked about tricks."

"Okay. How are tricks?" She realized too late that he was baiting her.

"Tricks? I think you're the authority on tricks, Johanna."

123

She slammed down the phone. War was officially declared between them.

She was too pent up to go to sleep. She asked Jeff to take her out; somewhere they could stay until daybreak.

"Just tell me where," he said.

She took him to a place called Le Bateau Ivre, after the poem by Rimbaud. It was in an alley in Montparnasse. Although the alley looked sufficiently threatening to make them think twice about walking the full length of it, the bar itself, once they got there, turned out to be respectable enough to cause them to despair. Johanna had been hoping for a room full of students and some painters down on their luck. And a melancholy whore leaning against the bar would have been just fine. But the place was empty and nondescript.

"It's unusually quiet in here tonight, isn't it?" she asked the bartender in French.

"*Non.*"

"Isn't this the place where about a year ago one student shot another in an argument about *The Flies*?"

"The flies, mademoiselle?"

"*Oui, The Flies!*"

"We do not have flies—"

"The play by Sartre!" she screamed in desperation while Jeff collapsed on the bar doubled over in laughter.

"Ah! Sartre! *Oui!*" the bartender exclaimed. But his enthusiastic grunts had nothing to do with furthering communication.

"Are you new here?" Johanna asked him.

"*Non, mademoiselle.* I am the proprietor."

"No student was ever shot in this bar?" She would not give up.

"*Non, mademoiselle. Jamais.*"

"Is there another bar in Montparnasse called Le Bateau Ivre?"

"*Oui,* there was until eight months ago. Montparnasse is changing rapidly. One day there will be office buildings only."

"That's what the taxi driver was trying to tell you when you couldn't remember the exact address," Jeff said through his laughter.

"What happened to the other place?" she demanded.

"The owner died while pouring wine. Heart attack."

124

"And you bought— Oh, shit." She finally gave up. "How much money do you have?" she asked Jeff.

"Why?" He began looking in his wallet.

"I want champagne."

"Enough," he said, counting.

They ordered champagne and played the jukebox and laughed until four o'clock, when the proprietor informed them that it was time for him to close.

The early morning air might have left them chilled. But the champagne and their laughter at the bar and their kissing and their handholding were a bulwark not only against the night air but against Conrad's rage and all their own uncertainty. They were lightheaded without being drunk.

They walked, unable to find a taxi. On the Boulevard du Montparnasse near the Boulevard Raspail, Johanna suddenly stopped and cried, "Look!"

Two *clochards,* men who'd been ragpickers for so many years they might not have been as old as they looked, were walking side by side, each pushing a baby carriage filled to the brim with the junk of their trade, bits of trash they'd picked up all over the city that they'd convert into enough money for a meal.

"Look in your wallet again," Johanna commanded Jeff.

"Why?"

"Just look."

"I have plenty of money. What's going on?"

She ran to the *clochards* and told them she'd buy everything in their carriages if they would give her and her friend a ride.

"What?" Jeff protested. "Are you crazy?"

"Yes, yes, I'm crazy!"

She began to bargain with the old men as they emptied their carriages of newspapers, magazines, wine bottles, odd bits of clothing, broken candlesticks, and an odd array of Parisian detritus, onto the street. Johanna flailed her arms while she arrived at a price. There was a ferocity in what she was doing that seemed to go beyond fun. Jeff wasn't enjoying any of it.

"Okay!" she called at last. "You take that one." She indicated one of the baby carriages.

"It doesn't look sturdy enough."

125

To satisfy him, she asked the *clochards* whether the carriage could support Jeff's weight. They reassured her that it could.

"Get in! We'll race."

"How far?" he wanted to know. "They're old men. Take pity."

"They're stronger than you are," she said. Then she asked them in French whether they were tough enough, and they confirmed that they were.

Reluctantly, Jeff climbed into the carriage she assigned to him. Johanna got into the other one. They sat cross-legged.

"Are we going home in these?" Jeff asked.

"We're not going home at all," she said. "We're going to have a carriage race."

"Antonia will be knocking at your door."

"Not for two more hours. We'll be back by then. Are you nervous about racing?"

"Yeah," he said. "I'm nervous about the health and welfare of these coolies."

"Go!" she shouted. And they were off.

The carriages were surprisingly sturdy. The original mattresses, filthy and rancid, were still in them. Their cushioning effect was certainly welcome as the two *clochards,* fully entering into the spirit of the race, began to push like a pair of galvanized maniacs.

The race began on the sidewalk. Jeff wondered how they would negotiate curbs without dumping their passengers out onto the pavement. The same thought had obviously occurred to the *clochards* because once they went over the curb they stayed in the street, at first close to the sidewalk, but then, as they had to contend with parked cars blocking their path, out into the middle of the road. At this hour there was very little traffic. Jeff began to enjoy the experience, but not nearly as much as Johanna, who had begun to wonder whether she could stand up in her carriage.

"Sit down!" Jeff shouted.

"I'll bet it's easier to stand up in this thing than it is to water ski," she called back.

For the moment the *clochards* were slowing down. They were actually trotting side by side, chatting with each other about the condition of young people demented by love. They'd sold all of their junk to Johanna; their day's work was over. They were in a grand mood.

"This is a contest!" Johanna reminded them. She hadn't quite got the hang of standing up in her carriage; she had managed to get up onto her knees and no farther. "A race!" she exhorted. "Faster!"

"How far? A race to where?"

"Can you go ten blocks down the Boulevard?"

The *clochards* looked at each other, discussed the problem, and decided they could do it if they went at their present pace, but if they were really expected to run, then no.

"Okay," Johanna said. "We'll go at a trot. But it is a race! Please! A race!" Suddenly she was standing up. Her balance was less precarious once she removed her shoes, but it never became steady or reliable. Once or twice she seemed to be going over the side. She was making Jeff extremely nervous, not only for her safety but because he now realized he had no choice but to stand up also.

After a struggle, he made it. He wondered for a moment how it would be to introduce baby carriage racing in New York. He could see it happening in Central Park. He could imagine it written up in the *New York Times*.

"Oh my God!"

Johanna fell out of her carriage.

"Johanna!" He leaped out of his carriage and ran to her. He knew she wasn't hurt. She was convulsed with laughter.

"It's not funny," he shouted, kneeling down beside her, taking her by the shoulders, pressing her body close to his. "Not funny! Damn you!" He kissed her forehead, her chin, her lips. She kissed him through her laughter. "Not funny," he whispered. "Not funny at all. Johanna, I love you. Johanna . . . Johanna."

"I love you, Jeff. Oh, I do."

"If monsieur and mademoiselle would like a taxi," one of the *clochards* offered, "I will be happy—"

"Yes. Please," Jeff said. And no sooner had he said it than he looked up and saw a taxi approaching, its bright headlights shining right at them. Jeff rose and then helped Johanna.

As they closed the taxi door and leaned back in the seat, a black Renault pulled away from the curb a short distance down the Boulevard. Its driver was Arthur Lamb, relieved because he guessed that they were going home at last, which meant he could go home also. He wanted to make love to Charlotte, his future bride, who was patiently waiting for him in his bed. He thought for a moment about the forthcoming event, the church wedding, and how from that day on she would share his bed forever.

Conrad did not return from London on the day he was supposed to, which struck Johanna as both odd and ominous. He had managed to telephone when she was out of the apartment, and the message he left with the maid was cryptic: Tell Mrs. Thornton there is one more problem for me to solve. It will take a few days.

Some of Johanna's paintings were being exhibited in a hastily organized group show that was a benefit for a maternity hospital on the outskirts of Paris. The idea for the show came about when plans for an elaborate charity dinner fell through. The cooking was to have been done by the chef of one of Paris' most expensive restaurants who, having learned that he was to be downgraded in the Guide Michelin from four stars to two, blew his brains out in a peremptory gesture that left the benefit committee bereft. In the wake of this tragedy, the committee decided that another form of fund raising was called for, and an art show was quickly deemed appropriate. Johanna was asked to exhibit because of Conrad's notoriety among aficionados of Parisian nightlife. Her marriage to Conrad made her sufficiently glamorous for the committee to consider her an asset. At first reluctant, Johanna soon agreed when she realized that it was a unique opportunity to show her work to influential people. Conrad had told her that he wanted approval of the canvases she selected. What he displayed in his nightclubs was one thing; what Johanna revealed in her pictures was quite another. He would be her censor. They'd been through it before, in other ways, in other situations. To make things easy, she said okay.

This had all been discussed in the privacy of their bedroom, and even as the day of the exhibition approached, Johanna hadn't mentioned it to Jeff. Now, as she told him about it, she kept wondering over the fact that Conrad had not returned to oversee her choices. The show was tomorrow night. Today was the day she had to get the paintings from her studio over to the space in a Left Bank warehouse that had been fixed up as a gallery.

"You're going to have to wear your blue suit again," she told Jeff.

"My white shirt is in my laundry bag."

"Give it to me; I'll have it ready for you in time. Does the suit need a pressing?"

128

"I'll look. Can I help you move the paintings?"

"No. It's all arranged. I want to surprise you when you get to the show."

"How many are you showing?"

"Six."

"Any Conrad would have objected to?"

"There's one," she said.

"Oh?"

"It's one I haven't shown you. You may not like it either." She shrugged, blew him a kiss, and went into the nursery to attend to Antonia, who was calling her.

When Johanna came out of the bedroom dressed for the exhibit, Jeff's heart sank. She looked monied, elegant, and self-assured in a way that suggested power. She had gone off to a hairdresser a few hours earlier, but the rich lady coiffure, which is how he thought of her new style, did not by itself explain the difference in her appearance. Jeff was stunned. The night Conrad's new club opened she had looked wonderful. But tonight she was transformed.

"Well?" she asked him.

"I don't recognize you."

"Do I look beautiful?"

"I don't really know. Are the diamonds real?"

"Cartier."

"And the dress?"

"Cardin. He'll be there tonight. I'll introduce you."

"I don't want to meet him particularly."

"What about Audrey Hepburn?"

"I'm too shy to meet Audrey Hepburn. I'll just gawk from a safe distance. Hey, Johanna, I had no idea—"

"Conrad and I are rich. Every now and then it pays for me to act the part. If you think I'm overdressed, well—call it show business."

"You look fine."

"Thanks. You don't look bad either." She came to him, and they embraced until they heard the maid's footsteps down the hall.

They said goodnight to Antonia together. Antonia had made them promise to come into her room so she could admire them in their finery. She kept planting kisses all over Johanna's cheek. She was wrecking her

129

mother's make-up, but Johanna let her go on doing it. Watching them, Jeff forgave Johanna for looking like a duchess. He had no trouble recognizing her now. Johanna repaired her make-up, and they left.

Cardin, as it turned out, did not show up. Neither did Audrey Hepburn. But Chanel did and so did Oleg Cassini, and it was rumored that Elizabeth Taylor might stop by. The women in the room were, for the most part, dressed with discretion, preferring simplicity of line to the flashy or the avant-garde. But here and there a woman did appear draped in a brightly colored abstract print that caught everyone's attention. These women were patrons of a new Italian designer named Emilio Pucci, who was in Paris and, according to rumor, might show up this evening.

When the crowd finally tired of scrutinizing itself and had its fill of champagne and milling about the long bar, it was ready to pay attention to the paintings, which were waiting in another room.

The first grouping, all together on one wall, was by a young woman who signed herself La Suicidée. On the wall there was a legend that explained the artist's intention to kill herself upon completion of a series of two hundred pictures dealing with the subject of death. The artist, it was rumored, was a victim of a terminal illness, and her heroic act was intended as an inspiration to those similarly afflicted. The legend ended there, but as Jeff finished reading it, he heard a gentleman say that La Suicidée had already sold the rights to her demise to the London *Daily Mail* for fifty thousand pounds. No French newspaper had as yet expressed interest, but an American television newscaster was in Paris trying to negotiate for a tape of her final moments. Her paintings were a huge success. Within minutes three of them were sold.

The next grouping was Johanna's incandescent nudes. The contrast between the somber mood of La Suicidée's work and Johanna's vibrant hymns to eros was powerful. The first viewers to arrive in front of them were noticeably delighted. But no one raced to the desk to make a purchase. Jeff wondered why. Then he saw that the crowd, having responded with spontaneous pleasure to the initial impact of Johanna's work, was now more carefully scrutinizing one particular painting. It was the one she had told him about, the one she thought Conrad would have made her withhold had he been there, the one she had hidden from Jeff the afternoon he visited her studio.

It was a male nude painted in an almost photographically realistic style, a style Jeff had no idea Johanna used. The model, in his early twenties, was posed at a kitchen sink drinking a glass of water. A clock on the wall said two. From the lighting, one knew that it was two in the morning. What was remarkable about the portrait, and what was causing a great stir, was that the young man did not have an idealized, athletic body. Johanna had chosen a model for his personality rather than his physique. The model's body was round in places, although never feminine. It was the body of a person who sat at a desk much of the day, and because he was not showing off the figure of an Adonis, he did not seem to be posing. Without the Greek demi-god perfection, there was no projection of ego. The result was a totally real, totally recognizable sexuality. Here was a man, quite possibly an intellectual, unabashedly naked in his kitchen. The impact of the painting came from its credibility. The women in the room seemed to find it erotic; the men were uncomfortable. Jeff watched each group of viewers go through the same course of responses before moving on to the work of the next artist. It was fascinating for Jeff to watch. But it upset him that Johanna was not selling any of her paintings.

"How do you feel?" he asked her.

"Fine. And you?"

"Nervous."

"Don't be nervous. There are some dealers in the crowd, and one or two of them look interested in me. Anyway, it isn't a matter of life and death."

"No," Jeff said, "life and death is a subject that belongs to La Suicidée. Tell me, why did you think I mightn't like the male nude?"

Johanna grabbed Jeff's arm. "Ask me that question another time. Conrad just arrived."

What happened in the next few minutes would never be clear to Jeff. Years later he would try to remember it, but there would always be some small piece missing. Conrad came into the room, greeted by everyone. He moved slowly, not at all like a husband navigating toward his adored wife after nearly a week's absence. He didn't seem to notice Johanna at all. Jeff wasn't aware of the exact moment Johanna moved away from him, but suddenly she was gone. Jeff watched her approach Conrad. Politely, they said hello. Conrad apparently suggested that they go into a small room at the rear of the gallery to talk for a moment. Apparently, she agreed. They entered and kept the door open. In a short time, Johanna

131

came rushing out. Jeff saw her heading toward the stairway. Jeff rushed to follow her, but the thickness of the crowd impeded him. By the time he got down the stairs, Johanna had found a taxi. Jeff hailed the next one that came along.

He got caught up in traffic and arrived a good five minutes after Johanna. The concierge let him into the building, and the maid let him into the apartment.

"Where is Madame?" he asked the maid.

"In the child's room."

Jeff went in; the door was open. Johanna was sitting in a chair in the corner, with Antonia, half awake, in her arms. Johanna was sobbing, saying over and over, "Everything will be all right."

"Why is Mommy crying?" the bewildered child asked.

"I don't know," Jeff said.

"Daddy was here," Antonia said through a yawn.

"Yes?"

"He brought me a present."

"Oh."

"Mommy, please don't cry. Jeff, why is Mommy crying?"

Jeff didn't know. But something inside his body seemed to know, because his body was shaking. He did his best to smile at Antonia reassuringly.

"Everything will be all right," Johanna repeated in a hoarse whisper while the tears continued to roll down her face. "Everything will be all right."

Chapter Nine

Conrad did not come home that night. Jeff sat up in bed listening for him. He had knocked on Johanna's door two separate times, but she hadn't answered. Either she was asleep or had withdrawn from him. He believed the latter, although he didn't really understand why. He realized there was danger lurking in that household and that Johanna had to find a way of dealing with it, but it disturbed him that she couldn't share it with him.

He had breakfast alone; Johanna didn't come out of her room. He inquired about Antonia. The maid said she was having breakfast with her dolls in her room.

At half past nine the telephone rang. It was for Jeff.

"Hello?"

"Mr. Winter?" It was an efficient female voice.

"Yes."

"I am calling for Mr. Conrad Thornton. Mr. Thornton would like you to see him at his office today. He was wondering whether three o'clock would be convenient?"

"That's okay," Jeff said.

"Do you know where his office is?"

"Oh. Well, Mrs. Thornton can—"

"I think you had better write this down," the woman said.

She gave him an address on the Boulevard de Sébastopol and abruptly hung up.

Jeff put the phone back in its cradle. He felt numb. All the adrenalin that had shot through his body seconds ago now dropped to a lower level. Suddenly he felt exhausted.

"Monsieur Winter, you look sad." It was the maid.

"Oh?" He smiled at her. "No, I'm fine."

"Monsieur Winter, Madame Thornton would like you to come to her room."

He was puzzled. This was definitely not Johanna's style, sending the maid for him. Christ! Was he suddenly a stranger in Johanna's court?

She was in bed. Her hair hadn't been combed. Her eyes were puffy from crying. Her nose was red. As he approached her he could sense her warmth, which he could imagine against his chest and arms. Her crying had overheated her body, and the air immediately around her was swollen with the scent of her hair.

"Johanna, what's happening?"

"Conrad wants to kill me," she said.

"Oh, come on." But he felt dizzy, ill.

"It's true."

"He phoned. He wants me to come see him."

"When I heard the phone I figured it was Conrad. I figured that's what he would ask. Where is he?"

"At his office."

"Conrad has as many offices as an octopus has tentacles. He keeps changing them. What's the address?"

"Somewhere on the Boulevard de Sébastopol."

"That's one I don't know. He must have borrowed it for the afternoon. Are you going?"

"Don't you think I should?"

"Yes. Might as well hear his proposal."

"Johanna, what do you mean when you say he wants to kill you?"

"Let him tell you himself."

"Johanna, what about *us*?"

"I'm married to Conrad. Haven't you heard?"

"That's not an answer."

"Go talk to him, Jeff. You'll have an answer then."

134

* * *

The building was disappointingly modern. Worst of all, the elevator, which was new, was designed as a replica of one of those glorious turn-of-the-century bronze cages. The effect was a disheartening obliteration of the past rather than a celebration of it. At least the elevator was efficient. In just a few seconds, or so it seemed, Jeff was lifted up to the penthouse suite, thirty floors above Paris.

The elevator door slid open, and Jeff stepped out into a large, airy reception room. The receptionist glanced up at him and knew who he was without having to ask.

"Mr. Thornton will be right with you," she said. "Please be seated."

But he preferred to stand. He went to the enormous sealed window, a floor-to-ceiling panel of glass, and drank in the view. He could chart the emotional high points of his trip to Paris by views, it seemed. He had met Johanna while admiring a view. Now their brief affair was ending. With a view.

The receptionist's intercom buzzed. She answered it and said, "Yes; I'll send him right in."

He acknowledged the signal. He moved to her desk, smiled, and waited for instructions.

"Straight down the hall as far as you can go, then turn right and right again. You can't miss it."

He wondered why Conrad hadn't sent out a secretary to convoy him. But he was pleased to be navigating on his own. It would give him a chance to look around as he went. There were no indications anywhere of the kind of business this was, but as he started down the hall he saw posters on the walls and names on various doors that indicated some relationship to cinema.

When he arrived at the office he'd been directed to, he found Conrad on the telephone, elegantly dressed, talking to Rome.

Conrad extended his hand, and Jeff did the same. Conrad motioned to a chair, which Jeff sat in, then covered the phone and said, "Trying to get Lollobrigida for one of my producers, but her agent says she won't act in porn."

"Is it really porn?" Jeff asked.

"It is in spirit. I don't know; I never go to see this shit, just put the

135

package together. Hello? Hello? Operator, I've been disconnected from Rome. Screw it, I'll call later." He put down the phone. "Jeff, how are you?"

"Fine."

"I've got to get back on the phone. I've got to reach Lollobrigida's agent in Rome. So I'll be brief. Okay?"

"Sure."

"Miss Leigh, my secretary, who is out on an errand but will be back in about five minutes, has your plane ticket."

"Plane ticket?"

"Yes; you're leaving Paris in the morning."

"I am?"

"I believe you are. Didn't Johanna tell you?"

"She said you'd explain everything."

"You have twenty-four hours; I thought I'd help you."

"Who's given me twenty-four hours?"

"I have."

"What if I don't go?"

"Johanna's life is in danger." He said it so matter-of-factly that Jeff might have asked him to repeat it hadn't he already heard it from Johanna. Jeff knew it was real now; he knew Conrad meant it.

"You're a lunatic," Jeff said.

"Maybe."

The intercom buzzed. Conrad flicked it on. A woman's voice.

"It's Miss Leigh," Conrad explained. "Back even sooner than I expected. She has your ticket."

Jeff couldn't move out of his chair. He felt that his legs wouldn't support him. "Conrad," he said. "I want to talk to you."

"Didn't we just do that?"

"Why don't you threaten *me*? I'm not afraid of you. Why do you threaten Johanna?"

"Because it's the best scheme I could think of. I gave it a lot of thought, you know. Listen, get it clear, okay? Don't ever attempt to see her again once you leave Paris. Don't ever attempt to contact her in any way. You behave, and everything here will be fine. Is it clear?"

"It's pretty clear."

"Listen, I've really got to get back on the phone. Miss Leigh has your ticket. Now go."

136

Conrad didn't come home that night. It was as though, having decided to destroy them, he found it appropriate to grant them the solace of an uninterrupted goodbye. Not as a generous act, but as a consciously sinister one. Their farewells were the tithe for his clemency.

They sat together on a small green sofa in a corner of Johanna's bedroom, prepared to spend a night without sleep. They would make love, but for now there were other things to think about. They had only this night to gather souvenirs, to create anniversaries. Tonight they would assemble the contents of future commemorations.

"What will you remember?" she asked.

"Your eyes."

"Everyone remembers eyes. No. Not eyes. Think again."

"Your voice, Johanna. Your walk. Your soul. The way you challenged me to understand what love is all about . . ."

"Better. Much better. I want to be indelible in your brain."

"I'll never forget you. Never."

"If you met someone who reminds you of me, what would you do?"

"Make love to her."

"Bravo! Make love to her. Do you promise?"

"Yes."

"I wish you many affairs."

"Will you write to me?"

"No."

"Why? You can mail a letter without Conrad ever knowing."

"It would make it harder for me, Jeff. It's not as though you could ever reply. I hate him. But my life is still here. I have to keep it tolerable. Oh, Jeff, find me something, some small gift, something of yours I can cling to."

"Wait," he said.

He went to get his duffel bag. He brought it into her bedroom and dropped it on the floor. He thought for a moment and then began to rummage.

"You'll never believe this," he said, removing some paperback books, a pair of rumpled blue jeans, and a variety of personal articles, until he found the thing he was searching for. "I just happen to have with me a totemic object I've been carrying around ever since my first Boy Scout overnight hike." Then he produced a small cardboard box, which he handed to her.

She opened the box and saw the compass inside it. She smiled. "You never had to fear getting lost?"

"Never. Now neither will you."

"Neither will I. Jeff?"

"Yes?"

"Take off all your clothes and come lie down with me. I want to memorize your body."

"Only if you undress too."

"I will." There were tears in her eyes. Her sadness was so eroticized for him now, it would always be a special ingredient in his feelings of pleasure.

He removed his shirt but hesitated about his trousers. He didn't want to encourage the demand building in his body. Then his own sadness became a kind of panic. The panic built. He was losing her. Too soon . . . He was losing her. He couldn't deal with the anxiety; he needed her to comfort him. "I want to hold you. Oh, God, I want to hold you, I love you so, Johanna . . ."

She held out her hand to him.

"Couldn't we just run away together?" he asked.

"He'd find us."

"It's so goddamn unfair! That sonofabitch can't just threaten us like that! He can't!"

"The reason he can threaten us is that he's made it all so simple. You leave Paris and your life goes on, which is really what you want it to do, and I stay here where I really want to be. And my life goes on."

"That's not the way it is."

"I think it is. In any event, I've had no fantasies about running away with you."

"Does Conrad really have enough power to kill you?"

"Yes. Why should that surprise you? What he's got going here isn't so different from the Mafia."

There were tears of rage in his eyes now.

"Your life isn't over," she said. "That's true, isn't it?"

"I won't ever forget you."

"Now," she said, "let me put my hands on your face the way a blind person would, so your face will be in my fingers."

"Yes."

138

She touched his brow and his cheeks and then his mouth and she got no farther because her mouth was suddenly covering his and her hands were on his back and then all over his body, and the urgency in her body was as poignant as the urgency in his, and they made love.

Afterward she said, "I've thought of a gift to give you."

She tiptoed into Antonia's room and removed from the wall a study of two women she had just hung there, acrobats in one of Conrad's cabarets, climbing a rope ladder. It was one of her recent paintings, and one of her best.

"I'll hang it near my bed," Jeff said, "so I can say goodnight and good morning to my memories."

"Until some woman in your life doesn't want it hanging there." She laughed. "Oh, I'm going to have to remind myself a hundred times each day not to think of you. I don't know if I can bear the pain."

"Is forgetting the best way for you?"

"It would be."

"Then I hope you forget soon. Remembering is the best way for me."

"I know." Then she laughed again.

"What's funny?"

"What if we're both wrong?"

"What do you mean?"

"What if it turns out that I remember and you forget?"

"It won't be that way."

"I'm going to paint something on your forearm," she said. She went to get a paintbox and some thin brushes.

"What are you doing?"

"You'll see."

She painted one small lotus flower on a long stem, directly on his skin. Then another, until there were six. Each was at an angle. Together they formed the shape of an open fan.

"What is that?" Jeff asked.

"It's a hieroglyph. Each lotus is a symbol for a thousand years. Six thousand years is an eternity. Will you remember me that long?"

"Yes," he said.

"But the paint on your arm will wash off. It may still be there tomorrow, and some of it the next day. But then it will be gone. That's how fast an eternity can go by."

"I can't lose you, Johanna!"

"Goodbye," she said, kissing him, holding him tightly, clinging. "Goodbye, goodbye, Jeff . . ."

"I can't say goodbye."

"Say it."

And then he said it. And they clung to each other until daylight, until they finally accepted that it was happening and that nothing would stand in its way.

He packed his bags and left Paris. For sixteen years, he didn't return.

Three

Chapter Ten

The Air France jet began to descend before he felt ready for New York. He was returning through two points in time, and his mind could not stop jumping from Johanna to Toni. From then to now. As the jumbo jet came closer to Manhattan, he looked out the window at the grid formation below. He perceived it as a maze.

He looked at his watch and saw six A.M. Paris time. He set it back to midnight, New York time. It was the beginning of Friday morning. He'd been flying for nearly eight hours against headwinds. He'd been gone only a little more than a day and a half. He was exhausted, but his body wasn't prepared to give up its tensions just yet. He couldn't remember what he'd said to Cathy except that he was coming home. He felt a desperate need to talk to her. But he couldn't possibly call her at this hour without disturbing her kids and her housekeeper. He had a feeling Cathy was still up. Maybe she'd call him. He figured it would take another ten minutes to land and taxi in. Then baggage. Then customs. Then about forty minutes more until he was actually inside his apartment. He figured somewhere between one-fifteen and one-thirty. Maybe Cathy would call . . .

His quick calculations didn't allow for resistance at every step. Baggage took forever. So did customs. So did getting a cab. He was home by two. And the miracle of it was that the phone was ringing. He dropped his bags and ran to answer it.

"Cathy?"

"You knew I'd call?"

"Hoped."

"Every ten minutes. Since midnight. God, you worried me. You sounded so awful in Paris. I knew it was more than the lousy connection. How are you?"

"Fine now. How are you?"

"I don't know. Upset. Did you just walk through the door?"

"Literally."

"Do you want to lock it? I'll hold on."

"All I want is to see you."

"Do you want to come over?"

"Is it all right?"

"Well, the kids and the housekeeper read the announcement of our engagement in the *Times,* so I guess they can handle finding you here when they wake up. Jeff, did the trip help in any way? Did you clear up anything? Or are we just in a lot of trouble?"

"You and me?"

"Yes. I've been thinking about us a whole lot. Most of my ideas about love and marriage, as it turns out, are pretty old-fashioned."

"You still want me to come over?"

"I didn't say I no longer loved you."

He took a deep breath and tried to clear his head. Maybe his need for her right now was too strong to be any good for either of them. He still loved her; he knew that. But he'd done something wrong that he wasn't ready to explain. And it wasn't over yet. He knew he would see Toni again. He still had to find Conrad somehow. The past still seemed in control of his destiny. He had to walk through it to the other side, to have some catharsis, before his relationship with Cathy could really work again. How much of this did he want to tell her tonight? If he saw her tonight, he'd spill it all out. Tonight he was too vulnerable, too exhausted. Too much in need.

"Cathy, you know what?"

"What?"

"I smell rancid, I need a shave, and I feel done in. Let's make a date for tomorrow."

"Tomorrow?"

"I mean today. Let's both get to sleep now. When can I see you?"

"Are you up to having dinner with my parents? The drive up there would give us an hour to talk. And I promise we'll leave early."

"That's fine. Listen, I'll call you when I get into my office. Are you going to be in your office in the morning?"

"Around eleven."

"Call you then. Cathy?"

"Yes?"

"I love you very much."

"I'm glad. Because I love you very much, too. Goodnight."

"Goodnight."

After he hung up, he locked the front door, went directly into the bedroom, pulled off his clothes, got into bed, and was asleep.

Jeannie Christopher and Max McClintock had stayed in bed together all day Thursday. As a result of Jeannie's sexual and medicinal ministrations, Max had a satiated feeling of well-being on Friday morning, combined with an exhaustion he attributed to the burning out of his fever. In any event, his temperature had returned to normal by the time the sun rose on their entangled bodies, and he decided to go back to work.

Jeannie, on the other hand, was feeling symptoms of a malaise.

"I think I've caught your bug," she told him.

"Oh, God, I hope not." Suddenly he was in a quandary. Would he stay home and care for her as she had cared for him?

"Where's that thermometer?" she asked.

"I think I put it in my shoe. Wait, I'll look for it." He stared at the chair on which her clothes had lain piled since Wednesday. He was on his way to the bathroom but dutifully detoured. The thermometer had to be nearby; he remembered the ease with which he had reached over the side of the bed and deposited it safely in the toe of his brown Bally. The shoes, however, were nowhere in sight. They must have been kicked under the bed.

Max got down on his hands and knees and in a moment let out a hoot of triumph.

"Here," he said, standing up, holding the thermometer, "open your mouth."

"Not on your life."

"Didn't you want it?"

"Not from *your* mouth, I don't. You've got to swab it with alcohol to get rid of your germs."

"But if you've already got my germs—"

"Do it!"

"Don't have any alcohol."

"That's right, you don't. But I've been managing nicely with your vodka while playing nurse to you. Get a cotton ball. Soak it in vodka. And swab. It's what I've been doing."

"Jeannie," he said in awe. "You're wonderful." He meant it. The vodka wouldn't have occurred to him in a million years.

He sterilized the thermometer and gave it to her. She took her temperature. For the three minutes the thermometer was in her mouth, Max sat on the edge of the bed studying her body, which neither of them chose to cover with the sheet despite the possibility of a fever. He watched the rise and fall of her full breasts, as beautiful as any he'd even seen. They were round, but what was especially thrilling to him was the way they curved to a peak at the aureola. The aureola itself had a remarkable fullness. Wonderful pink puffs. Spherical buttresses of erotic delight from which jutted her more darkly pigmented, now quite hardened nipples. His concentrated interest was not unappreciated by her despite the potential severity of her pending ailment. He hoped, however, that their byplay was not contributing to a rise in her temperature. In a combined act of friendship and charity, he forced his gaze in another direction.

"Okay," she finally said, removing the thermometer.

"Damn! I forgot to time it."

"Don't worry," Jeannie said, "I have a wonderful sense of time. I can tell three minutes so you could set your watch by it. Honest." She peered at the thermometer, having some difficulty locating the column of mercury, then finding it at last.

"Wow!" she said.

"Is it high?"

"No, it's normal. Wanta make love?"

He put his hand between her legs and felt a wetness there that so excited him he made her promise to make love twice because he didn't think once would get him through the day. Laughing, she agreed. They could have been puppies in some pet store window.

Afterward, she remembered that today was the day Ned Longworth was returning from London. She hoped her absence from the office yesterday hadn't created problems she would now regret. She showered with record-breaking speed, washed her hair, dried it with Max's dryer, put Wednesday's clothing back on, and helped Max fix breakfast.

While the whole wheat bread was toasting, she remembered something she wanted to do.

"I'll get your jacket from the dry cleaner," she said. "I'll ask him again about the letter."

"I'm sure it was still in the pocket when it went off to the cleaning plant."

"Max, do you still love me a little?"

"I love you a lot."

"Will you do me a favor?"

"Sure."

"Just tell Cathy Hayes about the goddamn letter, because I really don't want to deal with it any more. Okay?"

"Okay."

Cathy didn't wait for Jeff's call.

At seven-thirty, while he was sitting hunched over the *Times* at the kitchen counter, waiting for the coffee to perk, the phone rang. He didn't expect her.

"Hello?"

"I thought I'd check on a troubled friend," she said.

Her words were like warm hands on his bare back, doubly effective because they came as such a surprise.

"I love you," he said.

"Listen, going to my parents' place tonight is probably one lousy idea. Why don't I call that off, and you and I can plan to have a quiet dinner somewhere."

"I probably don't deserve you," he said.

"You probably don't. Is there any chance you'll change your wicked ways?"

"A pretty good chance, Cathy."

"Well, I'm a gambler."

"Listen," he said. "Don't call your parents. I can get through an evening up there, and then we'll have the rest of the night."

"And all of tomorrow," she said. "Don't forget tomorrow."

"And all of tomorrow."

"Can you really put up with Connecticut tonight?"

"I've done it before."

"Only once. They claim not to remember you."

"I must have made quite an impression. Listen, I think we'd better go tonight. What time are we supposed to be there?"

"Around seven-thirty. With Friday night traffic, I think we'll need more than an hour. I've got my car in the studio garage, and I can leave the minute I'm off the air. Can I pick you up six-twentyish?"

He had to think a moment; her driving made him nervous. He'd never told her that.

"Sure. That'd be fine. At my office. I'll be downstairs on the dot of six-twenty."

He was at the curb waiting for her. And when she came along so smoothly and stopped the car without a lurch, he had to acknowledge that she drove that damn Volvo with the same grace she did everything else. She and the car looked exquisite together; its deep maroon finish and matching leather upholstery and her brown linen suit and light brown, gently blonde-streaked hair offset by elegantly tailored gold earrings all came together in an ensemble of classy good taste. He opened the door and slid in alongside her. The car was cool inside, and the air conditioner kept recirculating her scent. He kissed her with a degree of self-consciousness, feeling like an actor in a play she was directing. But the kiss she gave back corrected his misconception. Underneath the surface gloss there was a woman who loved him. She would have gone home to bed with him even then if he'd asked her, telephoning Connecticut to say she'd just come down with diphtheria. Knowing that about her would add a pleasurable tension to the evening of small talk they would share at her parents' house. In her kiss was a wonderful promise for later.

"Do you want to hear something funny about your driving?" he asked her as they inched their way up First Avenue, heading toward an entrance to the jammed FDR Drive.

"I'm not sure I do. Is it sexist?"

"Probably."

"Do I have a choice?"

"You don't have to hear it if you don't want to."

"Oh, what the hell. Tell me."

"Well," he began tentatively, "you're obviously a very good driver. Beautifully coordinated. There's something almost balletic about the way you handle this car."

"That sounds like some sort of rubbish," she said. "What are you getting at?"

"It's not rubbish. I wish you'd just listen for a minute."

"Would you be more comfortable if you took the wheel? Really, I wouldn't mind. As a matter of fact I'm goddamn tired. There's a service station coming up, and we—"

"Dammit!" he roared.

"I beg your pardon?"

"I was developing a description of my feelings. You interrupted."

"Sorry."

"I was saying that your coordination—your oneness with the car—is almost— What's the matter now?"

"Oneness?"

"Oneness," he repeated emphatically.

"A word that makes me choke," she said.

"Your coordination—"

"You said that."

"Damn!"

"What is it you're trying to tell me?"

"I'm trying to tell you it makes me nervous to drive with you, for reasons I don't quite understand, but at the same time I get a hard-on just watching you behind the wheel."

"Not bad," she said. "On balance, almost a compliment. Essentially I have the same response sitting beside you in your white Mercedes, if you must know."

"You do?"

"Yes, sweetheart, I do."

They were bumper to bumper on the FDR Drive heading toward the Bruckner Expressway. She had squelched him so effectively he was momentarily speechless. But there was a smile on his lips that came from a heightened appreciation of her. She was special. This was no time to tell her that, however. Maybe on the drive home.

"What are you grinning at?" she asked.

"Nothing." He'd tell her later. He'd remember.

"Jeff, were you ever unfaithful during your first marriage?" She sprang it on him quietly.

"No," he said. "Why?"

"Just something I've been meaning to ask you."

149

* * *

Scott and Edna Powers lived in a twenty-two room stone house that was not of any significant architectural style and was hardly old enough to be of interest for its age. It had been built by a family of bootleggers as a wedding present to their eldest daughter in 1932. There had once been a fountain in the foyer. A tiny, ornate chapel off the dining room was still intact, untouched. There were both a library and a music room. The dining room walls were clutched by elaborate cornices carved into a semblance of hundreds of grapes. It was the least likely country house for retiring New York Episcopalians one could imagine. But it had been priced within reason, and its deflected ethnicity would give them something more to talk about. After living in it for six months, they remodeled most of it, leaving only the chapel and the carved grapes as signs of its colorful heritage.

As Cathy and Jeff pulled into the short driveway, Scott and Edna came out onto the porch.

"Hello there!" Cathy called out.

She stopped the car, and she and Jeff got out. She kissed them both. The time had come for them to greet their prospective son-in-law.

"Congratulations," Scott Powers spiritedly said.

"Congratulations," Edna echoed.

They all went into the house.

While Scott was fixing drinks and Edna was off in the kitchen getting some hors d'oeuvres, Jeff turned to Cathy. "We did this thing all wrong," he said. "We should have had some celebration with your parents. Taken them out to dinner. Something."

"I know, I've been through it in my head. I told my mother that since it's the second time around for both of us we're not making a big fuss. But it didn't feel right when I said it. I hate being so modern."

"Finally, so do I."

There was something unsettling about being here tonight with Cathy's parents. It was too normal; it didn't at all suit the bizarre circumstances of his life at the moment. God! Here it was again. A real family. And it *was* what he wanted. It had been what he'd wanted the first time around. It wasn't he who'd broken up his marriage. It wasn't he who'd been unfaithful. Not then. His answer to Cathy's question about fidelity was an honest one.

Then when had he crossed the threshhold? When had he let go of all of

150

his moorings? And how could he grab hold of them once more? It was easy. There they were in front of him. Cathy. Her mother and her father. There they were. Moorings. And his own parents in Scottsdale, Arizona, whom he vowed to telephone first thing tomorrow morning, before they left their condominium for the golf links. Here was his chance to reenter the reliable world. Yes, safety was what they were holding out to him. What was waiting for him back there in the maze was the remnant of a dangerous dream. The fact remained, however, that it was waiting for him. And he was going to have to deal with it.

"Will you try one of my margaritas?" Scott Powers was asking his daughter.

"Of course I will, Dad. I didn't know you made margaritas."

"It's one of the things I learned to do, living in the country. I find it a good drink for around the first of June, when we put away the bourbon."

"What ever happened to vodka and tonic?"

"We still drink it. Will you have a margarita, Jeff?"

"I certainly will."

"I do mean to propose a proper toast," Scott said. "We'll do that later over some champagne. Oh, my God—"

"What is it dear?" Edna's alarm system was set off.

"I forgot about the champagne when I made these margaritas. Champagne and margaritas will probably destroy us."

"We can drink champagne another time," Cathy said.

"Well, let's see how we feel after dinner. Maybe we'll have it after dinner. Anyway, my toast was to have been an elaboration on the theme of good luck to you both. So why not say it now? No harm if we repeat it later. All our best wishes." He lifted his glass.

"The very best," Edna echoed.

Then they all sipped.

"Cathy," Edna said, "I've been watching you on television with a compulsion that goes beyond maternal feelings. I just think you're so damn good! Really, I say this without prejudice. And your father, who wouldn't hesitate to be critical, agrees with me completely. Why, you seem to get better at it every time we watch. I think you're the best interviewer I've ever seen!" She was blushing by the time she got to her final exclamation. She felt a bit embarrassed, as though she'd paid too big a compliment. In desperation she looked at Scott and then into her glass.

"Darling, thank you," Cathy said to her mother. "You make me very happy. Listen, be sure to tell your grandchildren exactly what you've just told me. They're singularly unimpressed."

"And how are those grandchildren?" Scott asked.

"Well, Ted hasn't been thrown out of Trinity yet, and Beth seems to be holding her own at Dalton. But the best thing I have to say is that Jeff finds them tolerable." She extended her hand to him. He took it in his and squeezed it. She'd drawn him into their conversation, drawn him into their family. "Tolerable" was a risky word. But it had some overtones of lightness. Her father would find it witty. Jeff saw the involuntary smile on his face. Her mother, all aglow in the aftermath of her margarita, seemed to be smiling too. At Jeff? He hoped so.

"Those kids are adorable," Jeff said. He so much wanted to reach out to them, to make it all work. He turned inward while their conversation about the kids continued. He was going to be their stepfather, and he hardly knew them. He'd always wanted children of his own, but now with Cathy's career taking off he doubted that she'd want to consider having another child. Could he make a go of it with the two she already had? They'd never talked about it. They talked about the fact that they would *not* talk about it; that was their agreement. To develop no preconceptions about something that was beyond predicting. His relationship with the kids would be whatever it would turn out to be; and that would be that. No point in speculating. And as for Cathy's having another child? They would see how they felt about that, too, in a year. It wouldn't be out of the question for Cathy even if they waited two years. And then he thought . . . *Am I really here?* He could feel the perspiration trickling down his back. It all seemed so unreal. All of this everyday talk, all of these everyday thoughts. He had gone to Paris . . . only a few days ago. To avenge the death of a woman he once loved . . . To kill a man? Could that be literally so?

"Who's ready for another of my superb margaritas?" Scott was asking. He reached for the pitcher and began filling their glasses.

"I do hope you're all hungry," Edna said.

Jeff heard himself saying he was. He was trying, really trying. He heard Edna saying dinner would be in fifteen minutes. He watched her leave the room to check on something in the oven. Scott left the room a moment later. Then Cathy's arm was around Jeff's shoulders. She kissed him lightly on the cheek, asking, "Are you all right?"

"A little shaky."

"You've had a rough few days."

"Too much flying. Not enough sleep."

"Is that it?"

"There's more."

She took his hand. She told him she loved him very much. Scott and Edna came back into the room.

Cathy asked Jeff to do the driving back into the city. He remembered immediately that he had something to tell her that he'd been saving from the drive up. But it was taking the shape of a set speech in his head. Okay, Jeff. Now let's have the you're-very-special-Cathy number. Better do it. You might lose her. You might . . .

"Your folks are really okay," he said. "Better than okay."

"Yeah, I kinda like them, too."

"Cathy—"

"Darling, you seem so troubled."

"I'm pretty troubled," he said. "I—Oh, shit."

"What? What is it?"

"I wanted to tell you something nice. I can't seem to get the words out."

"Save it for when it's easy."

"I'm afraid of waiting."

"Why?"

"Afraid I might lose you."

"Oh, Jeff. There's very little chance of that."

"Your patience is driving me crazy," he blurted out. "Aren't there things you want to know?"

"Yes. But I'm not sure I'm ready to hear them."

"It's not that you're just being cool?" He smiled at her.

"I'm not that way, as it turns out."

"And not secretly a saint? Or even worse, a martyr?"

"Not that either."

"Well, thank God."

"Jeff, please. Either shut up for a while or change the subject." Her voice was tearful. "I told you I'm not ready for this discussion."

"Okay."

She paused, then added, "You're so full of guilt, you're bursting with it. You want relief. I'm not ready to give it to you. I know you've been fucking Toni Menard. It doesn't take a genius to figure that one out. And

153

now you want to explain to me that it's not over. Jesus! Just let me know when it's over! Will you do that for me?" Tears ran down her cheeks.

"It's over with Toni. That's not what isn't over."

"Sure, sure, sure. Damn it! I do not want to have this discussion with you! For Crissake, why do you think I haven't asked you about her? I don't even know whether or not she came back to New York with you."

"No, she went—"

"Shut up! Shut up! Shut up!" She beat her fists against the dashboard.

He bit his lower lip. They drove on in silence.

About twenty minutes later, she unbuckled her seat belt and shoulder harness and moved as close to him as she could get. He took his right hand off the wheel and gently put his arm around her.

"Now you know what a terrible temper I have," she said.

"I'm just so goddamn lucky to have you."

"If you really feel that way, don't abuse it," she said, "and everything will be okay. I understand that you're being driven crazy, but you're letting this thing take you over. It doesn't have to, you know."

"Except that there's something unresolved, a piece missing that I've got to find. . . . I'm sorry; I promised not to talk about it."

"That's right. You did. Jeff?"

"What?"

"I want to go to my place. I want the kids to see you in the morning."

"Are you sure about the kids?"

"No. But I think it's time to test the waters."

"Okay."

"Can you drive faster without getting a ticket?"

"I can give it a try."

"I want to make love to you," she said.

At the Aspen Dry Cleaning plant in the Bronx, Yvonne Smith was getting ready for her Friday night date with Jerome Sheehy. Ever since yesterday when he came to the Lost-and-Found department with the letter, she'd been thinking about him. What she thought was that she'd been foolish for treating him so disdainfully all of these months. Foolish and dishonest at the same time. Not to mention snobbish. After all, who did she think she was, anyway? She had the same job now she had seven years ago, hadn't even made it into middle management. Stuck. No, that wasn't true. She was lazy. She had a good mind, but she was lazy. Good mind? Change that to terrific mind. But lazy. She'd rather have the kind of job where you could sit and read magazines than the kind that demanded undivided attention. Anyway, getting back to Jerry Sheehy. He wasn't a bad sort, really. A blue-collar worker, that was true, but he was a member of a powerful union that guaranteed him a respectable living. And he had a remarkable set of medical and retirement benefits. God, what an unliberated way for a modern woman to be thinking. But, really, it was important! If she ever married and had a child, she wasn't likely to go back into the working force so soon. She would be the kind of mother who'd want to be at home with her child, even later on when the child was going to school. And to be at home meant being married to a man with a stable job and a stable set of benefits. Like Jerome Sheehy. She was thirty-two and never married. Jerome was—How old was he? Possibly a bit younger. Oh! That really turned her on. A younger man! Why, she began to speculate, I'll bet Jerome Sheehy isn't a day past twenty-nine. Oh, God, she was excited!

It was nearly half-past five. They were both on the same shift again today. Eight-thirty to four-thirty. Any minute he'd be coming by the Lost-and-Found office to pick her up. She was finding it hard to go on breathing normally. Calm down, she kept telling herself. Just stay calm.

She was applying a final bit of gloss to her lipstick when he came through the door wearing a dark blue, double-breasted suit, a white shirt with a button-down collar and a smart-looking silk rep necktie. She wouldn't have recognized him in a million years. He could have passed for a lawyer or stockbroker. All he needed was a copy of the *Wall Street Journal* tucked under his arm.

"Jerry, you look beautiful," she said.

"I'm also a terrific lay." He kissed her full on the lips and while kissing her cupped her rear end with both his hands.

She turned red. When men talked that way, it usually frightened her. She hated any situation in which there was some chance she might lose control. But Jerome didn't frighten her. She'd already made up her mind to let him spend the night in her double bed.

"Where are you taking me for dinner?"

"Mon Paris of Yonkers."

155

They went in his car; she'd leave hers in the Aspen parking lot until tomorrow.

Thank God she was in a dress, and a well-made one at that, she thought when they got there. Jerome had been there before and was quite familiar with most of what was on the menu. His self-confidence was picked up by Yvonne, always the quick study.

Over their first glass of wine, Jerome said, "Remember that letter I brought in yesterday?"

"I'll never forget that letter. It was the most important day of my life." Then she caught herself. She'd moved too quickly. But, what the hell, either it was going to be all right or it wasn't. Yvonne was a fatalist when it came to ongoing relationships. "What about it?"

"Well, did you notice who it was addressed to?"

"No. I didn't realize there was an address on it. Why didn't you just put a stamp on it and drop it in the mail?"

"There wasn't an address. Just a name written in longhand. You didn't look at it at all?"

"Not really."

"The name was Cathy Hayes. Does that mean anything to you?"

"No. Oh, wait a minute . . . the new Channel Seven newscaster? The one who does interviews mostly, and theater reviews? The one they're making such a fuss over? What makes you think it's the same person?"

"I don't know if it is. I looked in the Bronx and Manhattan phone books. There are a lot of Catherine Hayeses. We could call all of them plus the one on Channel Seven News and ask who's lost a letter. Except what if it's something they're not aware of?"

"Well, what do you want to do about it?" she asked. "It's not something I want to spend the night discussing."

"What do you normally do with things in Lost-and-Found?"

"Nothing. Just wait for someone to make a claim."

After they made love, he felt the need to talk.

All his guilt, confusion, sadness, conflicted memories, and the now terrible need to anchor his life—everything that had been building up in him throughout the evening—burst out of him. Cathy's closeness had touched him more deeply than any recent lovemaking he could remem-

156

ber; she had taken him far beyond sex into an emotional landscape he recognized from somewhere in the past, a place he thought he would never get to again. But he didn't tell her that. He was afraid.

What he talked about was his first marriage. It had lasted ten years and for a while had seemed a miracle of clever matchmaking. They gave smart dinner parties that made the columns and built a house in Montauk that made the Sunday *Times Magazine*. She was an actress. But her real talent, as she found out one summer in a stock company in Maine, was scenic design. When they divorced she went back to school and emerged two years later as one of the best set designers on Broadway. They had no children because she didn't want any, and he, ambivalent throughout, experienced no real difficulty in accepting her refusal. For the first month after their divorce he waited for the abyss, waited for the days of mourning, the pangs of memory, the sense of loss that would provoke him at four A.M. But none of those things happened. When anxiety came it was from realizing that in ten years of marriage they had lived parallel lives; divorce merely widened a gap that had always been there.

"What did she look like?" Cathy asked.

"Oh." He smiled. "You're so damn shrewd. You're trying to get me to say she resembled Johanna."

"Did she?"

"Yes. As a matter of fact, she did."

"I don't in the least resemble Johanna, do I?" Cathy asked.

"No."

"I'm glad I don't."

"So am I. I want to get on with my life."

"Are you through going back?"

"Almost through."

In the morning, he greeted the kids. Ted and Beth. Ted, who was twelve, was the older by three years. They made an extraordinary effort to be agreeable and sophisticated. They asked him all the questions they could think of about the legal profession; they told him their views on baseball, abortion, homosexuality, capital punishment, caffeine, and nuclear energy. The trouble was, it came out tense. He listened politely. Then he said, "I guess you were pretty surprised to find me here this morning."

They nodded. Cathy kicked him under the table. He shut up. But the

157

tension was broken, and the kids began to talk about their summer plans, which included a month at camp and a month in southern California with their father.

Jeff asked them whether they'd seen the new Woody Allen movie. They hadn't but wanted to. Suddenly Saturday afternoon was taking shape. He decided to treat everyone to dinner in Chinatown. Then, much later on, he and Cathy could wander over to the sidewalk cafe at the Stanhope and stare across Fifth Avenue at the Metropolitan Museum of Art while sipping a brandy and making plans.

Sunday was easy. They fell into the most familiar of routines. Brunch and the Sunday *Times* strewn all over the living room floor.

Jeff and Cathy went out to dinner by themselves Sunday evening. He invited her back to his apartment afterward, but she thought she should get back to the children.

"It's all gone remarkably well, Jeff. Hasn't it?"

"It has."

"We're almost a family."

He smiled.

"Is our romance being displaced by family habits?" she asked.

"No," he said. "I feel wonderful."

"Is it sexy enough?" she asked.

"Enough." He took her around the waist and pulled her close. "It's better than sexy," he said.

"Ouch. Can this marriage be saved?"

"I need to come back down to earth," he said. "Is it unflattering to you to say you offer me that?"

"No, my darling. Down to earth is where I want to be also."

"So?" he asked.

"We're made for each other," she giggled.

He kissed her. Then they said goodnight.

On Monday morning, at eleven o'clock exactly, a young woman stepped off the elevator on the forty-first floor and entered the law offices of Temple, Norton, and Winter. She told the receptionist she had no appointment but believed that Mr. Winter would see her. She gave her name as Toni Menard.

Chapter Eleven

She brought excitement into his quiet office; her walk was a definition of elegance; artifice was in command of her every gesture. She sat down in a nervous style descended from old movies and waited for him to sit opposite her.

"I'm in love with you," she said. "If you'll give me five minutes to elaborate, I'll leave."

Oh, God, he thought, where did you learn your act? Now the cigarette. Where was the cigarette? He noticed the quivering of her lips and that her eyes were misting over. She was going for the full treatment. Wasn't she afraid of parody? No, no, of course not. She had such insolence!

"Toni," Jeff pleaded, "don't."

"You think I'm a lying little bitch. Don't you?"

"I don't know. You were bad in Paris."

"Was I?"

"Yes."

"Are you sure?"

"Yes."

"Are you sure I didn't save your life?"

"What?"

"Save your life."

"What are you talking about?"

"There's something I haven't told you. I—"

The intercom interrupted her. He flicked the button and asked his secretary what it was. She told him Cathy was on the phone. He paused for just a second, smiled at Toni as though to say excuse me, and took the call.

"Darling," Cathy said, "are you as happy as I am this morning?"

"I am," he said. But his voice sounded flat to him. Don't do anything stupid, he cautioned himself. Don't, don't . . . "Let me call you back in half an hour," he said. "Is that okay?"

"Your secretary told me you're with someone, but I asked her to put me through anyway."

"Can I call you back?"

"Yes. Forgive me. I'll go now. I send you kisses."

"I'll talk to you soon."

"Soon," she repeated.

He turned back to Toni.

"What is it you haven't told me?"

"I know that Conrad killed Johanna," Toni said.

How could she know that? "What are you talking about?" he asked her feebly.

"You know exactly what I'm talking about."

"Damn you!"

"I saved your life."

"What's that supposed to mean?"

"The fat Paul Newman, remember him?"

"Yes, for God's sake. He was at the hotel with us. He and that blonde bimbo left when you did."

"He would have killed you if I hadn't left."

"Am I supposed to believe all of this?"

"It's true. Conrad knew you were in Paris. He could think of only one reason that you'd try to find him. He decided to have you killed if you became a real threat. He *would* have killed you. Don't you understand that?"

"Yes."

"The fat Paul Newman's name is Arthur Lamb. He was driving the car that hit Johanna."

"Jesus."

"Yes," she said. "Exactly."

"Why didn't you tell me all of this last week when you came to my office?"

"I don't know. I came there to tell you the truth and then found I was afraid of it. I screwed everything up; I got you to go to Paris with me to look for Conrad, then I—I made a real mess. I became very nervous. I was suddenly afraid of the situation I had created."

"Then you did deliberately interfere with my getting to see Conrad."

"Yes."

"And now what?"

"Now I'm in love with you."

"Toni, what do you want?"

"I think you know." She stood up.

"Do you still want to find Conrad?"

"Do you want me to?"

"Yes."

"Why?"

She screamed, "I hate him!" Then she screamed again, tears running down her face. She was out of control. Her face contorted into an expression of helpless rage; she looked like a hurt and terrified child. "I hate him! He killed my mother! My mother!"

"I—" Her speech was overwhelmed by her convulsive crying.

He left her alone. Her hysteria subsided into sobbing. Then she stopped. He offered her his handkerchief, which she accepted while she dug into her shoulder bag for a tissue. She took a long time composing herself. She dried her eyes but made no effort to repair her ravaged make-up. She looked tragic. He fought against his feelings; nevertheless, he was moved.

"What is it you would like me to do?" he asked her

In a voice no stronger than a whisper, she said, "Kill him."

A chill ran through him. He looked at her and wondered whether she'd broken down right there before his eyes; that was his first impression. But she hadn't broken down. And by the time her make-up was repaired with all the marvelous magic bits she hauled out of her handbag, he could feel revenge working inside him once more. Kill him? Was it possible?

Smiling, he asked her, "How would you suggest I do it?"

"I have a gun," she said.

* * *

161

He'd finally gotten her to leave by agreeing to telephone her at Streeter Cash's apartment at five. She had asked him to come to a party with her and Streeter tonight at a disco on West Fifty-third Street. When he declined, she suggested that he bring Cathy. He declined for Cathy and then said maybe he could drop by for a few minutes around eleven. She had thrown out a considerable amount of bait. For one thing, she told him that Ned Longworth would be there. For another, she promised that by tonight she could tell him for certain where to find Conrad.

He sat staring at the telephone. He had to call Cathy back. How much should he tell her? He dialed, got her secretary, and was relieved to find out that Cathy had gone into a meeting.

He met with a client who came to discuss revisions in his will, had lunch with a writer who wanted to bring suit against a publisher for holding royalties in an escrow account, returned to his office, tried Cathy again, didn't get her, went into a meeting with three Long Island realtors who wanted to break a contract they'd made for the sale of some land, called Cathy again, and this time reached her.

"Hi," she said. "Busy day?"

"Boring. And you?"

"Exciting."

"You're lucky."

"I know I'm lucky; I've been thinking about you all day."

"You're mushy," he said. "I didn't know there were any sentimental women still around."

"I'm the last of a dying breed. Hey, Jeff, did you ever hear of a lawyer named Ned Longworth?"

"Indeed I have. On his long list of high and mighty clients you'll find Conrad Thornton and Toni Menard."

"I know about Toni. Didn't know he did work for Conrad as well. I met him at a party last week after the Neil Simon play. He sort of grabbed hold of me. Anyway, he called to invite me—to invite *us*, actually; he specifically asked if you would come—to a disco opening. We had the oddest conversation."

"I'll bet you did," Jeff said. "I got the same invitation from Toni."

"She called?"

"Came to see me."

"Oh." Her voice was flat.

"Can you go with me?"

"No. I'm going out to Newark Airport to interview the released hostages."

He didn't know what she was referring to.

"The hijacking," she said.

"One of the nice things about an obsession is it keeps you from being depressed by the news. I haven't read today's paper."

"How would you like to come with me and watch me at work?"

"Will you give me a raincheck?"

"Sure. You're going to the disco?"

"I guess so. I hadn't really planned to until you told me about Ned Longworth's call."

"I think he has an interest in the place and would like some publicity for it. Anyone he considers really important from the press probably received an embossed invitation weeks ago. I'm obviously a last-minute idea."

"Maybe. But I think there's more to it than that."

"I guess that means we won't see each other tonight." She hesitated, obviously waiting for him to contradict her. "I'll miss you."

"Cathy, I'll miss you too. I'll miss you very much." And his face broke out in an enormous smile because he was able to feel deep down inside himself just how much he loved her, and he was so glad to reaffirm that feeling.

"If you aren't gay, go away." It was Streeter Cash answering the phone.

"Hello, Streeter. This is Jeff Winter."

"You may be straight, dear boy, but you're certainly not a bore. How are you?"

"I'm fine. Listen, is Toni there?"

"No. But she was expecting to hear from you. I'm the message bearer."

"The message is I'll be there."

"The disco?"

"Yes."

"It's all work and no play for poor Toni. Did she tell you?"

"No."

"We're shooting some layouts for *Vogue*."

"What time are you doing that?"

"No particular time. Informal shots. All through the night, dear boy."

"Doesn't sound too arduous."

"We're going to create a revolution in fashion photography tonight. Do you remember when Avedon horrified the fashion world with his photograph of a model on roller skates?"

"Can't say I do."

"Well, to tell you the truth, neither do I. But what we plan to do tonight is straight from Avedon. Pure theater, all nervous energy. Toni is going to be photographed high on tequila and cocaine."

"Sounds swell," Jeff said drily. "Is that really so innovative?"

"For high fashion photography I'd say it is. Bare tits, lesbian leers, even a bit of ass grabbing—I've seen plenty of that in *haute couture*. But a beautiful girl bleary-eyed, dancing in a disco, half crazed on cactus and coke? Man, that's news. I'm told she's a great fuck when she's high that way."

Recoiling from Streeter's voice, Jeff looked across his office at the wall of bookshelves filled with the volumes that were his rock, his foundation.

"Streeter, what do you know about Ned Longworth?"

"We had this discussion in Paris, didn't we?"

"Yeah, I guess we did," Jeff said. "See you later. Around eleven."

He'd been to places like this before.

This one was called the Plastic Lift. The advance publicity proclaimed the chief investor to be a Park Avenue plastic surgeon whose list of patients was described as legendary. The truth was that the doctor had been given some stock in exchange for the subtle exploitation of his fame. The real owners were Mafia. The Plastic Lift was a clever innovation, something to attract the attention of the bored folk who would otherwise be flocking to places that featured naked boys on trapezes, or dance floors that got snowed on by machines, or abandoned subway cars or any other bits of urban detritus that could become the decor of a club. The Plastic Lift had half a dozen different rooms, each based on body parts. There was The Face Lift, its walls all pink velvet, hung with photos of gorgeous and familiar people. Then came the room called The Breast Lift. Same idea, just a bit more erotic. Next came the room called Cheeks, replete with an impressive collection of buttocks, male and female, white, black, and suntanned, hirsute, and sometimes glistening with oil.

There were other rooms. One was called Lips. It featured mouths and labia. Another was called The Nose Job. The last room, for the most perverse and thrill-seeking, was called Accidents. Here one could see, in black and white, since color clashed with the decor, victims of every conceivable form of damaging trauma, before and after surgery. The results were consistently encouraging, but it was the before shots that were intended to turn on the dancers. Throughout all the rooms the music blared. There were dancers everywhere.

Once you got past the novelty, everything about the club seemed interchangeable with clubs Jeff had been to before; the crowd, the lights, the music, the bouncers at the door, the smell of marijuana, the presence of hard drugs, the transvestites at the bar and the dance floor. He looked at his watch. The music still blared.

He'd been brought up on a farm in Pennsylvania. His father had been a lawyer, and his mother had taught school until he was born. Respectable. Dull. Predictable. Stable. Good. Goddamn it, he thought, it *had* been good. Not liberal. Not overly intellectual. Not progressive. Not even particularly enjoyable. But good. Am I getting old?, he wondered. Those are the thoughts of an older citizen. Then he gave himself the answer. No, not getting old. Just being shot at in the middle of a battlefield. For that's what this place felt like to him. Alien. Dangerous. And when you're being shot at in the middle of a battlefield, you tend to romanticize safety, things of substance. That's all it is, he told himself. Fear. Yes, I'm afraid. He thought of Cathy. He wished he were with Cathy at home. He drank his scotch. He couldn't remember buying it or even getting anywhere near the bar. Someone must have put it in his hand. The first sip reverberated its warmth throughout his body. It wasn't the brand he was accustomed to. It was acrid. Peculiar. He drank more. His left hip bumped into something hard, and he realized he was standing against one of many bars. The music blared. He looked up. A slender black girl was dancing on top of the bar. She was wearing one of those micro mini skirts that had gone out of fashion for everyone but the whores who lined up along Eighth Avenue. Perhaps she was one of them. She was in her late twenties, he guessed. He really wondered what the hell he was doing guessing her age. But he understood what he was doing. He was doing his damndest to avoid looking up at her open crotch.

165

A flashbulb went off in his face. When he was able to see clearly again, he was looking at Streeter Cash.

"Are you planning to print that somewhere?" Jeff asked.

"Only in the *Columbia Law Journal*. How do you like this place?"

"Next time I'll bring my mother," Jeff said.

"Although you may think you see tremendous variety in this menagerie, I assure you they divide into two basic types. The molested and the unmolested. And it's the unmolested who can't be trusted. Because, baby, if no one's ever used you, you haven't learned a thing."

"Which am I?" Jeff asked.

"Dear boy, you have the saddest expression in this room," Streeter said.

Then Jeff saw her.

She was pale tonight, in an ivory-colored dress and wearing ivory earrings; ethereally beautiful. Heaven is having a sexy day, Jeff thought.

"Can you dance?" she asked. It was the same as hello.

He took her hand and led her away from the bar. Shortly after his divorce he'd taken some disco lessons as part of a self-imposed course in bachelor survival. He was good at it.

"Toni," he said, "you look smashing."

The crowd on the floor was very thick. He'd barely gotten started when they found it impossible to continue. But his looseness and grace impressed her.

"Can you stay around?" she asked. "I'd really like to go on dancing with you."

"For a while."

"You know, there's no correlation between how good a man is in bed and what he's like on the dance floor. Except sometimes. As I suspect in your case."

"Thank you." He pointed to the little pouch dangling from her shoulder. "Coke?"

"I've got some coke in there, and other things. Some excellent coke. The best. Does it tempt you?"

He laughed. "I grew up already. Can't you tell?"

"There's enough of the boy still left," she said.

"The boy came here to find out where Conrad is. Where is he?"

"Soon."

The music grew louder. A male voice coming from behind Toni pro-

166

jected over it. "Soon can seem like forever to an impatient man."

Toni took a deep breath and turned around. "Jeff, I want you to meet Ned Longworth."

They shook hands. They tried to talk above the disco din. Ned asked for Cathy, whom, he explained, he'd had the pleasure of meeting at a party less than a week ago. Charming woman, he said. He was ignoring Toni with a noticeable deliberation.

"Conrad is in New York," Ned Longworth explained. "He would like very much to see you. I would like to arrange it."

Jeff watched Toni open her pouch to find a cigarette. He felt his throat going dry. "When?" he asked Ned.

"Tomorrow afternoon would be most convenient. He's staying at the Pierre."

When Jeff was a teenager and wanted to learn the words of a new song, he'd play the record over and over, except not at first all the way through. He'd start with only a few phrases, until he'd learned them. Then the next few, until he'd learned them. And so on until the words were memorized and he could concentrate on the tune and the rhythm. Playing the record over and over, he would sing along, until he was ready to turn the record player off and sing without it, adding embellishments and improvisations. He would work up an act in front of the mirror, dreaming of the opportunity to give his performance with feigned spontaneity some Saturday night when a girl would ask him, oh, do you happen to know that new song, such-and-such, and he would nod, quite casually acknowledging that he did, and then he would sing it.

Of course the opportunity never came. The girls he chose for Saturday night dates talked about a lot of things, but rarely did they ask whether he happened to know that certain new song. And if they did ask, it wasn't because they wanted to be an audience for somebody else's production number. It was because for a short while, riding in a car through some summer breeze, they wanted to create a duet, and usually a bit off key.

He thought of that now, because what he was doing seemed to have something in common with that earlier time.

As soon as he had returned to his apartment, it had started. He had gravitated toward the bedroom, where he paused before his icon, the painting Johanna had given him. Then he loosened his tie and tossed his

167

jacket onto a chair, while vengeance, like one of the songs from his adolescence, reverberated in his brain.

Looking back at the chair on which his jacket had landed, he saw the tip of a pink slip of paper sticking out of one of the pockets. He knew it was something he hadn't put there. Instinctively he knew it was a note from Toni. He pulled it out and read it.

"Jeff, take a look in your briefcase," it said.

Where had he dropped his briefcase? He'd brought it home after dinner when he returned to shave and dress for the disco. Living room sofa, that's where. He went to find it.

A neat, small revolver lay inside, tucked among some papers. She'd placed it there in his office. She'd put the note in his pocket tonight.

At some level his mind wanted to express outrage, to say fuck this craziness. Just get on with your life. But the part of his mind that wanted to speak reason was overwhelmed by something else, by something simpler than reason could ever be. It was like learning those songs when he was a kid . . .

He couldn't decide what to do with the gun.

He thought of Conrad as he'd seen him in Paris. A sickly old man. Half blind. How was that possible?

The photographs . . . Where are they? He became excited, trying to remember. They were in a file somewhere, one of those heavy paper accordion files you can buy at any stationer's to keep your insurance policies in. In one of the closets, high up on a shelf. His first wife had hated photographs, so they had to find a way of saving them that would not offend her, that would not contradict her notion that prior to their marriage Jeff had not lived a life.

He went into the kitchen to get the step stool. He carried it with him from closet to closet until he came to the one where the paper file was stored.

He climbed up on the stool, reached up to the shelf, brought down the tangible evidence that his memories were true. He took the file into the kitchen. He wanted another scotch, a decent scotch. He looked at his watch. It was half past two.

He poured the scotch over some ice cubes. He sipped it. He removed the photographs.

Johanna . . . more beautiful than his memory had conjured.

Conrad . . . young and handsome.

Himself . . . so long ago.

"We all change," Toni had said. "Conrad is aging badly."

He stared at the photographs, concentrating on Conrad. How was it possible?

The answer to his question was, of course, Toni's secret.

Chapter Twelve

Four years earlier, in London in the fall of 1974, Conrad Thornton was pacing the floor of a suite in Claridge's. Youthful in appearance, physically in his prime, he was capable of a sensuous appreciation of his own powerful movements even as a dread, unlike any he had ever known, was building in him.

Impeccably dressed in one of the conservative suits he referred to as a money-making uniform, he strode briskly from the large, handsomely appointed living room to his bedroom and then across the small foyer to Antonia's bedroom. Occasionally he would pause and smile at the discrepency between his own chamber, which personal habits and the fastidiousness of maids left neat enough to appear unused, and his daughter's room which, despite everyone's best efforts, looked ransacked. But these momentary distractions did not alleviate a swelling anxiety he was finding it difficult to manage. He'd been foolish not to have gone with her despite her insistence that he not come. Waiting here alone this way was a form of torture he'd never before been forced to endure.

He looked at his watch. She'd left at noon. She'd wanted to walk to Harley Street. It was a beautiful day; she said it would do her good. Her appointment was at half past twelve. She'd promised to call immediately thereafter. He had told the switchboard to put no other calls through to him. He would not run the risk of tying up the line. There were emergencies in Paris he had to deal with, but they could wait. Oh, good God, where the hell was she? He'd promised not to call, to wait. But dammit, patience was not his style, and he'd already shown more patience than could reasonably be expected of anyone. He went to the phone.

As he picked it up, he sat down on the gold-toned sofa. Sunlight was pouring into the suite, and in its beams the sofa's arms were revealed as nearly threadbare. Nevertheless, the look of elegance remained. He thought momentarily of Johanna, who understood so well the seemingly irreconcilable split between his taste for contemporary vulgarity—hell, that's how he'd made his millions—and his need for attachment to something more stable. There were moments, like this one, when he still missed her. After twelve years.

When he heard the key in the door, he put down the phone. He crossed his legs and sat back, struggling for a pose of nonchalance while sustaining a further increase in tension.

Antonia came into the room slowly, her long hair flowing onto the shoulders of her Saint Laurent suit. He could hardly believe her incredible beauty. Each day he looked at her, he sought Johanna in her eyes, in her mouth. But this pursuit frightened him, and after a while he made a determined effort to see only Antonia, his daughter. My God, could she be only fifteen? He fancied that whenever they went to a restaurant or to the theater, they were mistaken for lovers.

He smiled at her very softly and said hello. There was no need to question her. She knew what the question was. But taking priority over the big question was a small one, no less urgent. Why had she violated her commitment to telephone him? She knew how he felt about such matters; a dependency on phone calls was at the center of his universe.

She was able to anticipate even that. "I didn't want to telephone. I wanted to come back here and tell you," she said.

He already knew what it was she had to tell him. He felt choked. He reached up to loosen his necktie, to open the top button on his shirt.

"The diagnosis has been confirmed," she said.

"Oh, God; Antonia," he gasped. "Then it's true?"

"Yes."

"All of it? Everything that son of a bitch told you in Paris?"

"He's not a son of a bitch."

"Heartless."

172

"Just honest," she said. Her voice sounded weary. She looked drained.

"I can't believe it," he said.

"Neither could I. Until today. Now I believe it."

"My darling Antonia," he said. "There's nothing in this world I won't do to make these last days as happy for you as I dreamed your entire lifetime would be. Nothing."

She smiled at him, a thin, wan smile. There were tears in her eyes now, and in his as well. They each needed to be alone. She excused herself and went into her room.

Her terror of death began at the age of three.

The day of the accident was not the worst day. Hope was still held out to her on that day. All she was told was that her mother had been taken to the hospital. No one said anything further. But the maid kept telling her that everything would be all right. And she believed it.

She cried a lot. She begged to be taken to the hospital to see Johanna. But the maid explained to her as patiently as she could that children were not permitted there unless they themselves were patients.

"What's a patient?"

"A sick person in the hospital to get better."

"I was in the hospital when I was born. Was I a patient?"

"That's different."

"I want to see my mother!"

"Perhaps we can telephone her. I'll ask your father's permission."

But Conrad, too distraught to comfort his daughter, made no effort at considerateness of any sort. "No," he told the maid, without a word of explanation. "She may not phone."

Three days passed, but Antonia had no concept of that. It seemed so immediate. It seemed to her that one minute her mother was going out the door with Conrad and the next minute she was dead.

Conrad didn't come home that night. In all the years since, Antonia did not find out where he'd gone. With some whore, she guessed, when she was old enough to think about such things.

It was the maid who told her about her mother's death.

The child said nothing for a long time. Then her small body began to shake all over. In the middle of the night she ran a fever and began to hallucinate and scream. She would fall asleep for a few minutes at a time and dream that she was in a boat, alone, in the middle of a lake, calling for Mommie, with no one to hear her.

The maid did her best not to cry in front of the child. But she couldn't help herself. She told Conrad how much the child needed him, and he nodded as though he understood what was being said. But, in fact, he did nothing to help.

The funeral was private. Conrad insisted on having it that way. How he dealt with Johanna's friends or with any of the people who'd become interested in her painting was something he never discussed with anyone. But then who ever questions the requests or motives of a man half crazed with grief?

None of his business associates came to the funeral. None of the entertainers from the clubs he owned; and not Arthur Lamb or his wife Charlotte.

When Antonia saw the wooden box being lowered into the ground and heard the cruel sound the earth made as it was shoveled back into the grave onto the coffin, she fainted.

Six weeks later, with the help of the maid and a very good doctor, she progressed from severe depression to a manageable grief, and Conrad was told his daughter's condition was no longer critical. He responded with a manic joy. After weeks of ignoring her, he could not spend enough time in her company. If he had to be away from her for a day, it was torment; for a week, it was unbearable. He showered her with toys, with clothing, with records and boxes of candy. Anything he spotted in a store window which he thought might amuse her, he impulsively bought. In the immediate aftermath of Johanna's funeral, while Antonia had still been swallowed up in her depression, the child had seemed like an enemy to him. Instead of following him back into the sunlight where they could recover together, she had retreated into the shadows, away from him. He had perceived her illness as rejection, even worse, as betrayal. Her recovery, therefore, was like an unexpected victory. The triumph of life over death, of love over denial. He had his daughter back. And he wanted her to know how much he appreciated having her.

Conrad's attention came as a marvelous change, something Antonia could revel in. She adored his gifts, even the silly ones. She no longer felt abandoned. Now she had a grown-up friend. A very strong man. Her daddy. His nearness filled her with an erotic delight that made her face glow with happiness.

174

Yet, every night, the terror of death returned. Every night she saw her mother's grave and coffin. And every night, in trying to imagine what her mother looked like lying inside that box, she envisioned some hideously awful distortion of Johanna's features that caused her to awaken and tremble. This same nightly trauma was endured by Antonia for more than a year. And even long after her nightmares stopped, she was unable to forget them. She could recall them even now. Death and those terrible images out of her childhood were still synonymous.

This was why, lying in her room at Claridge's, having come from Paris to London for a second medical opinion that would confirm the first, the terror was returning. Only this time, the terror came from the subject of her own death. And this time it was Conrad who would have to deal with being an abandoned survivor.

The diagnosis was lymphatic cancer. The prognosis was that Antonia had six months to live.

Gloom came into their suite with the darkness that evening at Claridge's. Conrad, the headstrong giant, had spent what was left of the afternoon sitting alone on the sofa, slowly draining a bottle of scotch, staring into space, silently weeping over his daughter's anguish. Giving in to a numbing drunkenness and morbidity, he protested that it could not be true. As he fell asleep, sitting there, he thought of being alone in a loveless world.

He awakened after sunset. The taste in his mouth was foul, but otherwise he felt refreshed. Stomach fine; no headache. Less depressed than before. The man of action had begun to take over. There was still time left. There were things he could do for her. He could feel his whole body reviving as his head filled with plans.

He got up and flicked the central switch on the wall, and all the lamps came on. Order was now somehow restored. He looked at his watch; he really ought to be phoning for a dinner reservation at Le Gavroche. Or should they go to the theater first and then on to the Savoy for supper? What would please her the most? The more he thought about it, the better the second plan appeared.

There was a new Tom Stoppard play he'd heard about. Was it something Antonia would enjoy? Then he hesitated. My God, he thought, I have no idea what Antonia's taste really is. A fifteen-year-old girl who could pass for twenty-three. A young woman still at school, off somewhere most evenings, just as he was off somewhere most evenings. Away weekends, just as he was away weekends . . . Someone he finally did not know. She has a *life*. But not with me. With whom? My God. This realization of how little he knew about her was almost as frightening as the news that she would die. They were strangers.

He called room service and asked for another bottle of scotch and some ice. He called the front desk and asked about tickets for the Stoppard play; he'd take a chance if tickets were available. He called the Savoy and reserved a table for after the theater. He was still on the phone when Antonia came out of her room in a long, silk Chinese robe, smoking a cigarette. He looked at her. Had he known before this moment that Antonia smoked?

"I feel better," she said. "How about you?"

"Better. I still have *you*."

"Are you taking me out?"

"I thought we'd go to the theater and have a later supper."

"That sounds fine; I'd like that a lot. Maybe you could get room service to send up some cheese and biscuits for me to eat while I'm bathing."

He said he would.

"Is there any scotch left?"

"I finished it. But I called for another bottle. Should be here any minute. Do you want to take that into the bath with you, too?"

"Yes; I love to keep a drink on the side of the tub."

"Your father's daughter." He smiled.

As he picked up the phone to order the cheese and biscuits, he asked himself whether he ought to be concerned about the fact that she'd begun to drink so young.

The play, called *Travesties*, turned out to be considerably more intellectual in its appeal than Conrad would have wished. It was a joy to listen to its language, but nothing much happened, and halfway through it he feared that Antonia was becoming bored.

"I'm having some trouble with it," she admitted during intermission. "But really, I'm having a good time. I hardly ever get to the theater in Paris."

"But why not?"

"Oh . . ." She let it go at that.

As they took their seats for the second act, he asked her whether she'd ever read James Joyce or had any familiarity with the ideas of Lenin; both of them were central characters in the play.

They walked from the theater to the Savoy. She took his hand. The warmth that spread through his body brought a smile to his face. The night air was damp and there was a chill in it, but they didn't mind. By the time they arrived, they had good appetites. Conrad called for the wine list and found a good champagne, which arrived sufficiently chilled so they could have their first glass while the bottle was further cooled in a bucket of ice. They looked at the menu, ordered, and looked at each other.

"I don't really know you," he said. "Isn't that amazing?"

"Not really."

"I seem to have missed the transition from child to woman."

"I seem to have missed it, too," she said. "And it all happened in *my* body. There was no transition, really. I just went from being one thing to being another. Overnight almost. I don't think it's all that uncommon."

"What world do you live in?" he asked her. "A child's or a woman's?"

"That's the big problem for me," she said. "I don't belong to either. I *am* a woman. But I still feel like a stranger in that territory. I don't really know my way around yet. You asked me how come I never go to the theater in Paris? Well, I have no one to go with, except for one friend. . . . I have one friend. He's older."

"You have a boyfriend?"

"Yes."

"Are you lovers?"

"Yes. But . . . I'm shocked at the way you—"

"At the way I what?"

"Nothing," she said. "Can we talk about *you?*"

"If we must."

"I don't see enough of you."

"I know that. We're going to make that up."

"We'd better hurry," she said. She smiled a small, sad smile that Conrad didn't miss. She sipped some champagne and said, "Thank you for tonight. I'm having a very good time."

"I'm glad. I am too."

"Tell me something. When did *you* change?"

"I don't exactly know what you mean."

177

"Whatever became of my gruff, scary father?" She laughed. He responded by laughing also.

"Oh, *him*," he said.

"Yes, all that raw energy. Of course, the energy is still there. But you've mellowed."

"Just getting older, getting richer. Just clothes and veneer. Don't be fooled. . . . Don't be fooled by something else, either. You may remember me as a wild man, but I'll bet that I read books, more books in a year than most people do in a lifetime. A bundle of contradictions. Your mother loved me for that." Then he realized that he'd made a mistake, hit a wrong note. No, Johanna had to stay out of their conversation. Johanna would not be a meeting ground between them. "Here comes our smoked salmon," he said.

She sat back and watched it being served from its gleaming silver tray. Watched the capers being spooned on, and the small bits of hard-cooked egg. Watched the broad gesture with which Conrad rejected the pepper mill, a reminder of an earlier image of him.

More champagne was poured. Then he asked her, "Who's the boyfriend?"

"Someone nice."

"Rich?"

"I've never asked him. You're rich. Which makes me rich enough, I guess. Conrad?"

"What?"

"Do you mind that I don't call you Dad?"

He thought about it. Then he said, "No, I don't mind. I sort of like it in an evil way."

"What do you mean?"

"Nothing."

But she knew.

"I have a secret," she told him suddenly.

"I have a feeling you've got more than one."

"There's one I want to tell you about."

"Okay. What is it?"

"I've started to work. Not seriously. But it's working nevertheless. I've been doing some modeling here and there."

The word modeling gave him a chill. His immediate association with it was sexual. He thought of his cabarets. He thought of lewd photographs in magazines. Silk stockings and whores. It was a momentary flash.

178

There was no misunderstanding of what she'd said. He knew she meant fashion modeling.

"Well, you certainly have the figure for it."

"My bust is too big, although someone said that idea is changing. But I've got the height. And I'm still growing. In another year or two—"
She stopped.

Was the evening over? What could they say to each other now? In a year or two she'd be a memory. In six months she'd be dead.

They returned to their suite at Claridge's after midnight.

Conrad immediately went in search of some brandy. He was sure he'd ordered a bottle of it when they first arrived, along with the scotch.

"Ah," he said. "Here it is. Would you like a little?"

"Yes, thank you."

He poured two glasses and gave her one. They sat opposite each other, he on the sofa, she in a wing chair. They said nothing for a long while. Finally, Conrad broke their silence.

"I meant what I said earlier."

"I hope you meant *everything* you said earlier. You said some nice things."

"I said I would do anything in the world I could for you. That's what I'm referring to now. What more can I do than offer you what money will buy? At least I have that power. And I'll *be* with you, Antonia. For however long you have, I'll be with you. We can cruise the Mediterranean, go to Tibet. Anything! But first I think we ought to get some sleep."

"Soon. I haven't quite finished my brandy."

"You must be exhausted."

"I am. You know," she said, "I *have* given some thought to what I'd do with the rest of my life if the first diagnosis turned out to be true. I began to imagine it in Paris. I guess I really knew what the verdict was then."

"Do you really want to talk about it now? Or should we wait until the morning?"

"Were you seriously offering to take me on a vacation somewhere?"

"Yes. Quite seriously. We can just keep going."

"I think I might like that a lot."

"I have to be back in Paris tomorrow," he said. "But I can arrange to

179

leave as soon after that as you'd like. We could start by going some place warm. We can follow the sun. . . ."

He stood up and left his brandy glass on the end table. He was desperate to get to sleep now.

"Ready?" he asked. She nodded, and he turned off the lights in the living room.

Their bedroom doors were opposite each other. They stood leaning on them, smiling a final goodnight.

"There's only one thing I really want," Antonia told him.

"What's that?"

"Your love."

"My love!" he said. "You *have* my love—"

"I want you to make love to me," she said. "That's the gift I want before I die."

She went into her room and closed the door behind her.

His hands were shaking as he closed his own door and prepared himself for bed.

He lay awake disbelieving it, denying she'd ever said it, wondering whether it was really possible. His head was too thick to think about it any more tonight.

In the morning he was able to put it out of his mind.

Only once, while he was shaving, did he think about it. And then he was able to persuade himself that Antonia, depressed by the blow she'd been dealt, had relaxed in his company, mixed champagne with brandy, and finally had no idea of what she was saying. She had responded to him physically, as teenage daughters do, but with an inhibition system weakened by exhaustion and alcohol. He let it go at that. There was something else that was bothering him.

He dressed hurriedly and joined her for breakfast. They discussed world events in that predictable way of people who see each other over toast every morning. The newspaper, brought with their breakfast, effectively allowed them to avoid each other without breaking the illusion of intimacy.

Afterward she said she was going to Regent Street to look at some sweaters at Jaeger. This provided the opportunity he needed. As soon as she left, he made the phone call.

"Dr. Kendrick's office."

"Is Dr. Kendrick there?"

"May I ask who is calling?"

"This is Conrad Thornton. My daughter, Antonia Thornton, came to see Dr. Kendrick yesterday."

"Oh, yes, of course, Mr. Thornton. You are a patient of Dr. Kendrick's also, are you not?"

"Yes."

"Well, I have been *searching* for you," the woman said.

"You have?"

"You are long overdue for a checkup. I sent you a card. You did not respond." It was clearly a reprimand, but he had no time for it. At last, the woman put him through to Dr. Kendrick.

"Conrad, how are you?"

"I'm all right."

"Well, I'm glad you are. You've got to be, you know."

"Should I come in? Should we talk?"

"Of course."

"Bill, listen to me. You're not listening. You're miles away."

"No. You're quite wrong. I'm right here. You see, we have a difficult—a really terrible situation. And the most difficult thing of all is how little there is one can say. Or do, for that matter. It was Antonia's choice to come here alone and to face the truth. Extraordinary, I thought, for someone so young. And she brought if off remarkably well. Remarkably. Your daughter is made of steel. She gets that from you. I told her the entire truth. And I will repeat it if you'd like to come in."

"There's nothing that can be done for her?"

"The answer to that question depends entirely upon what you mean by it. Can I save her life? No, I cannot. Prolong her life? Yes. But I'm not sure either of you wants that. I discussed that possibility with her. She rejected it. Quite frankly, I agree. She is a young and beautiful woman. She prefers dying whole to lingering. The difference in her case would at best be a matter of months."

"And without treatment? We're speaking of six months?"

"We're not dealing with a clock. What I told Antonia is that she can count on six months in which she'll feel essentially no different. And then, and only *approximately* then, since there is no way I can put a timetable on this with any real accuracy, she will undergo a more or less sudden decline. Her death will come rapidly, once that begins."

"Will she suffer?"

181

"There'll be pain toward the end. But we can control that. Conrad, I spent an hour yesterday talking to her. I tell you, she's remarkable. Now, I don't mean to be abrupt. But I am with a patient. Let me give you to my secretary, and you can tell her when you'd like to come in. I'd be only too glad to talk further with you then."

"Bill, one minute more—please."

"Of course."

"I should be getting back to Paris this afternoon. Is there any real point to my coming in?"

"No. Not really. If I could offer you some comfort, I'd say come in."

"I don't want comfort. Is there anything further you ought to be telling me? Medically, I mean."

"No. I assure you. There isn't."

"Aren't there any further tests?"

"No. Those were all done quite efficiently in Paris. I've scrutinized all the reports that were in her folder. No need to put her through any of the tests a second time. There was no need for me to do anything, really, other than corroborate the first diagnosis."

"All right, then."

"Conrad, I'm terribly sorry. I wish it were different."

"I understand. You're a doctor, not God."

"Quite true."

"I'll let you go now. Thanks for the way you handled it. I appreciate that."

"Take care of yourself."

"I will. Goodbye."

"Goodbye, Conrad."

Fatigue overtook him as he put down the telephone. His predicament took on a new finality. It had been real enough before; now it was irrevocable. And now he remembered more fully what she'd said to him last night. And he understood that she had meant it.

"I want you to make love to me. That's the gift I want before I die."

He could not deal with it. There was no energy left in his body or brain. He looked at his watch. Not quite eleven. Their flight was at four. He was due to see some bankers at noon and then have lunch with them. He thought of cancelling. But no, he couldn't really do that. Perhaps a short nap would help. He went toward the bedroom.

182

Her words were still ringing in his head. He felt the slightest bit dizzy. Stop it, he told himself. Stop it.

Okay.

He'd deal with it when he got back to Paris.

Chapter Thirteen

For the next few days, Conrad was in a tailspin.

He went about his affairs in Paris, spending very little time with Antonia. He justified the time away from her by the fact that they were planning a trip together, but he knew he was avoiding her. And so did she.

It wasn't that he was afraid she would repeat her words and that he would not know how to respond. He knew she would not repeat them; there was no need. Her words would not easily be forgotten. They had created a tension that would be there between them from now on. The next move had to be his. She would wait until he was ready.

He had seen everything there is in human behavior, or at least so he fancied. He had given up his religious scruples years ago. So it wasn't that. The ethics, in this situation, were all new, all different. The question was one he had never before confronted. A question about the essential nature of love.

Once he overcame his distaste for remembering her words, he became interested in them. He began to see himself as a player in a cosmic drama. He began to think he ought to seek advice.

There were three people he decided he wanted to talk to. Two of them were in New York; one was in San Francisco. Why not make these visits

185

part of their trip? He told Antonia they would begin their vacation in Manhattan.

She loved the idea. They left with only three suitcases. They would be gone an indefinite number of weeks. Anything they needed that they hadn't packed, they would buy. Anything they had packed that they no longer wanted, they would discard. "I'm going to teach you the value of being irresponsible with money," Conrad told her.

The first person he wanted to see in New York was Marcia Henderson, a woman who had worked for him years ago when he first started his agency in Boston. Although they always stayed in touch, Marcia had never met Johanna; she had quit the agency before Johanna came along. At the time Johanna and Conrad were married, Marcia was in Athens for a year; when they went to Paris, Marcia went to Edinburgh to medical school. And so it was. Conrad and Marcia would write to each other once every year or eighteen months, and they would meet when he was in Manhattan. Once, when they happened to be in London at the same time, they slept together without much emotional impact. Later he wrote to her about Johanna's funeral. Despite his knowing that Marcia had decided upon a specialty in psychiatry, he never mentioned in his letter the problem of Antonia's adjustment. That particular letter, in fact, had been startling for its factual and unemotional tone.

But now he needed her advice desperately. The fact that she was a psychiatrist suddenly meant a lot to him. What he had to tell her would not seem like some shameful secret.

"Where's Antonia?" Marcia asked when she greeted him at the door of her office in a large high-rise opposite Lincoln Center.

"In Saks or Bergdorf's. How've you been?"

They kissed each other warmly, but without any sexual tension; it felt safe and reassuring for both of them.

"I've been just fine," she said, closing the door. "You're looking well." She removed her reading glasses and scrutinized him more carefully. "Hey, I take that back. You look a bit frazzled. Is everything all right?"

They moved into her inner office, where he sat down in a well-uphol- stered chair aligned with an imposing hassock. He put his feet up.

"I could be better," he said.

"What's wrong?"

"I didn't invite Antonia to join us because I need to talk to you about

186

her. Can we go somewhere for a drink? Our dinner reservation isn't until eight. We've got lots of time."

"Do you really want to sit in some noisy bar? I've got some scotch here. Or we could go to my apartment. If we do that, I can put on something sexier than this tweed suit."

"I don't like to see you looking sexy, Marcia."

"Why is that?"

"You're the mother figure in my life."

"Yeah," she said. "I've always suspected." There was a good-natured prettiness in her face.

"How come you're not married?" he asked.

"I can't believe I'm hearing that question."

"Why not?"

"I hope you're prepared for this, old friend. I've been saving this to tell you later. I *am* getting married. Old Marcia makes it to the altar at last. He's a fellow psychiatrist. We're going to be Shrink and Shrink." She laughed, even though it was the joke she told every time she announced her engagement to someone.

"Congratulations. Where's the scotch?"

"Coming."

As soon as the alcohol relaxed them both, he told her about Antonia. "Are you much of an expert on the subject of incest?" he asked her at the end.

"Oh, Conrad," she said. "This is nothing to be glib about."

"I wasn't being glib."

"It's funny," she said. "All the while I've been listening to you, the word incest hasn't once come to mind."

"Well, then what the hell is it if not incest?"

"If that's how you really feel about it, then you've already got your answer."

"How do you feel about it, Marcia? Supposing I were a patient."

"You know how we work. We just help formulate the questions. Sometimes we don't even go that far."

"You're not shocked by what I've told you?"

"No."

"Is there some chance I would be giving her something important?"

"There's some chance of that," she said. "It's your own motivation you've got to examine. Death will purify Antonia. Only real love in your

187

heart can purify you. Please consider that philosophical, as opposed to professional, advice."

"And if I have real love in my heart? Are you saying then it would be all right?"

"All right? Conrad . . . only you can answer that question."

They talked about other things and then went to dinner. Over dessert and coffee, she asked him whether he'd like to resume their earlier discussion. He said no.

He took her home, kissed her goodnight in the lobby of her building, and hailed a cab. He went back to the Plaza, where he and Antonia were staying.

He thought of ringing her room to ask if she'd had a pleasant evening. But then he thought maybe she was asleep. He'd see her in the morning.

He got into bed depressed and thought about his mother.

Conrad's mother was short. Her spine was as straight as a dancer's. She had red hair, which she insisted was a gift from God, although logic suggested the alchemy of some expensive salon. Six months after Conrad was born, she cleared out the garage, turned it into a real estate agency, and became remarkably successful. She never referred to herself as Conrad's mother, not even on visiting day at his school. She would arrive at the registration desk and explain her presence by saying, "I'm Conrad Thornton's female parent."

Conrad did not love her. She was an essential force in his life, but he did not love her. She never smiled at him.

His teachers smiled at him, and he loved them. His father smiled at him, but he was rarely around. The maid smiled at him, but she was contaminated. Conrad heard his mother say that on the telephone.

The maid was nineteen years old. She had a full mouth and full breasts, and when she turned around you could see the fullness of her buttocks. Sometimes you could see the flesh of her thigh above her stockings. It was the flesh of her thigh, and the other flesh above that, that he dreamed about. He thought contamination must be the most wonderful thing in the world. Then, when he got a bit older, he began to wonder whether the maid had the clap.

"Does she have VD?" he asked his mother. He had learned about it in school and was probably the only kid in his class who could freely discuss the subject with his own mother. There was no subject too personal or too embarrassing for him to bring to her. She believed in trust, and total realism. She encouraged adult behavior.

"No," she responded, "the maid does not have venereal disease. If she did, she would not be in our employ."

"All right," he said. He was more puzzled than ever by what his mother had meant when she said the maid was contaminated.

He became obsessed by the maid.

He couldn't take his eyes off her. He studied her white uniform; his eyes became glued to it as she walked, trying to discern the line of her panties, the curve of her belly, the curved divide of her ass. Anything he could build on, could dream of, masturbate over. The mystery of her contamination only increased her erotic value.

"Is she still contaminated?" he asked.

"What do you mean?"

"I heard you on the phone."

"I see."

"I wasn't deliberately listening," he explained.

"I'm not angry."

"I'd just like to know," he said. "I mean, I think I'm entitled to know."

"She doesn't have an illness," his mother assured him.

"I kind of figured that out," Conrad said. "If she did, you'd have fired her."

"Now I'm going to have to fire her anyway," his mother said.

"Why?"

"Because I'm going to answer your question. Once I've done that, I'm going to have to fire her. Do you still want an answer?"

"Yes."

"She engaged in sexual intercourse with her brother when she was fourteen," his mother said. "I found her diary. That's incest."

"Incest," he repeated. It was a new word.

"Yes. It would be the same thing, Conrad, as if you and I made love."

That night he had a bad dream about the maid. In it she seemed shorter, and her hair was red, the same as his mother's hair, and her body much less full. She was lying on the living room sofa coughing; she couldn't seem to stop. And the doctor said she had a fever so high she would probably not live, and her cheeks were as red as her hair, and her thighs were open, and he was drawn to her, and the fever seemed to be even there, and he knew she was dying, and contaminated, and that he could become contaminated too, but still he was drawn to her . . .

He awakened in a sweat. He was wet all over. Sticky wet along his thighs and on his belly. He understood what had happened. His mother's words came back to him. "It would be the same thing, Conrad, as if you and I made love."

He felt his face getting flushed. His fists were clenched as hard as he could get them. He began to feel that he hated her.

But he didn't hate her. As he remembered it now, it wasn't hate he was feeling.

He bolted out of bed and was halfway across the room before he realized that he was vaguely disoriented. He had to remind himself that he was in New York, in the Plaza Hotel, in the present.

He turned on some lights, got his robe, and flicked on the television set. He looked at his watch. He didn't want to stay up too late. He had a breakfast appointment with Ned Longworth at eight.

"Oh, my God, Conrad, I can't believe it," Ned Longworth was saying.

They were in the Edwardian Room, seated near a window overlooking Central Park. It was a crisp fall morning. Their view of the city through the window made the world seem a fine place. Their view of life within the room was that personal power could solve any problem. So Ned regarded Conrad's tragic news about Antonia as a challenge.

"You've got to get her to John Saunders at Cancer Memorial," Ned was saying.

"No. It's beyond that. Believe me, we've been through it."

"You've got to try," Ned said.

"That's not what I asked you here for."

Ned was visibly upset by Conrad's rebuke. He misunderstood it.

"She's dying," Conrad said. "There's no question about that. The best thing I can do for her is take her mind off it. Give her six months of living that any other girl in the world would envy. That's what this is all about."

"Okay."

"We'll be here a few days. She's at Cartier's this morning. Buying emeralds. Why not? Next we go to the West Coast for a few days. Then

190

back here, to go to the theater. Then two weeks in Barbados. Then we'll see. Ned . . ."

"Yeah?"

"She's asked me to make love to her. It's what she wants before she dies."

Ned paused. Then he said, "That could be a very beautiful thing, Conrad."

"Are you sincere?"

"Do you know me?"

"Yeah, I know you. You can be an awful bastard in business. But you've got scruples about people. I think you're a kind-hearted bastard. That's why I'm here."

"I think it could be a beautiful thing," he repeated.

"It's incest. You're a lawyer. Doesn't that bother you?"

"The taboo about incest has to do with having children."

"It's a pretty strong taboo."

"I don't think of it as incest," Ned said. "It could be a loving act."

Ned would have gone on, but he was having difficulty finding the words. There was a look in Conrad's eyes he didn't think he'd ever seen there before. It was a look of deep pain. And love. But behind that expression there had to be a question. Conrad was not naive. He was bright enough to ask the obvious question even of himself. Was there a place in his head that was already responding to the opportunity to fuck his own daughter? That was the catch in all of this.

"You're the one who's taking the risk," Ned finally said. "Not Antonia."

"What do you mean?"

"You'll be acting out an historically deplorable lust. You may wind up condemning yourself for it. Even if it's lovely when it happens. Maybe especially if it's lovely when it happens. You're the one in danger."

"And you're still telling me to go ahead?"

"I'm not telling you anything. All I've said is it could be a loving act. Conrad, she's just a kid. She needs your love. In the closest sense. If that's what's going to get her through the end of her life, I don't see the harm. Not to her, if that's your concern. What I'm trying to tell you is that the risk can also save you, if you think about it. The risk means you're doing it for *her*. If you take the risk, it's already an act of love. No matter what happens in your head afterward, always remember that and you'll be all right."

"You really think so."

"Yes."

"I can't tell yet what I'm going to do. I'm not ready for it to happen yet. If it happens at all. But, listen . . ."

"What?"

"Thanks. Everything you've said really helps."

"It will be like a holy wedding, this gift of love," the guru in San Francisco said.

They were actually related. The guru, whose name had once been Norton Evans, was a first cousin of Conrad's. Although he hadn't seen him since they both were small boys, Conrad had been made aware of Norton's progress into oriental philosophy by his mother in the days when they were still corresponding, before her final illness. Oddly enough, those letters were never disapproving of Norton or condescending in any way. For a family that had little tolerance for the exotic in any form, they were surprisingly understanding. They thought Norton's behavior was odd, that he would have done better studying for the ministry. But they respected him. There was a spiritual quality about him, Conrad's mother had written, that was noticeable even when Norton was a child.

"Why did you come to me?" Norton asked Conrad.

"If we'd had a priest in the family, I would have gone to him, I guess. You're the closest we've got to that job description."

"But you're not religious, are you?"

"No. But where does one turn for permission to do the unspeakable, if not to a priest?" Conrad threw his head back in a reflexive gesture. He looked at the ceiling and winked at Johanna. She would have liked what he'd just said. That's the way they used to sit around and talk in the old days. Except it had never been a matter of life and death then. And now it was. There was a sinking feeling in the pit of Conrad's stomach. He looked at his cousin. What was his cousin really thinking of him? Was it stupid and unfeeling to be talking this way now? But his cousin was smiling.

"You're right, of course. That's really the essence of being a priest or wise man. Giving permission to do the unspeakable. I like that." He paused, smiling more broadly. "By unspeakable I'm assuming you mean heroic."

192

"Of course," Conrad said with heavy irony.

"But I see from your expression that you do not understand the true meaning of your own words. You can't accept the possibility of heroism in your present predicament?"

"I can accept it; I just don't see it."

"Afterward," Norton said. "You will be alone. And you will condemn yourself. Because despite your lack of religious feeling, you are conditioned to think of this act as a crime. And, afterward, if you once remember the beauty of her body or the strength of your passion, you will live in terror. That *is* the price you will pay for this gift you will give her."

"It's interesting," Conrad said.

"What is?"

"That you and my lawyer said almost exactly the same thing."

"Then he's a wise man, too," Norton said, laughing. "You've chosen well."

"You said it would be like a holy wedding."

"Yes. And it could also destroy you. The real trouble is you're not prepared. To do such a thing in a holy way would require years of a different kind of thinking."

"Then your advice is that I deny her request."

"No. That's not my advice. Is she here in San Francisco with you?"

"Yes. Would you like to meet her?"

"That would be nice. But under these circumstances I would feel peculiar. Conrad . . . you've come for my advice, and I haven't really given it. I'm not sure that I can. I have only one thing to say to you, and my words are going to strike you as odd. What I want to say is . . . There is no sin in this. As far as I can see."

They returned to New York, en route to Barbados.

He was afraid of her now, afraid of getting too close, afraid of touching. When they shopped for clothes together, he made a point of referring to her as his daughter. He knew what the salespeople were thinking. At Bergdorf's, before their relationship was clearly defined, a saleswoman with a deadly instinct invited him into a private dressing room with Antonia where she was trying on bikinis and one-piece bathing suits. The temptation nearly destroyed him. Then at Saks, in a boutique in the men's department, there were closet-sized rooms with louvered doors where she could have gone without embarrassment to watch him. A whole new world of erotic possibility suddenly opened. Couples together in department store dressing rooms. He wondered if anyone ever fucked in there.

All of his thoughts made him suffer. All of those raunchy flights of fancy with which he'd always entertained himself now turned sour, because they posed a threat. If he looked at himself in the mirror, he thought of her. He thought of her looking at him . . .

His only defense was to stop thinking of sex altogether. It wasn't something he planned or worked out. It just happened. All desire fled. He felt celibate and happy. The burden of virility was shed. He could touch her now, hold her arm or let her hold his. He could admire her now, advise her on this dress or that pair of shoes. He could put on his underwear without wondering whether that particular cut made him look fat. It was a welcome respite. Of course, it wouldn't last.

She fell asleep with her head on his shoulder on their flight to Barbados. The smell of her hair, mingled with the smells of her perfume and skin, would have been more than he could have tolerated had it not been for his self-inflicted ruse of chastity. In his own state of drowsiness he tried to remember scenes from her childhood, moments of family communion. His head bobbed onto hers, and for the few seconds in which he slept, he remembered the afternoon of lovemaking on the living room floor to which Johanna had always referred as the impregnation scene. She had always insisted that she knew for a fact the exact moment of Antonia's conception. He remembered the kiss he'd given her on that day on the thin, raised line between her vagina and anus. . . . He woke up. Suddenly. Pulled himself away from Antonia. All in one gesture. He hadn't meant to disturb her. But he did.

"Are you okay?" Antonia asked him.

"Yes. I—got a crimp in my arm. I'm sorry."

"Oh. That's all right. Why am I so sleepy?"

"Me, too," he said.

Antonia curled up in her seat and turned slightly away from him. He leaned back and closed his eyes. His mind was suddenly carnal now. Chastity had fled as unpredictably as it had announced itself.

They were staying in a cottage on the grounds of the Sandy Lane, on the Caribbean side of the island. The cottage was spacious and luxuriously appointed. There were two bedrooms.

194

The sky was cloudy when they arrived. Still they felt the heat. Antonia suggested that they go right to the beach, and Conrad agreed. They also wanted lunch. They decided someone could bring them a tray out near the water.

She complained about his remoteness even as he complied with her wish that he rub suntan oil on her back.

"I'm not being remote," he said. "Furthermore, there's no sun."

"It's there behind the clouds. You can get a burn in this weather."

"Okay."

He admired her supple figure. He admired her choice of swimsuit, her bangle bracelets, her backless beach shoes, her scarf . . . Everything she wore or carried seemed a part of her body. It was incredible. He could catch a glimpse of her terry robe draped across a beach chair and feel a sudden stab of desire.

When he finished applying the oil, he returned to his own chaise and lay on his stomach. She offered to apply lotion to his back, but he declined. He said his skin would tan. She contradicted him and laughed.

Her laugh was new. When had she laughed that way before? The sound was like some tiny oriental bell. He once slept with a waitress in Iowa City who wore an ankle bracelet on which she'd hung three of those tiny bells. The way they tinkled when he undressed her in the motel and when she sat on him in the straight back chair and when she stretched her naked body in some posture that reminded him of estrus in a cat was something he knew even then would be indelible. Antonia's laugh was like those little bells.

"You'll be sorry," she said. "You'll be as red as a lobster. You won't be able to dance with me tonight." She laughed again.

"When the sun comes out from behind those clouds, I'll let you do my back," he said.

Each sound she made only seemed to enlarge all of his senses. His eyes were closed now, because he didn't dare to look at her or at any of the possessions his rising desire had begun to personify. But there was no escaping her nearness. Her voice had become, in the last few minutes, an erotic instrument. He decided to go for a swim.

"That water is too tempting to resist," he said. "Want to come in?"

"And waste all this expensive suntan oil?"

"When you spot a waiter, you can order us some lunch."

"Anything special?"

195

"A sandwich. I'll let you surprise me."

Her hand reached out to him. He took it. She brought him gently to her. He lifted himself off his chaise and kneeled alongside her.

The clouds began to shift. He could feel the sun emerging, burning his back with its sudden heat as he bent over to kiss her just once on the mouth.

They went back to their separate bedrooms. They bathed. They napped. They drank scotch from bottles each of them had on a dressing table. They dressed for dinner. They were apart for nearly two hours. It was eight o'clock when Antonia knocked on his door.

She was wearing a black silk dress that outlined her legs and the rise of her belly and her pubic mound. But it also flowed, and it flowed so immaculately that it left the possibility of innocence an open question. It was a marvelous dress; its lines were meant for a dancer. Antonia wore it with grace and style. And to be admired.

"You look wonderful," he said.

"Thank you. You didn't turn into a lobster after all."

"I told you. I tan."

"You look healthy. And important. You *are* important."

"Everyone's important," he said.

"You know that's not true. You're important to *me*."

"Yes, I want to be important to you."

"Conrad . . ."

"What?"

But she couldn't bring herself to ask him the question on her lips. Instead she asked him to buy her a drink at the bar before they went to dinner.

To her surprise, he was not a good dancer.

He didn't really enjoy dancing. That was the problem. He tried to explain it to her, and for some reason it turned into a joke between them. His attempt at explanation just grew funnier and funnier to her. The more she laughed, the harder he tried to explain, and the more she laughed in response.

"I think one of my hips is higher than the other." And he howled as he saw her start to giggle again. "No, really," he went on. "I have that problem every time I go to get a pair of trousers. I always have them measure the length of each leg separately for that reason." They both burst out laughing again.

They were on the beach. Not far from the pavilion where the music and dancing were. They could see the lights and still hear the crowd and the beat of the music. But they were alone. Barefoot. At the water's edge. Laughing helplessly. Holding hands. Drunk. Closer. The moon was full. Directly above them. They fell into each other's arms. And he absolutely knew he would not let go of her again.

He tried not to think of the sexual details.

He tried not to notice hairs and smells and folds and moisture, but not noticing would have been a denial of his own arousal. And he could no longer make that denial. There were no more questions left in his brain. Except one. Would he cut himself loose from all control now? Would he be her lover in the only way he knew how to be anyone's lover, without inhibition? An elegant satyr, as Johanna once had called him? Did he dare? Could he abandon control? Part her legs; taste the honeyed spice between them, the condiments of sex? Respond to tendrils, fingernails, mouth, and tongue? Her nipples were burning; her thighs were wet from her own excitement. Her wanting him was a gorgeous song. She was singing that he *could* forget. He *would* forget. He let go of the last question in his brain. Let go of thought. Let go of . . .

She was having an orgasm beneath his hand, which was not really inside her but gently between her parted labia. Her hands were on the small of his back. He hadn't yet penetrated her. That was what she now wanted. *Now. Now.* As she began to come. He understood. He pushed himself inside her, and his stiff penis was stroked and kneaded by the spasms in her vagina. He began to move frantically. So he could join her. So he could come with her, urge her to further pleasure with the triggering of his semen. He rode her hard and grabbed her buttocks with his hands and lifted her. She moved like an acrobat then. They made enough noise to obliterate the crickets and the music that still came from the beach and the sounds of the ocean. When it was over, there was a smile on her lips that he would remember for the rest of his life.

In an hour they made love again. Then they slept.

They slept in the same bed, and he kept waking up erect and in need of her. By the morning he had to acknowledge to himself that the breaking

197

of the taboo was deep in his consciousness, that the content of his passion had some rapist element that could not be denied.

It did not bother him. They were lovers now. On vacation from the world of moral constraint. Having a marvelous time. Who cared?

She never once spoke to him while they made love. She said things like oh that's so good, or *yes yes*, but never words of endearment or I love you. He was grateful for that.

But then he began to wonder. What had happened to the holy wedding? How had they managed to have so completely lost the meaning of their lovemaking? The father's gift to a dying daughter?

He no longer cared. He no longer wished to think about it. It was carnal now. Not pure. It was a raging passion, not tender. He was wild. Too wild to think clearly.

He had to have her. He knew how much she wanted him.

Their affair continued.

It continued in Barbados. It continued in London. It continued in Paris.

It continued through the winter and into the spring, well past the six-month limit put on her life.

She was in his blood now. He wanted no other woman. She seemed to live for him alone. If she had a boyfriend somewhere, she most certainly never saw him. She spent all of her free time with Conrad. There were some modeling assignments every now and then, and Conrad finally took an interest in her career. He used his influence where he could to help her. But how long would it go on?

She seemed to be in perfect health. Had some miracle occurred after all? Were all the doctors wrong? It had been known to happen before in medical history.

One thing began to seem certain. Antonia was not dying.

Chapter Fourteen

Conrad had always harbored an irrational distrust of French doctors. And so, when Antonia had come to him more than six months ago to say she'd been suffering from fatigue and a general feeling of malaise, he had wanted her to fly over to see Bill Kendrick in London.

But she refused. The glamor of a world-famous clinic in Paris had much greater appeal. She preferred to go there. When Conrad asked her what she knew about this place, she answered in a vague way—her usual style—that she'd read about it in some magazine. Conrad was busy; he had business affairs to attend to. He didn't believe for a moment that her problem was serious. He shrugged and told her she was an adult as far as he was concerned. Go to any doctor you like, he said.

When she called the clinic, she gave them a made-up name. She said she was coming in for a checkup, that her specific complaint was headache. On the day of her appointment, she sat in the waiting room hoping she'd be lucky. And she was.

The doctor assigned to her was Pierre Lazarre. He appeared to be about thirty-four. He was nice looking without being strikingly handsome. He was shy. Unmarried. His attraction for women was largely based on his failure to comprehend that women responded to him.

Her introduction to him was proper, the examination discreet. He could find no apparent cause for her headaches. Her health, he said, was excellent. He recommended that she come back in a few days if the headache persisted.

Two days later she was back, aware by then that Pierre Lazarre, young as he was, enjoyed a fine reputation both in hematology and oncology. He was famous as a specialist in cancer.

Pierre could not make sense of Antonia's symptoms as she described them. When he challenged her, she readily admitted the truth. "I came back to be touched by you," she told him.

She had lied about her age as well as her identity. Her chart had said nineteen, an exaggeration her well-developed body confirmed. Looking at her first in the examining room and then in his small office, Pierre could not hide his interest. She proposed dinner that evening. He accepted. She said she wanted to sleep with him. He blushed. Then she told him that the hairs on the back of his hands would feel wonderful against her thighs.

He asked her to sit in the waiting room until he finished examining his last patient of the day. "Just as there is no cure for my shyness," he said, ushering her out, "there is probably no cure for your blatancy. You appear to be an intelligent young woman. I would like you much more if you were better behaved. Do you mind waiting one hour?"

"No," she said. "I don't mind."

"Or you can meet me at twenty-six Rue de Montmorency, where I have most of the meals I don't cook at home."

"I'll wait here," she said.

She returned to the waiting room and thumbed through every issue of *Paris Vogue* she could find.

When Pierre emerged an hour and a half later, he told her his car was parked in a lot in the rear of the building. He offered to pull it around and pick her up at the entrance. But she chose the adventure of going with him.

Darkness had not yet set in, but it was late enough for the parking lot to be deserted except for Pierre's Renault.

"I'm more starved for sex than I am for dinner," she told him.

He laughed. But she saw his eyes narrow. She thought she knew how to play him. It excited her.

"Have you ever made love in your Renault?" she asked.

"Yes." He called her Denise since Denise Bruxelle was the name she had given. She had given a fictitious address in Lyons. "But I also make love in my bed. I much prefer to go there."

200

"Take me there now," she said.

"Do you read a lot of erotic books?"

"Why?"

"Because your exaggerated behavior is imitative of pornography. I've been wondering where you learned it. Not from a lover, I hope. If I didn't think you were joking, I would suspect a real pathology."

"Do you really think I'm joking?"

"My dear," he said, "do not misunderstand. I have every intention of fucking you." There was a barely perceptible thickness in his voice that had not been there a moment ago. "I have never before met anyone like you. In just five minutes we will be home and in bed. You are very beautiful."

"After you fall in love with me, I have a favor to ask of you," she said.

"I never fall in love after sex. If it's love you wish from me, we should go directly to dinner."

He parked the Renault on a side street in Montmartre.

"There is where I live."

They both got out of the car.

Pierre Lazarre was in for a surprise.

The powerful experience Antonia held out to him did not come from anything as mundane as technique. The number of things one could do with mouths, fingers, orifices, and erectile tissue, although seemingly infinite, were, for all practical purposes, already within his repertoire. So the impression she would have to make would be on the mind.

Never having so aggressively gone about the task of seduction, Antonia had no way of knowing how stimulating it would be to her. Her scenario was based on a classically potent sexual fantasy, a patient's seduction of a physician. But even more powerful was its reversal, a physician's molestation of his patient. It was this change that was taking her so by surprise. As Pierre responded, so did she; her excitement stimulating his in return. A synergy was building. By the time they were in bed, each intent on the nakedness of the other, freed from tenderness by a pact of deliberation, it was no longer clear who the aggressor was. The heat came from the game.

She triggered in him a revival of fantasies from his early student days. So he was much more than fucking her; he was abandoning himself to older temptations. As a student he had practiced a thousand ways of distracting himself from sexual arousal during the examination of a patient. But now that forbidden dream could be acted out in his bed. She had set him up for it very carefully. Even during the initial examination there had been a tension, an intimation. And during the second visit to his office, she had said it all very clearly. "I came back to be touched by you."

His penis was too hard now to remain comfortable inside his shorts. He stripped them off and knelt over her body, his knees digging into the mattress somewhere along the remarkable line from her knee to her hip; her curves seemed to be swelling before his eyes. Deep inside his head he was giving her orders.

She looked up at him. Her smoky gray eyes suggested, in their intensity, shades of blue. What is it you wish? Her eyes were asking. She knew that in this game she was supposed only to *ask*. And to wait. He would tell her what to do. He would conduct the examination, as it were. The metaphor of doctor and patient was potent still.

She could see from the set of his face that he was ready now. By swinging one leg over her, he could straddle her at a point between her belly and diaphragm, his penis pointing upward between her breasts. And from the tension in his thighs she imagined that that was what he was going to do. But she was wrong. It was wrong to anticipate anything. She hoped he hadn't noticed.

Could he read her thoughts by looking at her face? She tried to be impassive. He would give the orders; she had to remember that. The whole process of victimizing herself in this way almost gave her an orgasm. If he so much as touched the underside of her stiff nipple with his fingernail now, she would come. But she waited. He still looked down at her. He was unquestionably ready to articulate his orders now.

Nothing debasing. Humiliation was already implicit in his total power, so the need to defile her with cruelty would have been totally superfluous, even anti-erotic. Although the inordinate intensity of his quivering erection demanded constant reinforcement, stimuli were still relatively easy to find. He would issue commands in a low voice, keeping his sadism subliminal. The metaphor of the examination continued.

He told her to roll over onto her stomach very slowly.

When she did he watched the way her panties, as yet unremoved, rose into her crotch and anus, folding over into damply delicious flesh where the round mounds melted into a hot rear and frontal feast. He had never experienced such an erection in his life.

She rolled over onto her back again. This was his second command. Her nipples were so stretched they hurt; her vagina so fevered she would have begged him to enter her had she not been afraid of making the wrong move. She was thirsty everywhere, but still she waited. As he watched.

Now he was ready to touch her.

He told her to remove her panties. And although she would have done it reflexively, he added the directive that she open her legs. He added *wide*. He added *please*. He wanted to hear himself saying the words. Extending the metaphor continued to be important.

He watched her bring her knees up toward her chest, lift her head, reach down and push her panties toward her ankles, working them with her feet so they dangled from just one foot, until she kicked them off onto the floor. He stared at them. A tiny heap of nylon. It was amazing; they too had a potency.

"After you fall in love with me, I have a favor to ask of you," she had said. She remembered that now, thinking she had failed at her task. She was well beyond the point of having any advantage over him. The very idea of trying to enslave him began to appear ludicrous. It was she who was being melted. It was she who was the specimen. The experiment was his. All she could think of was how much she wanted to have his fingers inside her.

It was what he wanted too.

Her mucus was warm and smoothly textured. When his fingers were inside her, they quivered the way his erection did. He stroked the walls of her vagina, turning his fingers this way and that, crossing and uncrossing one finger over the other, causing currents inside her that were fiercely hot, satisfying and teasing all at the same time. He kept on doing that even as his tongue gently found her. But even the gentleness of his tongue was motivated by the metaphor. The time had come to produce a climax in the patient.

After she came, screaming in her frenzied pleasure, wildly disoriented from her original plan, flung over some mountain in an ecstasy beyond anything she had ever experienced or dreamed, he mounted her.

With Pierre on top, they fucked for a long time; the prolonged teasing of his penis had a reverse effect, as he suspected it might. Instead of causing him to ejaculate immediately, it caused a long delay that suited his purpose better than anything he could have achieved deliberately. She came again and again as he rode back and forth and in a circular motion, at first sliding, and then as she tightened, forcing his way inside her. When he finally came, he felt wonderfully satisfied.

The question of who was in charge would not be answered for another several hours. "If it's love you wish from me, we should go directly to dinner," he had said earlier.

But in the end, he was the one to be fooled. They had not gone directly to dinner. But he fell in love with her anyway.

As long as the metaphor had remained effective, he could think logically within its context, even in the heat of sexual excitement. But once the satisfying of their passion effectively destroyed it, his detachment crumbled. His coolness turned to ardor, his resistance to surrender, his mastery to submission.

Antonia's plan was working out after all.

"What is the favor you want of me?" he asked.

"Soon." Why hurry now? She might as well get to know him better.

"You are trying for a career in modeling, Denise, and you do not live in Paris?"

She had made a mistake. She should have invented a job in a beauty salon to go with her false identity.

"As you can see, I'm not too serious about it," she said.

He was studying her; not as before, no longer with even a pretense of detachment. Now he was searching for clues that would rationalize his sudden need of her. Was she in any way intellectual, artistic, or sensitive? Did she, for example, have the sophistication to properly appraise this restaurant, which was so very special to him? Would she understand that despite the humble surroundings they were in an expensive little gourmet paradise wherein the chef produced a marvelous hot truffle pie, a pudding made of pike, and a magical foie gras of duck carmelized with pepper?

"Would you like an aperitif?" he asked her.

"I've had one," she said, smiling so wickedly that she instantly destroyed her innuendo.

Modeling would be the best career for her after all, Pierre thought. She is always posing. Perhaps he could help her meet some of the right people. He began to make suggestions.

"Modeling is not really my major interest," she said.

204

"Oh? Then what is?"

"Journalism," she said.

He was stunned. And delighted. Suddenly he saw that there was a true intellectual depth beneath the sensuality. Of course. How could he have become so enamored without that? What a marvelous creature!

"Journalism?" He repeated the word as a question. He was lost in rapture.

"Yes."

"Oh," he said. "I want to hear about it. But first let us decide on something to eat, or the chef will retire for the night before we are fed. They have already made an exception for us."

"I'd like the duck," she said.

"Nothing first?"

"No."

"Me, too. The duck and nothing first. And a marvelous wine? Yes?"

She nodded, entrusting him with the selection, caressing the knuckles of the hand that held the wine list, withholding in her breath and eyes further news of her interest in journalism. The erotic bond was perfectly welded now. She shared his appreciation of food; she was obviously intellectual enough to be introduced to his friends; and she reminded him with her caress that she was an incredible fuck. She was stimulating all of his appetites simultaneously. She would get from him everything she wanted.

In the Renault, on their way back to his apartment for an hour of slow lovemaking and a night of delicious sleep, she explained to him the nature of the favor.

"You see, through my interest in journalism, I have gotten to know many writers." She told Pierre about odd jobs she'd taken at various newspapers just to gain experience. She told him that last summer she'd studied at the Sorbonne. "And naturally I've become friendly with some of them."

A pause. Was she about to tell him she had a lover?

"Naturally," he repeated. He felt a twitch near the corner of his mouth.

"One of them is writing a novel. I would like to help this writer."

205

"What sort of a novel is he writing?"

"She. The writer is a woman." Out of the corner of her eye she watched him relax. She had played it expertly. She was improving.

"She is writing some sort of a medical novel?" Pierre asked.

"Yes. A medical thriller to be exact. And she requires some authentic information that I have agreed to research for her."

"Well fine. I can certainly help you with that."

"Could you show me the file of some young woman, say someone of about my age, dying of something unusual?"

"Maybe not precisely what you have described," Pierre said. "But close enough. There is in my file an interesting case. The woman is older, but not by many years. Your friend could make her younger and use the information. It would be accurate. All the results—bloodtests, scintillation scans—would be the same for your friend's purposes. The specific illness in this case is lymphatic cancer."

"Is that fatal?"

"Oh, yes."

"When can I see the file?"

"Come tomorrow after my last appointment. I will explain it to you. You may take notes."

"What would the symptoms be?" she asked. They were in his office. The file was on top of his desk, spread out before them.

"Initially the patient would complain of fatigue, headache perhaps but not necessarily, and weakness. Mostly a feeling of weakness."

"And how would the diagnosis be made?"

"In two ways," Pierre explained. "First the doctor would palpate the patient. If he could feel an enlargement of the spleen or enlarged lymph nodes, he would already suspect a great deal. Then he would make blood tests. Probably he would order a bone marrow biopsy. You can see the results of such a procedure in this particular file. The biopsy confirms an abnormally high white count in the blood, as well as the presence of immature white cells. You see, what happens usually is that the white cells which do not mature remain circulating in the system and this causes a proliferation. Do you understand?"

"Yes," she said. She was listening so intently she was gritting her teeth. She was concentrating with all of her power; she *had* to understand. "Yes," she said again. "What else?"

206

"Well, the blood results are in the chart. We've just talked about those."

"Oh—" she interrupted. She just thought of something. "The bone marrow biopsy. How is that done?"

"It is a simple procedure, really. It's surgical, but quite simple. Done in the doctor's office. The hip bone is used as the site. Long needles are pressed into the bone, and the marrow is aspirated. The marrow is then put onto slides and examined in the laboratory."

"Does it hurt?"

"Not when I do it," Pierre said. "The patient is anesthetized in the area. The patient feels a great deal of pressure but no pain. The first injection, the anesthetic, may hurt just a bit. But this is a procedure we usually describe as painless."

"What else is in the chart?"

"The results of a scintillation scan. Do you know what that is?"

"No."

"It is a technique for seeing, in this case, the spleen and liver. The patient is injected with a radioactive dye, which travels to the area we wish to visualize. We use a special camera to make a picture which shows up on something that looks a little like a television screen. We then make a photograph of this for a permanent record. Here." He reached into the chart for the Polaroids. "Here are the photographs of this patient's scan. They show a much enlarged spleen as well as an enlarged liver. This is an advanced case of lymphatic cancer from which the chances of recovery are very slim."

"The patient is so young," Antonia said.

"This disease rarely strikes older people," Pierre said.

"May I borrow the file?"

"You have made notes."

"Oh, Pierre, please. It would be so much more authentic for my friend if I could have everything photocopied. Please."

"I am not sure it is ethical," he said.

"I am not interested in who the patient is. I'll mask the patient's name on the photocopy, I promise you. Please?"

For the sake of journalism, and for his own pleasure, he agreed.

She borrowed the file. She had what she needed to trick Conrad. Now all she needed was to find a way of getting rid of Pierre. That would not be so easy, she realized. She would have to go on sharing his bed for a little while longer.

Now, months later, she was able to smile down at Conrad in triumph.

At first Conrad did not understand. He mistook her smiles for gratitude. But he knew there was something else. He sensed something wrong.

"How are you feeling?" he began asking her. He knew she was not dying.

"I feel wonderful; I have your love," she would say.

"Of course you have my love."

"You're the best."

And that was how she got at him. That was the innuendo that threw him off balance. It could, of course, have been the most innocent of remarks, as in you're the best daddy in the world. But it was not too likely somehow that that was what she meant. He'd begun to feel, weeks ago, that they should stop being lovers. But he didn't know how to end it. Night after night she would seduce him. And that was what he'd begun to live for. She was the most incredibly effective seductress he'd ever known.

Antonia planned her triumph most carefully.

She would tell Conrad nothing until the truth occurred to him. Slowly. It would occur slowly. But there *would* come a moment when he would understand. Until then, she would smile down at him, his head on the pillow, hers propped up on one elbow. She would smile at him in a way he alone would have to interpret.

The night finally came when, in a drowsy, post-coital state, he said, "There is nothing wrong with you, is there?"

"No," she whispered hoarsely.

"Oh, my God," he said, as hot tears began to roll down his face.

"I am not dying," she said.

"You're not even ill. You've never been ill."

"No."

"How did you fool Bill Kendrick?"

"That was easy."

"How? Didn't he examine you?"

"I had already been examined by one of the most widely respected doctors in the world. I had all of my test results. I was going to Bill Kendrick only for corroboration. I begged him not to put me through

208

those tests again. I was so upset emotionally I wouldn't even let him touch my body. He's a nice man; he understood. He looked at the chart I brought him from Paris. That was all he needed."

"And the chart you brought him from Paris? Where did you get that?"

"That's my secret. I got it."

"You fucked somebody for it, didn't you?" He sat up. He was shouting so loudly the blood vessels in his neck were popping out.

"Yes," she said. "Just as you fucked me."

"Bitch!" He screamed. He struck out at her with his hand. She ducked. His hand connected with her right breast and made an ugly slapping sound. He hurt her enough to make her cry. The whole idea of hitting her there made him feel sicker. Can you give someone cancer that way? Your own daughter . . . A cluster of irrational thoughts, fears, disgust . . .

"You fucked me because you wanted to," she spat at him between her tears. She was out of bed now, a safe distance away.

"Shut up! I'll kill you, Antonia!"

"The way you did Johanna?"

"What?" His body seemed to collapse on the bed, folding over, his head falling onto his knees. So that was it. So that's what this was all about. Well, there was one surprise left. Yes, he thought, he'd been smart after all. Very smart. A smile was on *his* mouth, this time, a smile Antonia could struggle with. There was still one secret left. The triumph would still be his.

What neither of them counted on was that Conrad would start to go berserk.

His last scruples were God-fearing after all. Night after night he had dreams and visions he could not tolerate. Visions of angels coming to torment him, to demand his punishment. Now he broke. He had spent too many years of his life building up guilt and not knowing he had a conscience. All at once, guilt crashed down on him. He literally became crazy. In his craziness, he began to search for a path toward expiation.

The story of Oedipus blinding himself began to haunt him. In Conrad's madness he decided that that was the way . . .

He had no difficulty acquiring the acid. Lye was a simple enough thing to obtain. The deliberateness with which he poured it over his head was the aspect of the act he would think about later, after the plastic surgery,

209

after the bouts with the psychiatrist, after the madness would leave him. The deliberateness was sculptural; he remembered watching his arm raise up, he remembered watching his hand before it poured the scalding, disfiguring liquid down upon his head from the pot that was its container, its holy vessel, its amphora.

It was crazy. But it would make him sane.

His eyesight would be ruined. He would require the thickest of lenses and be considered lucky that he hadn't gone blind. His face would eventually be restored, but in the process he would age twenty years.

In the end it would lead him to think of Johanna. She would understand that what he'd done had a vivid beauty all its own, a violence that was poetic. An expiation after all. But he would never be the same again. And Antonia's hold on him was still not broken.

Conrad was hospitalized for a long time, nearly four months. After six weeks he was well enough to resume his business affairs from his bed. No morsel in his ever-expanding empire was lost. Loyal servants and the telephone were all he needed.

Arthur Lamb came to see him every day. Conrad told Arthur it was a freak accident. That he'd knocked a pot of lye off a shelf while reaching up for something. Arthur didn't believe him but wouldn't dare ask questions. Arthur understood that Conrad had given him the official story and that was the accounting he passed along.

Ned Longworth was told the same story. Ned didn't believe it either. But Ned had more information than Arthur Lamb. Ned knew of Antonia's illness and of Conrad's dilemma over her request that he make love to her. Ned concluded that Conrad's charitable act temporarily unhinged him. Ned saw it as a great tragedy. He accepted Antonia's recovery as a blessing from God, a direct effect, he believed, of Conrad's unselfish love for her. He knew, of course, that there was no cure for lymphatic cancer. But Antonia's remission, he thought, with luck, might last for years.

Conrad did nothing to disabuse Ned of any of his ideas. Conrad had no intention of telling him it was all a trick. There was no way he could tell Ned that much without also telling him about Antonia's motivation. And Conrad was not about to reveal any of those secrets to Ned. As far as Ned knew, Johanna had died in an accident. And that was that.

Ned flew into Paris, came to the hospital, flew out again, returned in a week, repeated the round trip, and finally saw that Conrad was making slow progress and that it would take time for him to heal. After a while he stopped coming. He did wonder though about the fact that he never bumped into Antonia at Conrad's bedside. And there was no evidence in the hospital room, no little gifts or flowers, to indicate that she'd been there at all.

The model's life was suddenly the only life that counted, to Antonia. She was telling that to Pierre one night over a dinner he had cooked for her in his apartment.

"What happened to journalism?" he asked.

"I am fickle. What can I do?"

He smiled. But he sensed something more. He still called her Denise. He still believed she came in from Lyons to be with him. "Nothing, I guess. Women are that way."

"Sentiments such as those die hard, Pierre, don't they?"

"If they die at all."

"I am leading a whole new life now. You won't like me any more."

"Perhaps you are right," Pierre said. "I will be sad if our love affair is over, but such is life."

"I'm moving to Paris. I'm going to change my name from Denise to something more suitable for a model. You'll see my picture in magazines, Pierre, and you will pine for me."

"I will not pine. Pining is for those whose sex lives are unsatisfactory."

"You're pontificating again. You can't be feeling all that sad."

"Truthfully, I am not," he admitted.

"Then you will not be mad at me? We will be friends?"

That night Antonia got rid of Pierre.

She was still Antonia Thornton. But she was ready to become Toni Menard.

Four

Chapter Fifteen

Yvonne Smith's attitude towards the small, gray envelope began to change after a pleasant night out with Jerome Sheehy. By the following afternoon, Yvonne persuaded herself that the letter was worth further consideration. The fact that it bore no address made it clear that it was meant to be hand delivered. The more she thought about it, the more the probability that it was intended for the Cathy Hayes who was on television was reinforced. Ordinary people get their letters through the mail.

Retrieving the envelope, she paid attention to something embossed in low relief on the back flap. Although there was no return address, there was a logo. Six long-stemmed flowers arranged in the shape of an open fan. It was beautiful.

Jerome had wondered why Yvonne didn't just open the letter. It seemed to him a legitimate and logical means of trying to identify the person it was meant for. Yvonne had protested. It was something Lost-and-Found never did. She even thought it might be against the law. But now her adrenalin was beginning to flow. Why *not* open it? Jerome was right. She reached for her scissors, then slit the envelope.

The note itself was brief. It was written in a bold, almost calligraphic script. It said: "Dear Cathy. I am in New York for just a few days. I

215

think it would be worth your while to phone me at the Carlyle. I have something to tell you that will affect your forthcoming marriage." It was signed "Sister Love."

Yvonne's hands were shaking. She decided to telephone Channel Seven immediately.

She couldn't get through to Cathy Hayes. But a man who identified himself as Max McClintock got on the phone.

She took a deep breath, prepared to spew out a dramatic story. She only got as far as mentioning the letter when Max jubilantly interrupted her with a thousand thanks. Yes, it was Cathy Hayes's. Yes, this was the right Cathy Hayes. Yes, yes, thank you. What a relief. Please mail it to Channel Seven News.

Success created a terribly let down feeling. It was as though the bottom had fallen out. Yvonne shouldn't have undertaken this task alone. She should have shared it with Jerome after all. Then he would have been there, supportive, at the moment she most needed him. She felt so disappointed she wanted to cry. She couldn't understand her emotions at all. She looked at her watch. It was five-thirty. On top of everything else, the butcher would be closed before she got there.

"No! Oh, no! It must be shot again!" Streeter was shouting, frenetically dancing his way through blazing white light and the crowd of people who were there either to assist him, to observe the proceedings, or because they were part of Toni's entourage.

Streeter's studio was in a renovated brownstone in the West Eighties just off Central Park. It was the place—or more accurately the space—in which he lived as well as worked. Sought after by editors, models, and other media people for enough years now to own both a townhouse and two Jaguars, Streeter had also become an object of interest to rival photographers. They came to watch him work, to record his technique, to document and comment. At the moment, Streeter was photographing Toni for a sequence requested by Channel Seven News for the interview with Cathy Hayes scheduled for Thursday. While Streeter photographed Toni, other cameramen were making a film of Streeter. So in addition to the pandemonium created by more than thirty people running around inside a limited space, there was the confusion of mirror images. "I am a film within a film," Streeter muttered to no one in particular. "Toni. I'm

216

sorry, dear. But we must do it again. Oh, Jesus, look at your make-up. Where's that cunt who does your make-up?"

"She won't come near you, Streeter, if you talk that way," Toni said.

"I don't want her near me. I want her near you. *Who* moved that plant?" he shrieked. "Some oaf has pushed that marginata three quarters of an inch to the left! The composition is ruined!"

Everyone in the room who could hear him above the din knew that this was no moment of low comedy. Nor was there any element of the ludicrous in Streeter's carrying on. Streeter had the eye, as they said in his profession. When you had the eye, you could tell at a glance if a composition had been disturbed or if the elements of a design would fit together as perfectly as one had imagined. Streeter's living quarters, in the basement below the studio and offices that occupied all of the upper floors, contained several antique armoires that he had bought in England. Without ever measuring either the armoires or the space he intended them for, he had moved them into place. They fit perfectly, thanks to his having the eye. That anecdote had become a legend.

Having finalized the arrangements for Toni's appearance on Cathy's show, Ned Longworth decided to join the observers at Streeter's studio this morning. The object of the shooting was to illustrate the entire process a high-fashion model must go through. So Toni was to be photographed from the moment of her arrival, through the application of a new make-up, a change of costume, a rearrangement of hair, resting between takes, handling other business on one of the half-dozen telephones scattered throughout the studio, and so forth.

Ned had been hoping for an opportunity to see Toni alone. But Toni's schedule during her brief stay in New York had become so full, she suggested that Ned come to the shooting where, she said, there would be enough noise surrounding them to provide a blanket of privacy. She was right.

Ned still worried about her health, still marveled at the remission of her symptoms, still believed in the miracle of her recovery. He never suspected that it was a hoax. If someone had told him the truth, he would have despised that person forever and still not believed him. Nevertheless he had begun to distrust Toni.

Ever since her liaison with Conrad four years ago, Toni had an exaggerated sense of her power over the lives of others. She viewed herself as

217

dangerous. She reinforced her fury by detaching herself from its consequences. At the same time, she became obsessed by a need for expiation. She thought about it. She waited for it. The way to expiation was through Conrad's death.

"Have you seen Conrad?" she asked Ned.

"I was up there this morning. We had breakfast together."

"Did he actually leave his suite?"

"We had breakfast in his suite."

"He's become a regular recluse."

"Not really," Ned protested. "He just likes his privacy. He gets good service at the Pierre."

"There she is! There she is!" Streeter was shouting at the make-up artist. "Please, please do Toni's mouth over. And the eyes! The eyes!"

As tribute was paid to Streeter's ruthless search for perfection, Ned stepped back to allow the work on Toni's face to be continued.

"Do you want to buy me a drink around five?" Toni asked Ned.

There was a look in her eyes he had never seen there before. He had a quick premonition, which receded; he lost it. Or maybe he didn't want any part of it. In any event, some fear had stabbed at him, then stopped.

"Five o'clock?" Ned asked, thinking about it.

"I need a joint," Toni whispered.

"No!" Streeter shouted. "That's not the look I want today."

"He's got the hearing of a rabbit," Toni said as tears, for some reason, came to her eyes.

The make-up woman flew into action, ready to prevent serious damage. "My dear, are you okay?" she asked.

"I'm fine," Toni said, clenching her teeth. "I just need a joint. One toke."

Streeter repeated his loud refusal.

"Okay. Just watch me have a breakdown," Toni warned him. "Right in front of your fucking camera. I mean it."

"I'll try to make it at five," Ned told her. "Okay?"

She didn't respond. She was concentrating on gaining control. You're a big girl now, she told herself. She closed her eyes and thought of Johanna. When she reopened them, they were sparkling, and she was able to smile for Streeter and the camera again.

As soon as the session ended, she would telephone Conrad to say that Jeff was on his way with a gun.

218

Arthur Lamb was surprised to find that the simple lie he told the security guard worked. He said he was there to repair Cathy Hayes's air conditioner.

Whoever had done Conrad's research was good at it. Conrad had assured Arthur that despite there being central air conditioning, Cathy's office had a window unit. Conrad told him to dress up in overalls, carry a large toolbox, and proceed with authority.

When Arthur reached Cathy's floor, a receptionist explained that Miss Hayes wouldn't be along for at least an hour and that he could work there undisturbed. Arthur smiled and proceeded.

He was on a reconnaissance mission. All Conrad really wanted him to do was to look around. This was part of a phase Conrad described as early exploration. He was simply gathering information on Cathy, in no particular fashion. Information was a form of power; there was nothing specific he was looking for. Not yet. He was just spying in the hope that a random sweep of her office would produce something interesting, something to build on. Arthur's instructions were to take away anything small that looked interesting.

Floor-to-ceiling bookshelves lined one wall. They were filled with books sent over by publicity directors hoping to get their authors a five-minute interview on Cathy's show. There were also some framed photographs of children, a house in the country, and a man Arthur recognized as Jeff.

Cathy's desk was neat. No clutter. Her large appointment book was open to today's business. Nothing there worth reporting to Conrad.

There were no locked cabinets in the room. The closet seemed empty except for a black cardigan sweater on a wire hanger and an old umbrella. The only other furniture in the room was the chairs and the sofa.

Arthur would have left in five minutes if it hadn't been for the early delivery of the mail. A stack of it was carried in by the receptionist and put on Cathy's desk. Later in the morning, a secretary would determine what needed Cathy's attention and what didn't. When Arthur was once again alone in the room, he went through the mail, trying to guess whether anything there might be of interest to Conrad. Most of it appeared to be junk.

He came upon a small, gray envelope. Cathy's name was written in one handwriting, the address in another. The envelope had been opened and resealed with tape. Arthur had no idea why he thought this was something he ought to take, but there was nothing else in that office to make his search worthwhile. So he took the letter.

Then he left.

Jeff's apartment was filled with the aroma of freshly brewed coffee.

Cathy had changed her mind. She wanted to know all about Toni's recent place in Jeff's life now. Everything. All of the things she had thought she couldn't deal with. And all of the small details he had omitted about the past. For nearly an hour they had been sitting close to each other on the sofa, waiting out the early part of this strange afternoon.

"You know what I find so completely unbelievable?" Cathy asked.

"What?"

"The fact that we're calmly talking in this book-lined room and you've got a gun in your pocket. I never understood before how *possible* killing really is."

"I know."

"Could you really pull that trigger on Conrad?"

"No. I mean, not in the sense that I could go up there and deliberately shoot him."

"But once you saw him and began to recriminate about the past? Then?"

"I don't know. I really don't. Last night, I had such dreams. I'm not even certain I was asleep; you know the kind of night I mean? My heart never stopped pounding all the while I dreamed of killing him. And when I woke up—" He looked at Cathy.

"What?"

"I thought I heard Johanna's voice. I thought I heard her call my name. I began to shake like a frightened child. I felt lost, bereft. Isn't it stupid?"

"No, it isn't stupid." She drew closer and touched his shoulder.

"I'd been looking at old snapshots before going to sleep last night. Pictures of me and Conrad and Johanna . . . Always a mistake, before going to sleep."

"I want you to leave that gun here."

"I know you do. I want to also."

"Does that mean you'll do it?"

"Yes."

220

He removed it from his pocket and put it down on an end table.

"Most of all it means I love you very much," he said.

She reached out her hands, which he took in his. She was frowning.

"What? What, Cathy? Tell me."

She looked up at him. "Will Conrad try to kill you? Would that gun do you any good? Could it protect you?"

"I don't know how to use a gun," Jeff said, laughing. "I'd probably shoot my toe off instead of killing him. Conrad is a trained gangster. I'm just a soft Manhattan lawyer." He was kissing the back of her neck.

"I want you to come back from there alive," she said. "Do you promise me you will?"

"Yes."

"I want to keep us safe. Please . . . protect *us*."

"The way I protected Johanna?"

"Oh, Jeff, don't start lacerating yourself all over again now."

"Why not? It heats up the blood. All the better to fulfill my murderous mission."

"*Stop* it! Can you?"

"Okay." He took a deep breath. "You had wanted to look over my apartment. Still want to do it?"

"Yes. Although I'm sure I've got it memorized."

"Come." He took her by the hand.

They went from room to room, tourists among his possessions, reconsidering the notion that after their marriage they would go on maintaining his place as well as hers. Jeff's apartment was to have been the hideaway, the rendezvous. The concept was wonderful. But there was an element in it, they both recognized, that denied the reality of a marriage. Not that romance had to die. But the growth of a marriage was in a different direction. They would always want their private weekends; they would always hope to make love in the afternoon. But somehow, maintaining Jeff's apartment as a separate place seemed to be a contradiction of the integration marriage was intended to provide.

"I'd be willing to sell it," Jeff said. "I never thought I'd hear myself saying that. But, I'd be willing to do it. The cooperative market is peaking; it would be a good time to sell. We could buy a place in the Hamptons with the money."

"Or in Vermont, for less money. I'm not dying to be in the Hamptons."

"Okay. Whatever. Shall I sell it?"

221

"Well, let's think about it for a few days. There are so many things here, Jeff, in addition to your library and paintings. Things you care about that I've begun to love. I can't see putting any of that in storage."

"There's an awful lot of detritus here that I don't want to drag along with me into our marriage." He thought of the painting Johanna had given him. It had become his icon. He remembered Johanna telling him that some woman in his life would want to remove it from his wall. Maybe, he thought, it was time to remove it.

The phone rang.

Jeff answered it.

"This is Arthur Lamb," the voice said.

"Yes?"

"I'm calling about your meeting with Mr. Thornton."

"It's this afternoon at five," Jeff said.

"Mr. Thornton has decided to go to the country. He'd like you to come there."

"How far?"

"Not far at all. Bedford. He asked me to apologize for the inconvenience. Can you still make it?"

Jeff became irritated at the impertinence of that question. Could he still make it? Of course he could still make it. He would have gone to the ends of the earth. What difference did a forty-minute drive to Bedford make to him now?

"Yes," Jeff said, "I can still make it. Just give me the address."

"I'll pick you up," Arthur said. "Is three forty-five convenient?"

"Just give me the address. I'll drive there myself."

"This is the way Mr. Thornton would like to do it, Mr. Winter."

"Okay," he said. "Three forty-five."

Arthur hung up abruptly.

Jeff put the phone back in its cradle. His face was flushed. He was staring straight ahead, somewhere else in time.

"Who was that?" Cathy asked him.

"Arthur Lamb."

"Has there been some change?"

"Conrad's up in Bedford. He doesn't want me to have the address. Arthur's going to drive me there."

"Jeff!" Cathy was beside herself with fear.

"I know." He put his arms around her.

"You don't have to go," she said.

"Don't I?"

She hugged him hard and held him for a long time. Then he walked over to the end table on which he'd left the gun. He stood over it, staring down at it. He picked it up.

When he looked at Cathy again, she was crying.

Chapter Sixteen

A growing fear began to discomfort him as he stood in front of his apartment house waiting for Arthur Lamb.

It was a peculiar, disorienting sensation. He was waiting for an evil emissary from the past to reveal himself; he expected to see dried blood from Johanna's mangled body on the front bumper of Arthur's car. It was the morbidity of his situation more than any danger that was getting to him. He didn't really expect that Arthur Lamb had come to take him for a ride in the old gangster-movie sense. If Arthur's orders were to kill Jeff, that matter could have been worked out long before today and with much greater efficiency. No, there was no doubt about it. Conrad wanted this confrontation as much as Jeff did. So Jeff's safe arrival was pretty much guaranteed. The trip homeward might be another matter.

A Ford Fairmont stopped for a red light about a block south of where Jeff stood. But even from that distance, Jeff had no difficulty identifying the driver as the fat Paul Newman. The light turned green. The Ford pulled up to the curb where Jeff waited. Arthur Lamb rolled down his window, smiled, and reached behind him to unlock the back door. Jeff got into the backseat without a word. Arthur rolled his window back up and sped away.

By the time they reached the Henry Hudson Parkway, Jeff felt a bit more relaxed, although his breathing hadn't quite returned to normal. In a little more than half an hour, he'd be seeing Conrad.

Jeff looked out the window and saw a handsome young couple jogging along the service road. She was blonde. He was dark. They were so healthy looking. So happy. Her blonde hair flying. The graceful lines of her body. Enough to feed his confused emotions. He was remembering again. Images flew at him quickly, fluidly, easily. He was back in Paris. Shortly after his arrival. With the two of them, the two people he loved then. Until it all turned sour. Johanna and Conrad. They were all involved in washing Johanna's hair . . .

There was a party that night. At Harvey Blados's apartment. Harvey was an independent filmmaker whose last three movies, neo-realistic soap operas combining heavy sex with heavy doses of social message, had made a fortune. Because Harvey kept insisting that some of the most exciting people in the world were expected at his place tonight, Johanna had decided to take her hair a bit more seriously.

"I like your hair exactly as it is," Jeff had said to her, in front of Conrad, just before lunch. "How much more serious can hair be?"

"I think it needs to be a little more blonde for tonight's party."

"Jesus," Conrad said. "The natural woman succumbs to pollution. Isn't that against all of your principles?"

"Yes. But it's against all of *your* principles to be going to Harvey's party. Yet you're going."

"I enjoy Harvey's parties. It's Harvey's movies I can't stand. Besides, I wouldn't let you go to one of those orgies alone. Just the idea of going has already made you crazy. What the hell do you want to bleach your hair for? It's blonde already."

"I want to be blonder. It's just the way I feel. Now, are the two of you going to help me or not?"

"Oh, shit," Conrad said. "Just the way I wanted to spend the rest of the morning."

"Afternoon," Johanna corrected him. "First we'll have lunch. Then we'll worship beauty."

Having lunch meant drinking wine. So by the time two o'clock rolled around, Conrad and Jeff were both feeling more agreeable about participating in the further blonding of Johanna.

"The instructions on this fucking bottle are complicated," Conrad complained. "If you're going to wind up looking anything like the picture on the label, forget it."

226

"Let me see," Jeff asked. He took the bottle. "Oh. Yeah. It's a real churchgoing blonde."

"That's it," Conrad said. "Anyone who buys this stuff has got to be aware of the call of the whore in her soul. So the churchgoing blonde gives reassurance with her angel's smile. Good merchandising."

"Okay," Johanna said. "What's the first step?"

"Shampoo your hair," Jeff said.

"Aren't you going to help me?"

"Can't you shampoo your own fucking head?"

"You promised to help!"

"Shit!"

"Well, where do you want to do it?" Jeff inquired, hoping this wasn't going to turn into another free-for-all. "Bathroom or kitchen?"

"In the bathroom sink," Johanna said. "Everybody ready?"

"All right," Jeff and Conrad said in unison.

"Then, let's go. Follow me."

They got her head soaked and well shampooed. She was seated on a low stool with her back to the sink. They had rigged it so it all worked pretty comfortably. They were all warm from the wine, and when Johanna said it would feel wonderful if both of them massaged her soapy scalp at once, they complied as she cooed, and Conrad said it was such fun to be jerking off all together this way.

They rinsed her hair and applied the bleaching mixture they had produced from the bottle. The argument began when they all realized they had twenty minutes to wait before the next step in the process.

"I think Harvey is a turd and that his movies are shit," Conrad said.

"That's because you don't understand the esthetics of junk," Johanna retorted. "If you did, you would know that Harvey's movies have soul. That's why they're so commercial."

Conrad was about to counterattack when Jeff interceded, suggesting that Johanna probably had an interesting point to make, so why not give her the chance. There'd be time for rebuttal afterward.

"Okay. Go ahead. I'm listening." Conrad felt he was making a huge concession.

Conrad and Jeff were sitting on the rim of the tub. Johanna had put down the lid of the toilet seat and was sitting there.

"The difference between junk and turd is that turd doesn't report to any true emotion. Junk does. That's what makes it work. When Harvey

227

says he laughs or cries over a scene as he directs it, I believe him."

"Harvey's some slob," Conrad said. "Slobbery bastard."

"Maybe he's a slob," Johanna conceded. "But that doesn't deny his energy or willingness to take risks. He *gives*. The way a— Oh! Ouch! Help! Help!"

Johanna's scalp had begun to burn. She screamed at them to shampoo her head a second time.

It was then that the feeling Jeff would always remember granulated through him like a giddiness in his bloodstream. Jeff's fingers and Conrad's fingers side by side in Johanna's soapy hair. Ludicrous and loving. A smile on her mouth as she faced up at them, her head thrown back, her eyes closed against the assault of the soap but bearing an expression of passion . . . The three of them were in harmony then. There was a feeling between them that nothing could any longer contradict. Maybe that was the key to their relationship after all. The three of them locked into something they'd never escape . . .

They applied the bleach one more time. Now they argued past the deadline printed on the bottle. By the time they remembered to wash the stuff off, it was too late. They would not know the results until her hair was thoroughly dry. But they suspected, correctly, that it was a wreck.

In an hour they all convened.

"You look like hell, Johanna," Conrad said. "I've seen hair like that on two-dollar floozies. I'm not letting you go to Harvey's tonight looking like that."

She had to agree.

"A lesser woman would break into tears," she said.

"That's true," Jeff nodded. "But, Johanna, I'll cry with you if you want to have a good cry." He meant it. He remembered the recent winter's day when he first saw that wonderful mane of hair flying in the wind high up in Notre Dame Cathedral.

"Who's the best hairdresser in this town?" Conrad bellowed.

"I don't know. I practically never go to a hairdresser anymore," she protested.

Research. That was the next step.

Conrad telephoned a few whores. They would know about the classiest salons. It was what they all aspired to. When two of their recommendations turned out to be the same, he felt confident that he had the name of the best place.

They all piled into the Citroën and drove to an establishment on the

Rue du Faubourg Saint-Honoré so intimidating they didn't believe they could go inside dressed as they were, which was essentially correct. A receptionist at the door explained that an appointment had to be made and at present there was a two- to three-week wait for new customers.

"Bullshit!" Conrad roared. "We're going to a party tonight!"

"I am very sorry," the receptionist said. "Besides, it is already almost tonight."

Johanna and Jeff were beginning to feel more than a bit uncomfortable. They tried to nudge Conrad toward the door. But Conrad wouldn't be nudged.

"Who runs this place? Who's the boss?" he demanded.

"The boss is in the United States at the moment opening a branch." But then the receptionist softened and agreed to make a phone call.

She was on the telephone for a full five minutes. Then she hung up and told them she'd made an arrangement for Johanna's hair to be done at a small shop a short distance away, a few blocks off the Champs-Elysées, by a friend who was very experienced but just getting started in his own business.

The place was called Monsieur Pygmalion. Jeff and Conrad waited at a nearby cafe. They waited three and a half hours.

When Johanna came to get them, they were drunk. Johanna looked gorgeous in a fake, astonishingly glamorous way. But when she walked through the door, their recognition, already dulled by alcohol and thrown off balance by her transformation, was so slow that her heart sank. She was thinking she was about to meet with further disapproval, and although not normally vulnerable to male criticism, she had, by that hour, gone through enough of an ordeal to make even the strongest woman weak. As she came nearer to their table, she realized that it was not their disapproval but their distance she was feeling. They were in awe of her.

"My God," Jeff said. "You're the most beautiful woman I've ever seen."

"Shit," Conrad said. "I ain't takin' you to no party lookin' like that." He smiled. "Somebody else would steal you away, Johanna." There were tears in his eyes. "Some bastard would come and steal you away."

She put her arms around both of them then, standing between their chairs. She bent over and brought their faces close to her own so her face was sandwiched between them. She stayed that way, holding them, swaying gently from side to side, comforting them.

They sobered up. And they did go to the party. They got there at midnight.

The memory faded as the Ford turned off the parkway onto a side road. Jeff looked at his watch and figured it couldn't be much farther. Reflexively, he touched the gun in his pocket.

They drove through wooded hills banded by low stone walls and planked fences until they came to a long driveway lined with maples. Ahead of them loomed a huge Georgian mansion. It had to have forty rooms at least, Jeff thought, wondering whose house it was and why Conrad had chosen it as the site of their meeting. Jeff couldn't imagine living in such a place without a staff of crisply organized servants. He'd only been inside one house like it before, a house owned by a client whose family had made millions in textiles. He was still musing about the opulence of the estate when they reached a point beyond the wooded area where there should have been an enormous expanse of manicured lawn on either side of them. But what Jeff saw was evidence of grass grown too tall and burned out by the sun. Neglect. One answer to the servant problem. As he looked more carefully, he saw that the hedges hadn't been cut in months and that the flower beds were ruined. When they drew closer to the house, he could see broken shutters. He was beginning to imagine the formation of cobwebs inside, when the car stopped.

"Wait here," Arthur said.

Jeff watched him walk up the path to the heavy oak door. Arthur took out a key, used it, and went inside.

Jeff sat in the car listening to the stillness that hovered over the premises, a stillness that was growing increasingly oppressive. Restless, he leaned over the front seat, idly curious about the pile of junk Arthur had left there. Overalls, a toolbox, boots. And on the floor, where it had fallen, a small envelope.

Jeff leaned over as far as he could from the back seat, but there was no way he could reach it. His heart was beating faster than he imagined possible. What was it on the flap of that envelope? What was he seeing? The light was peculiar. He was sweating. He felt as though he were going out of his mind. He opened the back door and ran around to the front. He opened the front door, bent over, and grabbed the letter.

That logo had once been painted on his arm . . . He ripped open the

230

envelope and read the note to Cathy. He still recognized Johanna's handwriting after all these years.

"Give me that!"

Arthur had reappeared. He was grabbing at the letter.

"No," Jeff said, pulling away.

"Okay." Arthur took a swing at him, but his corpulence slowed him down. Jeff had plenty of time to duck. And to decide not to swing back. Jeff's business was with Conrad.

"Shove it," Arthur said. He got back into his car and drove down the driveway until he disappeared.

The front door of the house opened quietly. Standing there beautifully tailored in an Italian-cut double-breasted suit, elegantly thin, a bit stooped, white-haired, scarred, wearing thick eyeglasses tinted a medium shade of brown, was Conrad.

Jeff had no difficulty recognizing him now. The features were clearly there; the square jaw, the high forehead, the heavy, sensuous mouth that Johanna had always proclaimed had been cast from the same mold as her own.

"Johanna's alive!" Jeff shouted, waving the letter wildly.

"Of course she's alive," Conrad said. "Come inside. I don't enjoy the fresh air anymore."

"Sit down," Conrad said. "Let me get you a drink."

They were in the living room. It was fifty feet long and had a fireplace at either end.

"For God's sake," Jeff exploded. "Don't insult me with amenities! Talk to me!"

"Why don't you have a drink and try to calm down."

"I don't want to calm down."

"All right. I appreciate your quandary. You came here with a gun in your pocket. And now you have no reason to use it."

"Toni told me you killed Johanna!"

"There's an element of truth in what she told you. I tried to kill Johanna. As it happened, she didn't die."

"Maniac! I kept my part of the bargain; I left Paris as you—as you *ordered* me to! Why did you want to kill her after that?"

"Don't shout at me you bastard! I trusted you as a friend! Once!"

231

"Your idea of a friend was someone you could run. But . . . I'll tell you something, Conrad. For all that, I *liked* you. I really did. Sweet Jesus! Did you really try to kill Johanna?"

"You were never a match for either of us."

"No. I never even understood that it was all a contest."

Conrad laughed. He sat down, and Jeff sat opposite him.

"I guess I wouldn't mind a bourbon," Jeff said.

There were whiskey bottles and a bucket of ice cubes on a low table placed between them. Conrad began to fix Jeff's drink. "Bourbon's new for you, isn't it? In Paris you drank scotch."

"Could we get bourbon in Paris?"

"We had anything we ever wanted in Paris. Don't you remember?" Conrad handed him his drink.

"Is this your house?" Jeff asked.

"One of them. I just bought it. I think it suits me, don't you agree? A once-powerful estate? Of course, unlike me, these premises can be restored."

"What happened to you, Conrad?"

"I've turned into an old man."

"But what happened to you?"

"Finish your drink. . . . I'm going to tell you."

"Where is Johanna?"

"Slow down! I'll get to that, too."

"Aren't you having a drink?"

"Alcohol doesn't work for me anymore. But," he said, pouring himself a straight scotch, "I still enjoy it." He took a sip, then another. "Revenge can make you crazy. You wouldn't argue with that, would you?"

"No."

"And everyone wants it . . . Antonia—Toni, as she's called now— has apparently wanted to destroy me from the time she was old enough for all the poison in her life to take effect. When she was fifteen, she persuaded me that she was dying. Without going into detail, let me assure you it was convincing and that she had the help of some highly respected doctors who were too dumb to understand what she was up to. My dying daughter came to me with one final request. Can you guess what it was?"

"I don't know."

"That I make love to her."

Jeff stared across at Conrad blankly. He felt disoriented. He suddenly

232

couldn't remember where the real world was, although he was sure he'd been in it not too long ago. He didn't have to ask Conrad anything more. Jeff knew; he understood everything—almost everything—now.

"Months later," Conrad continued, "she turned on me and told me it was a trap to prove my vileness. I tried to blind myself with lye. A crazy thing to do, but I *was* crazy for a time. There was no chance I would tell her her mother wasn't dead after that. For all those years until then, I kept Johanna and Antonia apart to punish Johanna. But now I was doing it to punish Antonia. Can you understand?"

"You arranged the car accident? You actually told Arthur to run Johanna over?"

"Yes."

"And when the accident didn't kill her, you still told Toni her mother was dead? I can't believe anyone could be so inhuman!"

"Johanna had no trouble understanding it. She knew how much I had to have hated her, then. Each day she was in the hospital, she grew more terrified of me. She thought I would try it a second time. I let her believe it, encouraged her to believe it. I made a deal with her. I told her she could leave Paris provided she would make no effort to get in touch with you. I told her she had to leave Antonia behind. With me. She agreed. When they got ready to discharge her, I had some of her things brought to the hospital. She never came home again. I arranged a mock funeral that Antonia attended. That, in the end, was my way of killing her."

"Then Toni still believes Johanna's dead. Which is why she set me up to kill you."

"Not exactly. Johanna and Antonia were finally reunited nearly a month ago. I think it must have been Johanna's idea that Toni come to see you. I think Johanna set you up to kill me."

Jeff pounded his fists on the arms of his chair, spilling his drink. "I was so in love with her!" he cried out. "I was so in love!" His voice grew hoarse.

"We were all in love! *Once!*"

Jeff took a series of deep breaths and closed his eyes. In a moment he asked, "Is Johanna all right?"

"What do you mean?"

"She isn't crippled, or anything?"

"No. Except by her discovery of religion. She's Sister Love!"

"Where is she?"

"I don't know."

233

"How can you not know?"

"I don't know *exactly*. I have no reason to be in touch with her. You'll have no trouble finding her, though. There's a woman called Cima Wein who runs a gallery in SoHo. Cima handles Johanna's work. Under the name of Sister Love, of course. Cima will have her address. It's somewhere in Dallas."

"You could have told me all of this in Paris."

"I wasn't ready to tell you in Paris."

Jeff found it hard to go on looking at Conrad. He hoped Arthur would be along soon to take him home. And then he thought he heard the sounds of a car pulling into the driveway.

"Oh, before I forget," Conrad said, "I'd like to have my gun back. Toni stole it from me to give to you. May I have it please?"

"I wish I had used it on you," Jeff said, handing it to him.

"This way you get to see Johanna again. Listen, when you do, tell her for me to go to hell. Soon! Be sure to add *soon!*"

Jeff walked to the front door alone.

In the car, he leaned back and closed his eyes once more. Johanna was alive. . . . He tried to feel something. He couldn't. But her presence hovered over his life.

The car pulled onto the main road and headed toward the parkway. Jeff didn't notice the limousine passing in the opposite direction. Even if he'd noticed, he could not have seen that its sole passenger was Toni Menard.

Chapter Seventeen

The limousine had been Streeter's idea. A reward for good behavior.

The shooting finished on time. Everyone got through it, finally, in reasonably good spirits. Ned Longworth called to say he couldn't have drinks with Toni after all, which was fine with Toni, since she'd already decided to break their date.

On an impulse, while relaxing over a joint after the shutters stopped clicking and the brightest of the lights were turned off, she decided to drive up to Conrad's house in Bedford. He had told her about it on the telephone a few days ago, and now she wondered what she'd find there.

"How the hell am I going to get to Bedford from here?" she asked Streeter.

"By limo, darling. I've decided to spoil you rotten. I may even stake my entire future on that mouth of yours." He went to the telephone and hired a limo. She heard him shout that he wanted it at the front door immediately. Later, he explained that that was quite possible, since the livery service's main garage was just around the corner. "These limos come equipped with a full bar. And they stock tequila," he told Toni. "Sure you don't want me to come along for the ride?"

"No, darling," she said. "But thank you for a beautiful present."

They went from grass to cocaine. Then she got her things together, kissed everyone who was still left at the studio, and went to the limo.

She touched the upholstery in the backseat. It was some sort of fake suede, but it felt good. She looked out the window and realized that she could see into other cars although no one could see her. The windows were made of that specially tinted glass. She could do anything at all back there and no one would know. Except the driver.

She wondered whether Conrad would turn the house in Bedford into a corporate mansion, an executive retreat for the staff of that empire of slick porno magazines he now controlled. No, she decided, Conrad was not about to have a mansion like Hugh Hefner's. Besides, the base for his publishing venture was in England, not here.

"How do I turn the radio on?" she shouted at the driver.

"You can talk to me through the intercom," the driver said. "You don't have to shout."

"I want the radio."

"There's a panel on the door."

She found it. She wanted hard rock. And another joint.

Why the hell *was* she going up there? Then something occurred to her.

She began to laugh.

When he got home, he phoned Cathy to tell her he was all right.

She said thank God and didn't question him. Something in his voice told her he needed to be alone for a while. When he asked her to meet him at the Russian Tea Room at nine, she decided to wait until then to find out what had happened in Bedford. She would have felt foolish asking him whether he'd shot Conrad. Reasonableness seemed to have returned to their lives; Cathy felt reassured.

Then why did Jeff sound so awful? It wasn't the awfulness of a man who'd committed murder. Of that she was certain.

"I love you," she said.

"I love you," Jeff repeated. They said goodbye.

He walked away from the phone repeating the phrase: "I love you." He said it into the living room air. It sounded hollow.

What if Cathy were dead? He shouted the question up at the ceiling. How much would he weep? How much pain would he feel?

Johanna was alive! Why did he feel nothing? Was it simply that time had finally erased his yearning? But *when*? Why could he no longer remember the feeling that had once been so overwhelming?

He ran toward the bedroom. He wanted to see the icon, the painting of the women acrobats, their flesh rendered in hot pink paint thickly applied, the heat of their bodies radiating off the canvas, the warm cabaret lights softening their hair and their perfumed skin, causing it to glow. . . . What? Could he smell their perfume? Yes, yes, he could. . . . What fragrance did Johanna use? Hadn't she told him? Hadn't it clung to his body, to his pillow, to his sheets? The magic of Schiaparelli, she had said, laughing. Love is so commercial, she had said, still laughing. Love comes with a label just as perfume comes with a label, she had said . . .

Jeff lifted the painting off the wall. It was so light. . . . Why did its lightness surprise him? He smiled at his surprise. He sat on the bed with the painting in his hands. He kissed it. . . .

Then he broke the canvas over his knee and stared at it long and hard, knowing that this was the murder he had awakened this morning to commit.

When he told Cathy that Johanna was still alive, her smile collapsed, and she said, "Well, Jeff . . . goodbye."

"What do you mean?"

"Isn't it the greatest love story ever told? You and Johanna?"

"Except that it's over."

"Oh, no, you're wrong about that. It looked like it was over. But that was when we still believed she was dead and you were finally going to accept that fact after sixteen years. Remember? But now we see embers."

"Maybe you do. I don't like anything you're saying."

"Well, you don't have to like *everything* I say. Not if you love me."

"Jesus, Cathy! What is it?"

"You tell me! You're smart. You tell me what it is that's bugging the hell out of me right now. Mucking up my life. I'm so sick of all this."

"Cathy . . ." He tried to put his arms around her. She pulled away. "God," he said, "at the moment when I need you the most—"

"That's not fair. Goddamn unfair! Don't feed me that! I've been

237

through a lot with you. And I'm going to go through this with you, too. Because, dammit, I do love you very much, and I still hope we have a future. But I'm angry! Angry at your naiveté. Angry at Conrad and Johanna and Toni for being so rotten. And finally angry at myself for being such a fool."

"You haven't been a fool."

"Are you sure?"

"Yes."

"I want to believe that. I'm just so damn insecure all of a sudden. Oh, Jeff, do you think about Johanna a whole lot?"

"No. Oh, I wonder what she looks like now. I wonder whether she's begun to hate me. I wonder why she waited so many years before trying to find Toni. I wonder what it was like for her in Paris during those last few days."

"That's all!" She began to laugh.

"I love *you*, Cathy. Don't you understand?"

"Not completely. But maybe I don't have to."

"I swear to you—"

"The oath I want is in your eyes. I see it there. I'm okay now."

"Will you help me find Johanna?"

"Why do you want me along?"

"It may be the only chance you'll ever get to watch me walk through fire."

"That's not something I especially want to see. Fire frightens me."

"I *need* you."

"Okay," she said. "Jeff . . . I'll go with you."

But it would have to wait until tomorrow.

It had begun to rain at about five-fifteen. Jeff had his secretary phone a service he sometimes used, to provide a car and driver. He didn't want to waste time trying to pick up a cab.

He called Cathy and asked her to be waiting in front of her building as close to six as she could make it. He had the car pick her up first and then get him. But despite all their frantic consideration of logistics, they were defeated by traffic, and it began to look as though they'd never get to SoHo before the gallery closed.

They got to the address at six forty-five. There were still lights on. The

238

gallery was of the storefront variety. The front door was open. They walked right in.

The tall gray-haired woman swathed in antique velvet and American Indian shell jewelry had to be Cima Wein.

They began too rapidly.

"I'm sorry," the woman said. "But I don't know who you are. You can't just come in off the street and expect me to confide in you. This is extraordinary. Please leave."

"I'm Cathy Hayes of Channel Seven News."

"Oh. So you are. You look younger in person."

"Miss Wein," Cathy broke in, "forgive me. But we have an urgent reason to locate Johanna Thornton. We think you can help us."

Cima Wein looked into Cathy's eyes. All of her years of experience with people told her that Cathy was okay and to believe her.

"Come with me. Both of you," Cima Wein said. "Back here. The paintings I want to show you would normally be sold at the gallery uptown, but I've decided to try to develop a market for them down here as well. They're priced a bit higher than most of the things I will sell here. But they may have some downtown appeal." They were following her as she spoke. "They are of a religious nature, as you can see. But hardly orthodox."

The group of canvases Cima Wein was showing them treated the subject of lilies of the field, except that the petals of the flowers were rendered in human form. Clusters of naked children being drenched by the sun and all the energy of the heavens.

"This is the work of Sister Love, the evangelical artist," Cima Wein explained. "She no longer calls herself Johanna Thornton."

Cathy and Jeff begged her to tell them more.

"Sister Love has promoted a form of pop religious art into a million dollar business," Cima Wein continued. "Maybe multi-million dollar, for all I know. I'm not the only gallery representing her. And quite frankly, it's not to my taste at all. But she sells. She may even help pay the rent here in SoHo. It's not only the paintings. There are ceramics, Bible boxes, even items of clothing. I carry only the paintings here. All of this stuff comes out of an enterprise housed on twenty-five acres of expensive real estate in suburban Dallas. Sister Love's studio, art school, ceramics factory, and church are all located there. She's married to some rich Texan. He backed her in the beginning. Now she's made a fortune."

"Can you give us her address?" Jeff asked.

"It's a town called Warrensville, Texas. Just outside of Dallas. Any cab driver at the Dallas airport will know how to take you there."

They were flying Braniff to Dallas. But there was a delay in takeoff, and they were killing time at a bar in the terminal at LaGuardia.

It was Thursday, the day Cathy would have been interviewing Toni Menard on Channel Seven News. Cathy had gotten another member of the news team to fill in for her, but then the studio received a call from someone saying that Toni was canceling out. There was no explanation.

They were drinking Perrier. They were both on the verge of depression and were afraid that a hard drink would push them right into it.

"Were Johanna and Conrad ever divorced?" Cathy asked.

"I doubt it. A divorce would have added confusion to the lie."

"But she's remarried?"

"Who knows?" Jeff said.

"It's curious."

"Nervous?" he asked.

"Very. Aren't you?"

"Yes. Very."

"Oh, the hell with it," she said.

"The hell with what?"

"Let's take a chance on a drink. How much more in the dumps can we get?"

"Scotch?"

"No. A vodka martini."

"Two vodka martinis," he told the bartender.

"They're never as good at any bar as the ones you mix," she said.

"That's because *I* mix 'em. I'll teach you how, if you're nice."

"If I'm nice?"

He thought she was about to cry again.

"Oh, shit," he said. "I can't even make stupid jokes anymore."

"Not for the next two days. That's all. After then, you can make all the stupid jokes you like." She stopped herself. She kissed him lightly on the cheek.

Their drinks arrived. The first sip made a difference. It helped.

"Should have done this an hour ago," Jeff said. "That feels good."

240

Then Jeff saw him.

He nearly spilled the rest of his drink.

"What is it?" Cathy asked.

"There's Arthur Lamb," Jeff said. "Heading straight in our direction."

He was walking toward them with the deliberateness of a bulldozer.

"I don't mean to intrude," Arthur said in a genuinely apologetic tone, "but Mr. Thornton wants you to know that his daughter Antonia is already in Texas, reunited with her mother."

He paused long enough to determine whether or not there were any questions. He shifted his glance from one to the other. There was a hint of a smile on his well-chiseled mouth; Paul Newman grown fat and mean.

Arthur turned on his heels and left.

They finished their drinks. They walked to the gate to get some further information about their flight

Sister Love's Studio, School, and Church of the Soul was not as well known in Dallas as Cima Wein had imagined. It wasn't in the telephone directory, at least not under that name. And the woman at the Hertz counter had never heard of it, nor had the taxi dispatcher. They decided to rent a car, drive out to Warrensville, and make inquiries there.

In Warrensville, a suburb made up of small ranches and expensive estates, they stopped at a gas station, where they were handed a map. The attendant said the place they were looking for wasn't really in Warrensville, but up in some hills just beyond.

After a good bit of driving around, they found their way. They came at last to a dirt road that led to the secluded campus.

At the point at which the dirt road became a gravel driveway, there were stables on one side and tennis courts on the other. Just beyond, there was a modern-looking two-story structure that could have been a dormitory, and another identical building alongside it that might have contained studios or classrooms. Farther along the driveway there was a chapel, at which point the driveway looped around. At the center of the loop was the main house.

Jeff stopped the car, and they got out.

They heard the sounds of choir practice resonating from the chapel. But the predominant feeling was one of quiet. They listened to their footsteps as they approached the front door. Then they heard a shot ring out.

"Jeff!"

Reflexively they grabbed each other and crouched to the ground. But the shot had been fired inside the house, not at them. They got to their feet. Jeff rang the bell.

Some static came out of a speaker above the peephole. Then a voice.

"Your timing is lousy, Jeff." The voice—the silk shirt with the stabbing pin—was Johanna's.

"Is she going to let us in?" Cathy asked.

"I don't know."

They waited, staring at the door for what seemed an interminable time, until it opened.

Dressed in a floral caftan, her carelessly pinned-up hair now strawberry blonde, a bit heavier, burdened with the tragedy of her life, she still measured up to his memories of her. But there was something new in her face, some element that time alone could not account for. Whatever it was wrenched his heart even before he could identify it. An addition . . . an erasure. The light of defiance that had once radiated so brightly from her eyes was now veiled in sadness.

She broke the silence between them. "Would you buy it back if you could? The dawn of our lives?" she asked him.

He didn't answer.

"You'd be a fool even to consider it. Come in," she said.

They followed her into a large foyer and then into a parlor that was apparently her office. Johanna closed the double doors and invited them to sit down.

"This is Cathy Hayes," Jeff said.

"I know."

Cathy nodded.

"We heard a shot," Jeff said.

Johanna's mouth twisted. "Antonia is dead," she said. Then the corners of her mouth turned downward, pouting, before her lips began to tremble. Her face was suddenly wet with tears, and little black mascara blotches appeared below her eyes.

He went to her. He would have put his hands on her shoulders, but she hunched over slightly and backed away. He realized that Cathy was standing there, and he no longer knew quite what to do.

242

"What happened?" Jeff asked Johanna.

"She shot herself."

"Why?" he pleaded.

"She was *disgusted* with her life."

"She was enjoying her life! She was on the verge of a career bigger than Lauren Hutton's."

"There was another part of her life. Do you know how much she hated Conrad?"

"I have a pretty good idea. She set me up to kill him."

"That was *my* idea." A self-mocking smile—he remembered that smile—broke through.

So Conrad was right.

The extent of Johanna's fury made him feel ill, and numb with sorrow.

"About a month ago," Johanna continued, "I decided to find her. I—"

"How could you have kept yourself from her all that time?" Jeff interrupted.

"I'll tell you how. I was comforted by knowing that each year as she grew older, without me, believing me dead, she would hate her father more and more. I wanted that hatred to grow. Can you understand that?"

"No." His throat was so dry he felt himself choking as he said it.

He'd had it all wrong . . . everything.

For sixteen years he'd been clinging to his youth, not to his love of Johanna. How well had he ever known her? To have been so completely hypnotized he had to have been under his own spell, not hers.

"When I came to New York," Johanna went on, "I happened to go to the theater. And Cathy, you were there. Someone pointed you out to me. I sent you a note."

"I know," Cathy said.

"It was an impulse, that note. I don't know—I began to think maybe my plan wasn't according to God's will. I wanted to tell you to stop Jeff from going to Paris."

"Why didn't you just stop Toni from taking him?"

"When you didn't call, I decided it might be God's will after all." She was crying again. "I didn't think it would be His will for Antonia to be lying dead in the next room."

"Shouldn't we go in there? Shouldn't we call a doctor?" Jeff asked.

"Why? She's dead. . . . Do you want to know about the final disgust that killed her?"

They were silent.

"She went up to Conrad's estate in Bedford sometime after you were there, Jeff. And they made love again. Which is to say they went at each other like two reptiles playing with each other's bodies. She came here. . . . It *was* disgusting. Disgusting to God. She had to die. What other way was there for me to help her?"

"Help her?" Jeff asked.

"Yes. I helped her die. . . . Haven't you ever seen it? Death? Oh, surely . . . Jeff, do you remember all those conversations in Paris? We talked about death; we tried to imagine it in relation to art. Do you remember?"

"Yes." It was part of the nonsense of being young, he thought. Hadn't they left all that behind?

"Well . . . it *is* like art . . . when it happens the way it did to Toni," Johanna went on. "My creation . . . Her eternal rest. The wound was well placed! It didn't mar her. Her blood was *not* disturbing to see . . ."

Jeff put his arm around Cathy as though to protect her from what she was hearing. She was shivering and welcomed the shelter he provided. But what Johanna was saying was beyond Cathy's understanding. She didn't want to hear any more. She had to get out of there. It occurred to her that they ought to call the police, but she didn't care.

"Jeff," she begged, "let's leave. I'm going to even if you're not. I can't stay here."

"Okay," he told Cathy. Then he looked at Johanna. For years to come he would return to this moment in his dreams; he would say then the things he was unable to say now. He wanted to comfort her. But the pity and anger he felt cancelled each other out, and he felt nothing at all. He was numb, and Cathy was urging him away from there. He had no choice but to go.

At the door he stopped. He was going to turn back.

Cathy waited.

He couldn't do it; he couldn't turn back. Not ever again.

Chapter Eighteen

The sound of jet engines was the perfect accompaniment to his need to withdraw into himself.

He sat hunched over a cup of coffee the stewardess had handed him, his back supported by a pillow that had slipped from behind his head to somewhere around the base of his spine. In the next seat, Cathy was sleeping. Across the aisle, someone reading *Newsweek* had just come to a story about Toni's rising star in the tough world of modeling. Out of the corner of his eye, Jeff caught the spread of color photographs. They weren't meant to have been her epitaph.

Epitaph . . .

He had been seeing his life as a choice between recapturing his past and burying it, as though the events of his youth were really a thing he held in his hand, a thing he could either bring back or forever entomb. But that wasn't the way it worked.

Epitaphs should be written in chalk, he thought, not cut in stone.

Can the truth, once it has been revealed, also recede? Not in law. But in life? Maybe. Could he restore innocence to his dreams of Johanna?

When he fell in love with Cathy, he knew his life was going in a new direction. That was the point to return to, to start from, now. He was still young. Still strong. Cathy was younger. He turned toward her and smiled. Her eyes opened.

"Were you smiling at me just then, or did I dream it?" she asked.

"I was smiling at you."

"I think it began as a dream. You just started smiling at me, right?"

"I've been smiling at you since we met."

"No, no seriously. You just turned toward me, right?"

"Yep."

"But I've been dreaming it ever since I closed my eyes."

"Well?" he asked. "What do you suppose it means?"

"It means my dream came true. Oh, Jeff, is it awful of me to be feeling so happy right now? So soon after all we've been through?"

"Awful? It's marvelous that you can, after all I've put you through."

"You'd do the same for me, wouldn't you?"

"Yes. Of course I would." Then he paused. He felt a surge of good feelings returning to his body. "But what did you have in mind?"

They both laughed.

An hour away from New York, they asked the stewardess for two splits of champagne.

The funeral was private.

Toni's body was cremated. Her ashes were brought in an urn to the campus, where Sister Love received them, and a service was held in the chapel. Sister Love presided while thirty-two artist-novitiates assisted her. They chanted prayers, sang songs of devotion, and called the roll. Each of their names was read off by Johanna, and each in her turn responded with the words "Present, Sister Love." When Toni's name was read, thirty-two voices cried out in unison, "Absent, but only from this tangible circle. Present in eternity. Present before the Lord. Present forever."

The chapel doors opened. The youngest of the novitiates took the urn and carried it down the aisle while all the others waited. The doors remained open; the room remained silent. Minutes later, the young woman returned and announced to the room, "It is done."

They understood. Slowly they disbursed. Toni's ashes had been scattered in the wind.

* * *

Newsweek managed to get a follow-up story out of it. The wire services put together a story. The *New York Times* ran an obituary of considerable length, which included a few memorable quotes from Streeter Cash. And news of Toni's death was published abroad. Everywhere, it was reported as a suicide.

Jeff read everything he and Cathy could get hold of. But with each passing day, he dwelled on it less. It was all safely behind him now. Finally he understood that he was free.

Conrad went into a deep depression, which lifted periodically. And then he would have insane rages. Toni would not have taken her own life; Johanna had to have been behind it. It was Johanna who had taken Toni away from him. Johanna who had finally beaten him. All right! Let it end here! He grieved for Toni. He wept. And he could find no peace. It would not end here. His rage of sixteen years had come full circle.

Johanna went into seclusion after the funeral. The man she called her husband made little effort to comfort her, since he had reached that unfortunate state at which most of his life was lived inside a bottle of bourbon. He was aware that a great commotion had been stirred up around him by Toni's death. And he realized that Johanna was suffering. But hell, why shouldn't she be? She was the kid's mother, after all. Nevertheless, he meant to say something consoling to her. But soon he was under a haze, and the stupor was not far away.

One morning, about three weeks after the worst of it, Johanna decided to pull herself together. She told her secretary she was taking the day off to go into downtown Dallas, get her hair done, and do some shopping at Neiman-Marcus. Her secretary said she would inform the chauffeur. But Johanna said no, she would drive herself. The secretary smiled. It was a wonderful sign of recovery. She could hardly wait to spread the news among the novitiates.

At ten minutes to three, a crowd formed outside the main entrance to Neiman's. In the street a woman lay critically injured, both her legs mangled, blood running out of her mouth. Her eyes were open. She

247

hadn't yet lost consciousness. The police and an ambulance were on the way. But for now, she was being looked after by passing strangers.

The crowd was angry. The woman had been hit by a speeding car. Some maniac had plowed into her just as she had started to cross the street. Sent her body flying. Then ran right over her. The crazy son of a bitch sped away. But there had been a witness. Someone in the crowd had seen every detail, had even managed a glimpse of the driver. The witness was still standing nearby, talking to people at random, repeating over and over the story of what he had seen. There was one part of his set speech that particularly interested his listeners. "When I first got a look at the driver, I said to myself that has to be Paul Newman. But then I figured that couldn't be right. Unless, by God, Paul Newman's put on forty pounds."

The crowd didn't know who the woman was. The police would arrive at any minute and find various bits of identification in her wallet. They would know soon enough that she was both Sister Love and Johanna Thornton. But by then she would be dead.

She managed to utter one last sound. It took all of her strength. But she articulated the word so there was no misunderstanding what she said in the end.

"Bastard!"

Then her mouth moved again to form what looked to everyone there like an affectionate smile.